# THE MAYORS OF
# NEW YORK

# THE
# MAYORS
## OF
# NEW YORK

### A BILL SMITH / LYDIA CHIN MYSTERY

# S. J. ROZAN

PEGASUS CRIME

NEW YORK LONDON

THE MAYORS OF NEW YORK

Pegasus Crime is an imprint of
Pegasus Books, Ltd.
148 West 37th Street, 13th Floor
New York, NY 10018

First Pegasus Books cloth edition December 2023

Interior design by Maria Fernandez

Library of Congress Cataloging-in-Publication Data is available.

ISBN: 978-1-63936-525-8

10 9 8 7 6 5 4 3 2 1

Printed in the United States of America
Distributed by Simon & Schuster
www.pegasusbooks.com

*To my cousin Elaine*
*Wish you were here*

# 1

I don't like the mayor," I said. "Or her kids."

"Oh, I didn't realize you were acquainted." Aubrey Hamilton, in a familiar move, tossed her golden hair back off her brow. For the brief time, centuries ago, when we were together, that honey color had come out of a bottle. Now it was no doubt the result of a three-hundred-dollar-every-three-week touchup at some exclusive salon.

"I'm a New Yorker. I have a God-given right to dislike politicians. Personal experience is unnecessary."

"That right extends to politicians' children?"

Sitting across the marble-topped café table, Aubrey poured herself tea and gave me a conspiratorial smile. Not my kind of see-and-be-seen café. Not my kind of flowery tea. Not my kind of smile.

"And New Yorker or not, your accent is still Kentucky," she said, putting the pot down. "Used to be stronger, though."

"So did I. What do you want, Bree?"

"The mayor has a problem."

"I don't care."

"Her son's run away."

"Good for him."

"Come on, Bill. He's fifteen."

I rubbed a curl of lemon rind on the rim of my double espresso. According to the menu, Meyer lemons. They don't make espresso taste better than other lemons do. But they're expensive.

"I told the mayor I knew the man for the job," she said.

"Then go ask him. Seriously, Bree, you think flattery will work on me? Have some respect."

"Mark's a kid," Aubrey pushed. "Out there in the big bad world."

"Fifteen's not such a kid. A couple of wars ago he could've lied about his age and joined the army."

"Can't do it now."

"I bet he regrets that. I ran away half a dozen times before I was fifteen."

She arched her right eyebrow. Also familiar. She can't do the left. "And what happened?"

"My father beat the shit out of me each time."

"So you went back home."

"They found me and dragged me back."

"If you find Mark no one's going to beat the shit out of him. I promise."

"I'm sure they won't. Her Honor will lock him up in Gracie Mansion and go back to ignoring him."

"What makes you think—"

"I'm Dr. Spock. If the mayor's really worried about her kid why doesn't she go to the cops? Conclusion: she's not worried. Either she's pretty sure she knows where he is and as soon as I sign on she'll tell me and I'll go fetch him, keeping her out of it—"

"And you'll collect your fee for doing very little." Aubrey set down her cup. Her coral lipstick—probably this year's hot color; Lydia would know—left not a ghost of a stain on the rim.

I took a sip. The espresso was good. "Or she doesn't actually know but she's pretty sure he's safe. Or she doesn't know and doesn't give a damn, but she can't have him running around loose in case he holds a press conference or something and embarrasses her."

Mark McCann, the dark-haired, brooding male half of the mayor's unmatched-in-every-way twins, had, as far as I knew, never held a press conference. His public presence was, generously put, negligible. But his ash-blond drama queen sister Madison Guilder—she still used their father's name, while her brother had switched sides—had summoned journalists to an event simultaneous with their mother's inauguration last winter as New York's mayor. To those who showed—and every news outlet sent someone—she denounced New York City's woeful lack of leadership on the world stage in seeking solutions to the existential threat of climate change and expressed an urgent hope that the new administration would do better. It was great political theater and one of the biggest birds I'd ever seen a child flip a parent, even including myself.

"What's wrong with that?" Aubrey said now. "Nobody wants to be embarrassed."

"Don't be coy. You don't wear it well. Or," I went on, "there's one more possibility. She *is* worried about Mark, but she's at least as worried about why he ran away. What an investigation might find. Which is why she wants private talent and not the NYPD."

Aubrey sat back, silent for a moment amid hushed conversation and the refined ding of tiny silver spoons on porcelain. "No. She *is* worried, but none of that is why she wants you."

"What is, then?"

A sigh. "Every second year the City enters contract negotiations with the municipal unions. First up is the Detectives' Endowment Association. Those talks just started. Carole went to the opening round with the City's team and she's promised to go personally as often as necessary."

I said nothing, just circled my hand to get her to the point.

"The big shot across the table is the DEA president," she said. "A lieutenant named Herb Straley. 'Bulldog,' they call him, because he's got a face like one and a personality—if you can call it that—to match. He's got a whole Dog Pack in there with him. Honest to God, that's how he introduced them, the DEA negotiators. The Dog Pack. Hand-picked by him. His right-hand man is a Sergeant Alex Bozinski. More of a Doberman, that one. Straley and about half the others have done these negotiations three times already."

"If you're trying to tug at my heartstrings—brave little lady facing down a ravenous dog pack—it's not working. All I get is that picture they have in dive bars of dogs playing poker. The bulldog has a cigar."

"You have no heartstrings. And I don't know what goes on in dive bars."

"Since when?"

"Oh, for God's sake, can we knock this off?"

"If you come to the point."

She tightened her mouth and lifted her teacup. Without sipping, she said, "The point is this. Whatever agreement they come to will be the benchmark for everyone else. There are parities and ratios, by law. It's dominoes. The Sergeants' Union, the PBA, the FDNY, Corrections, Sanitation. . . . The city's budget for the next two years depends on this." Now she sipped.

"Okay, I see where you're going."

She went anyway. "If Carole has the NYPD chasing after her runaway son the first thing that happens is her political capital takes a hit because she looks like a bad mother. Then her position as a tough negotiator

4

evaporates. How's she going to refuse to raise the salaries of the people who're literally working overtime trying to save her child?" She let out another sigh, this one hissing of suppressed irritation. "Yes, she's worried, yes, she wants him back, but she can't afford to have the police involved. This is bigger than one kid and his mom."

"Sounds very self-sacrificing," I said. "Except for the part about political capital."

"And personal capital. Yours. You want your taxes to go up because Carole can't hold the line? No? So take the damn case."

"Ah, now we get to the extortion part of the morning. If I turn the case down, it'll cost every New Yorker, you're saying. But no pressure."

"Pressure. As much as I can apply."

I looked around. Populating the place were men in suits, elegant women, children with their hair brushed taking a break for treats on a trip to New York, New York. The silverware and china glowed in the warm lighting. People spoke softly and smiled knowingly.

I turned back to Aubrey. "What actually happened?"

Her smile went beyond knowing, to border on smug. "Okay. The details. For one thing, Mark's bank account has been nearly emptied. He left something like twenty dollars, I don't know why."

"Because it's easier than closing it. Leave money behind, it's just a withdrawal. Take everything, there's paperwork. When?"

"When did he take the money? Tuesday afternoon."

"How much?"

"About five hundred. Birthday and Christmas money."

"Does he have another account? Credit cards?"

"He has a college savings account but he can't access it without a co-signer. He has the use of one of his mother's Visa cards. I told her to cancel it."

"Why?"

5

She missed a beat. "So he couldn't buy a plane ticket to Abu Dhabi, I don't know."

"Did he take his passport?"

Head tilting, she said, "I don't know. You're thinking to let him keep using the card because you might be able to track him through it?"

"If I were actually taking the case I might. What else?"

"Nothing. He took the cash and some clothes in a backpack."

"How about his phone?"

"It's not in his room. But the GPS is off. We assume he has it with him but he's keeping it off because he knows it can be tracked."

"You've tried calling?"

The look she gave me could've frozen lava. Well, it was an obnoxious question. To keep my streak going I asked, "Is there tracking software in the kids' phones beyond the GPS?"

"Oh, come on! If there were I promise you I wouldn't be sitting here watching you holding yourself back from going all bull-in-a-china-shop."

"It's that obvious?"

"You're that obvious. Security suggested trackers to Carole but she wouldn't have it."

"Why?"

"She didn't want the kids to feel like they're on leashes."

"But they have bodyguards?"

"Of course. But only when they're out. To protect them, not to make sure they don't escape."

"This one escaped. Did he leave a note? 'I hate you people, don't try to find me, so long, suckers'?'"

"Is that the note you used to leave?"

"I never left a note."

"Mark didn't either. But the money, the clothes, the backpack—it's pretty clear he ran away, and wasn't the victim of something."

"'Victim of something.' You mean you don't think he's been snatched by a perv with a taste for politicians' kids?"

"Jesus Christ! Could you be more coarse?"

"Yes."

She pursed her lips and nodded. "I remember. That's one of the reasons I left you."

"You didn't leave me. You cheated on me and lied to me. I kicked you to the curb."

"The first time I cheated on you, that was when I left you. It just took you a while to figure it out. Can we go back to Mark? He hasn't been seen since the night before last. He didn't come down yesterday for breakfast but he sometimes sleeps in, so that wasn't unusual. It was when the bodyguard on duty—Danny Rodriguez—showed up to take Mark to school that they discovered he was gone."

"But you waited until now to do something about it."

"The police say twenty-four hours until they consider someone missing."

"Not a kid. Especially a celebrity's kid. And if you didn't call the police how do you know what they say? Oh, wait, I bet you watch *Law And Order: Politics*." I drank more coffee. "And I have no twenty-four-hour time delay but you didn't call me yesterday either."

Aubrey paused. The April sun, hidden behind gray clouds all morning, suddenly glowed through the sheer curtains. "Carole thought he might come back."

"Based on . . . ?"

She gave me a rueful smile. "I don't know. Hope?"

"Obviously false."

"Apparently." The smile faded when I didn't respond to it. "The alarm system hadn't been triggered. The readout shows it was disarmed, off for just under a minute, and rearmed."

"The mayor's kids know how to work the alarm system at Gracie Mansion?"

"The mayor doesn't live at Gracie Mansion. A lot of mayors haven't. She uses it ceremonially but they live in the townhouse she bought after the divorce."

"And there's no security detail there?"

"Of course there is. Inside and outside. They stay downstairs, though, not on the bedroom floors. Again, the point is to keep the bad guys out, not the good guys in."

"How did the kid get out?"

"Through a first-floor window in the back. Close to the rear alarm panel."

"But the inside security guy was there."

"In the living room, apparently. Possibly asleep, though he says not. He's been reassigned."

"So your theory is Mark tiptoed downstairs, turned the alarm off, opened the window, rearmed the panel, slipped out and closed the window in the twenty seconds the system gives you to leave?"

"Why not?"

No reason why not, actually. "So I'm right. Her Honor figures the kid has money and a change of underwear. She's not worried."

"She still wants him back. I'm asking you to do a job. Not make a moral judgment."

"I throw the judgments in for free. What about his friends? His dad?"

"I called around his friends yesterday morning. Said he'd left something behind that he needed. No one could tell me where he is."

"You believe them?"

"I don't have a reason not to."

"Except they're teenagers. They have a romantic sense of loyalty."

"I'm glad someone has a romantic sense of something."

"Jesus. Can I smoke in here?"

"Of course not." She offered me that conspiratorial smile again.

I took a breath, looked around—the sunlight had faded again—and came back. "What about Mark's dad?"

"His dad's a shit."

"Shits don't get to see their kids? Wish someone had told my father that."

"Mark wouldn't go to him."

"Have you asked him?"

"Jeffrey? Carole doesn't want him to know there's a problem. He'll jump right up on his 'unfit mother, unfit mayor' soapbox." She paused. "I called him anyway. I said I must have gotten the custody schedule wrong. He told me not to be stupid, that it wasn't his week and, in any case, Mark's been refusing to go over there on Jeffrey's weeks since last fall. Which was fine with Jeffrey."

"Did you know that?"

"That Jeffrey doesn't want him, or that Mark doesn't go? I knew both. Madison, the sister, spends a lot of time with her dad but he and Mark have a mutual dislike."

"How about that, I have something in common with Mark."

"You know Jeffrey? Or are you exercising another God-given right?"

"The latter. So, what happened?"

"I threw Jeffrey off the scent by saying someone had just slipped me a note about a school trip. Apologized. He said it figured Carole would hire an idiot aide. What's funny?"

"You're actually asking that?"

"Fine. Whatever. We still want Mark found."

"But quietly so no one's embarrassed. Even though he's out there in the big bad world."

She bit her lower lip. The lipstick didn't come off on her teeth, either.

"Tell me something," I said. "Why did you take this job?"

"What job? Working for the mayor?"

"When I knew you, you had your own PR firm."

"With a partner. She decided to go in another direction. I think she's in Namibia saving elephants." Bree stirred her tea idly. "I ran the firm alone for a while and discovered something."

"And that was?"

"I'm a better lieutenant than I am a general." She looked up at me. "And I like it better. Carole's smart, principled, and going places. She's a visionary. I'm a detail woman, a planner. I plan for myself, I run a PR firm. I plan for Carole, I work for the mayor. Maybe one day the governor. Or the president."

"I hear the racket of a bandwagon."

"I'm the one choosing the music. Are we done analyzing me? Can we get back to Mark?"

"I just like to understand who I'm dealing with. Apparently I didn't, before."

"I think you always did."

"You never had any idea, did you? But okay, as you say, let's get back to Mark. Why did he pick now to leave? Trouble at school, at home, any issues? Does he have a drug problem?"

"A drug problem? I don't think so. He probably smokes a little weed, they all do. But he's not withdrawn—at least, not more than usual—or hostile or any of the things druggie kids are supposed to be. His grades are good."

"Anything else? Girl trouble? Boy trouble?"

"Not that I know about."

"What about that anyone else knows about? His sister?"

"Madison says she has no idea who Mark hangs out with because they're in different schools but that he's been talking about running away for a couple of weeks, at least."

"But no one paid attention."

"He has a therapist."

"Oh, there you go. Nobody in your family has time for you, but they'll get you a shrink so you can talk about it."

"You're one hostile bastard."

"To the mayor because she's a politician. To her ex because he's as scummy as his clients."

"You know that for a fact?"

"You want to contradict me?" She didn't. "And to you because after everything you have the balls to come ask me for a favor."

"It's not a favor. You'll be well paid. And the other thing was a lifetime ago."

"I hold grudges."

"Does that mean you wouldn't want me to . . . make it up to you now?" Her smile was sweet and playful.

I stared, then laughed. "Oh, Jesus. You're still a helluva piece of work, Bree."

She gazed steadily at me. I finished my coffee.

"So, I'll tell the mayor no?" she finally said.

A waiter in a white apron wafted past carrying a tiny pitcher of almond milk to a dairy-free patron. "As much as I'd like to hang you out to dry," I said, "you can tell yourself no, but tell the mayor I'll do it."

"But—" She shook her head. "Bastard. You were just pulling my chain?"

"No. I meant every word."

"Then why?"

"Because," I said, standing, "I ran away half a dozen times before I was fifteen." I turned and walked out of the tea shop, sticking her with the bill.

# 2

I called Lydia as soon as I hit the street.

"How did it go?" she asked.

"She made it clear she'd sleep with me if I took the case."

"Old school. What did you do?"

"I took it anyway. She can't scare me."

"I thought the point was she did scare you."

"Different point."

"What's the case?"

"I'll tell all. Did you take that one you had the meeting on this morning, or are you free for lunch?"

"Amber Shun? I'm going to turn it down. Just waiting for another couple of details. We going someplace fancy?"

"How can you afford fancy if you go around turning down cases?"

"You're buying."

"You should've volunteered this time, you'd have gotten off cheap. We're dining al fresco in City Hall Park. That tearoom filled my fancy quota for the month."

I stopped at a deli for sandwiches and soda, and subwayed downtown. Lydia was waiting for me on a bench by the fountain. "What a relief," I said. "Cloudy sky, crapping pigeons, honking traffic, and you."

"That bad?"

"The place had flowered wallpaper and petit fours. When was the last time you saw a petit four?"

"I don't know if I'd recognize one if it tried to mug me. What are we eating?"

"I'm eating salami. You're eating sardines."

"What if I want salami?"

"Then I'm eating sardines."

I held out both foil-wrapped sandwiches. As we ate—she took the sardines—and watched the fountain splash I laid out the case.

"The mayor's son," she said. "Wow. And we're buying the idea he ran away, no foul play involved?"

"I'm not ready to go that far. Out-and-out kidnapping, no. I guess it's possible he was persuaded, or even coerced. But I do think he took himself out of there. The alarm system had been disarmed and rearmed by someone who knew how to do it."

"He locked up after himself? Conscientious. So what's the plan?"

"We have an appointment with the mayor at one."

"An appointment? Her son is gone, we're supposed to find him, and we have to see her by appointment?"

"Adding weight to my theory," I said, "that she's not really worried."

"Because she knows something, do you think, or she doesn't care?"

"You mean, is she a close-to-the-vest scheming politician, or a negligent parent?"

"Kind of."

I shrugged. "Do you have a preference?" I wadded up our trash.

"No. But if I'd known I was going to see the mayor I'd have dressed up a little."

"You look gorgeous." She wore hunter-green slacks, a white shirt, a short swingy tweed jacket, and brown Oxfords, and she did look gorgeous. "Besides, I knew I was going to that fancy tearoom this morning and I didn't dress up."

She looked over my jeans and bomber jacket. "You wore that to be annoying. I'd rather wait to annoy the client until I know them."

"It's that delicacy of judgment that makes you so admired in the profession." I stood and she did too. "What was the case from this morning, that you're turning down?" I asked.

"Also a teenager, but worse, because dead. Amber Shun, one of those model-minority over-achievers. Straight A's, Drama Club, voice. Found hanged. The medical examiner says suicide. The parents say no way."

"In Chinatown?"

"Chinatown kid but going to a ritzy Upper East Side school on scholarship. Macauley Prep. Chris Chiang sent the parents to me."

Chris Chiang, a high school friend of Lydia's, was a Fifth Precinct detective. "He caught the case?"

"No. She was found uptown, in a park near the school. But it's Chinatown, Jake. You understand that's a racist line?"

"Hey, I didn't use it."

"Just don't. The point is, Bing Lee called Chris."

"And Bing Lee is?"

"Head of the Chinatown Improvement Association. Kind of the unofficial Chinatown mayor, I guess." She nodded through the trees, in the direction of both Chinatown and City Hall. "The Shuns went to him because they felt they were getting the brushoff from the cops. Bing called Chris because Chris is a cop and his mother and Bing are close. Chris comes from Chinatown royalty, you know."

"I didn't even know Chinatown had royalty. Your mother must be the Dowager Queen."

"I don't know what that means but it better be a compliment. Anyway, Chris can't touch the case himself, of course, which Bing may or may not understand, or want to understand. But Chris thought I could do some looking around and that might satisfy Bing and make the parents feel better."

"They give you a reason, the parents?"

"Nothing except she was a good daughter, she'd never leave them like that, she was doing well in school, had friends, had summer plans. Looking back, they say these last couple of weeks she was quieter. Spent a lot of time in her room. They thought she was just studying hard for finals. I said I wouldn't take their money to start with but I'd look into it and if there was anything, we could talk about them hiring me. After they left I called the NYPD detective on it. A guy named Joe Lenz."

"Don't know him."

"A cop you haven't irritated? I'd say he must be new but actually he's close to retirement."

"He told you that?"

"By way of saying he's been around forever and he's seen it all. He can tell the sheep from the goats."

"And the suicides from the homicides."

"That was the implication. He said there's no reason to suspect she didn't do it herself but did I have anything new?"

"And you don't." We headed around the fountain.

"Only brokenhearted parents saying over and over, 'We worked so hard, everything for her, for her future. She'd never do this to us.' I asked him about the autopsy. He said he'd call me, though it seemed to make him tired just thinking about all the extra work that will involve.

Unless there's something seriously funky there, I'll call the parents and tell them sorry. And you know what? I will be sorry."

I threw out the trash and we walked off to find out what another parent didn't know about her child.

City Hall Park, of course, is at the feet of City Hall. We mounted the meant-to-impress steps and showed our IDs to the guard, who very somberly looked at her list, back at our IDs, back at her list, and finally nodded. After passing through the obligatory scanner into the marble lobby we were met by a plainclothes security officer, taken up more grand marble stairs, and, in what I took as a sign of the mayor's hopes and dreams, steered to a second-floor suite called the Governor's Room.

The lemony aroma of furniture polish sharpened the air. A lustrous heavy-legged conference table stood firmly on the thick carpet, with four bottles of water—two on one side and two on the other—waiting on coasters with the New York City seal on them. The security guy who'd brought us up took a position at the door. Lydia and I seated ourselves on chairs that had never been comfortable in all their hundred and fifty years. Coffered ceilings, ornate moldings, heavily-framed portraits, and tall curtained windows did their best to daunt us into insignificance.

Within a minute of our arrival Aubrey breezed through the grand paneled doors. "Bill," she said. "And you're Lydia Chin? Aubrey Hamilton. Thank you for coming."

Lydia stood and shook Aubrey's hand with a friendly smile, as though she knew nothing about her aside from the fact that she was the mayor's top aide. Aubrey gave her back the same smile as though she believed that. Before anyone could say anything else, Carole McCann, Mayor of the City of New York, strode into the room. I gave her points for not keeping us waiting.

I stood, as I hadn't for Aubrey, and Aubrey introduced us. The mayor's no-nonsense handshake matched her expression and her reputation.

Appraising Her Honor, I decided the room's attempt to intimidate was unlikely to succeed.

A tall, dark-eyed, richly chestnut-haired WASP—I wondered if she and Aubrey got their touch-ups done side by side—wearing black wide-legged trousers, a white silk shirt, a long gray jacket, and black-and-white wingtips, New York's first female mayor carried herself like the athlete she was renowned to have been: track, lacrosse, and crew at Harvard and at Columbia Law, with medals to prove it. A member of the hyper-exclusive New York Athletic Club—as useful for high-level networking as for working out—to this day she regularly sculled with an all-female crew out of Columbia's boathouse on Spuyten Duyvil Creek. I imagined her security detail for those workouts earned its keep.

"It's okay, Mike," said the mayor with a smile at the bodyguard who'd come in with her. He got it and went to join his compatriot outside the door, closing it behind him while we all sat, McCann and Aubrey across the table from Lydia and me.

"Thank you for coming. Aubrey says you're good." McCann swept our side of the table with a searchlight look, as though examining us for proof or refutation of that claim. She wore minimal makeup, or maybe color so expertly applied I took it for natural. Small gold earrings matched the chain at her neck. She opened a leather-covered notepad, took a gold pen from the loop in it, and slipped on a pair of half-glasses. Looking at us over them, she asked briskly, "How can I help?"

I opened my own drugstore notebook and took out my Paper Mate. "I was hoping you could tell us about your son."

"Tell you what?"

"Who his friends are, what he likes. . . . Where he's likely to go."

"Aubrey can fill you in on the details. As to where he'd go, I have no idea."

"I doubt that."

Her dark eyes flashed. "Aubrey told me you think I know something or I'd have sounded the alarm sooner. But you're wrong."

I didn't answer. She didn't go on. Through the open window I heard the whine of a truck shifting gears.

Lydia said, "He's done this before."

Carole McCann turned to her. More silence.

"That's why you thought he might come home. Because the other time, he did."

After a few more moments, the mayor said, "Three other times."

I caught a tiny change in Aubrey's face. She hadn't known that, then.

"When?" said Lydia.

The mayor took a pause, then said, "The first time was seven years ago. Just before the divorce. There was a lot of stress in the household."

Oh, really? I thought.

Blandly, Lydia asked, "Where did he go?"

"He was only eight. He didn't get far. We were living on East End Avenue. I was councilmember for District Five." Arguably the wealthiest of the city's fifty-one districts. "He took the tram to Roosevelt Island. The week before, I'd taken the children there, to a rally I spoke at to preserve the hospital ruin. Madison was bored but Mark was enamored of the place. She's a realist; he's always been a romantic." The mayor smiled. "He was planning to stay there, live there, in the ruin, until things calmed down at home. But after the rally they'd locked the gates again. He couldn't get in. And he'd only brought a peanut butter sandwich. He ate it and then came home at supper time when he got hungry."

With a flick of a glance at me, Lydia asked, "Did you punish him?"

"For running away? God, no. Why would I? I feel like doing it myself half the time."

"Have you ever?" I asked.

"Punished Mark? Mark gets punished when he deserves it. That time I felt he didn't. Or did you mean, have I ever run away? A patronizing question." Her look was steady. I'd meant both and I didn't answer. "As you might guess," she said in a sardonic tone, "politics is not a profession that takes well to sabbaticals."

"And the next time?" Lydia intervened. "That Mark ran away?"

McCann turned her attention to Lydia. "He was ten. Both children were staying with Jeffrey in Watermill for the month of July. That was the custody arrangement. I don't know what set Mark off but he took sandwiches—three this time, plus a couple of Cokes and a box of cookies—and rode his bike to an abandoned house the neighborhood children always thought of as haunted."

"The neighborhood children," I said. "Including Mark, but I'm betting not Madison."

"Of course and of course not. Mark loved the idea of ghosts. Madison could never see the point. What use would a ghost be if they were real, except to scare you? Why would you want to believe in that? Mark went to the house, but not only wasn't it haunted, it wasn't really abandoned. The place was tied up in a nasty fight over a will so it hadn't been used for years, but it had a caretaker. He saw Mark's flashlight." She smiled, this time, it seemed to me, with a touch of maternal pride. "Mark gave him one of the sandwiches and a Coke. They ate the cookies, they sat and talked, waiting for the ghosts, and then the caretaker drove Mark back to Jeffrey's."

Lydia asked, "Did Jeffrey punish him?"

"Jeffrey," the mayor said icily, "was out for the evening. Neither he nor the housekeeper had any idea Mark had been gone. Madison told Jeffrey the next day, but he was distracted by work, as always, and brushed it off. No one told me about it until the children came back at the end of the month."

"And the third time?"

McCann sighed. "Two years ago. After school he took Metro North to Storm King. He wanted to see what it was like to live off the land. This time he was better prepared. He had a tent and a sleeping bag."

Aubrey gave me a quick, appraising glance. I was sure she was less interested in how I was taking all this information than in what I thought of her for not knowing it. I kept my eyes on the mayor.

"How long did that last?" Lydia said.

"It rained that night. The tent was new and hadn't been tested. Very like Mark. It turned out it leaked. Local police found him, damp, cold, and at Burger King the next morning. I sent one of my people to pick him up. And before you ask, again, it was Jeffrey's custody week and again, he hadn't noticed Mark was gone. To be fair to Jeffrey, though I don't know why I should, Mark had said he was going home with another boy after school."

"A criminal mastermind," I said. "And Jeffrey—"

"Is not the most attentive of parents," McCann interrupted me. "He is also not the subject of this meeting. Mark was staying with me when he left this time."

I looked at Lydia, didn't look at Aubrey just to annoy her, and went back to the mayor. "All right. Specifically, each of those times, why did he take off?"

McCann nodded, acknowledging my return to base. "The first time, Jeffrey and I had been fighting. In retrospect I can see why the atmosphere in the house might have upset a child. Though Madison was taking it all in stride."

"When you say fighting—"

"Raised voices. Anger. Recriminations and long, frozen silences."

"Nothing physical?"

"My God—!"

"It happens in the best of families."

"*Not* in mine." More definitive words were never spoken.

"Okay, fine. And the times after that?"

She narrowed her eyes. After a moment, with the I'm-the-mayor tone back in her voice, she said, "The times Jeffrey had custody, I don't know what specifically set Mark off, but afterward he said, both times, that he'd needed to get away to think. Which is more or less what he'd said, in eight-year-old words, the first time."

"If that's what he's doing now," I asked, "what's he thinking about?"

"I have no idea."

Lydia, who'd been watching in line-judge silence, now spoke up again. "I'm sorry to have to ask this, but is there any possibility your ex-husband was, or is, behaving inappropriately with your children?"

McCann swung her narrowed eyes to Lydia. "No," she said. "There's not. Jeffrey Guilder is many abhorrent things, but he is not a child molester."

"Though he's defended a couple," I said.

"For God's sake. He's also defended thieves, embezzlers, and corporate raiders. It's what lawyers do. If you told me he was shouting at the children for minor—or imaginary—misdeeds I'd believe it. Or demanding complete silence while he was working, which would have been all the time. Or refusing to buy them pizza and ice cream and making them eat kale salad. He's a health-food nut, mostly because it gives him another way to control people. More likely than any of that, he was probably just ignoring them. Why Madison continues to spend time with him I can't fathom."

"Why did Mark stop?"

"Because he has better sense than his sister."

Neither Lydia nor I said anything.

McCann sighed. "Mark running away to Roosevelt Island was the final straw in the marriage. I told Jeffrey to move out. That caught him by surprise. He told me I was being precipitous. He said that just because an eight-year-old couldn't handle the situation didn't mean adults had to cave. That I should take time to think about what I was doing. I said he should take time to pack a suitcase and I'd have the rest of his things sent."

"And you think he blames Mark for that 'precipitous' end?"

"Mark, running away from the situation, showed more understanding of reality than Jeffrey did trying to stay." The mayor drew a breath. "But yes, I think he does blame Mark. That might well make Jeffrey's home less than welcoming for Mark, even all these years later. And Mark's a sensitive boy." She glanced at her Cartier watch. "I can give you ten more minutes," she said. "Make them count."

Ten minutes, when your son, a sensitive boy, is missing. "Has he been having trouble in school lately? Or with anyone in particular? Is he bullied? Does he have a girlfriend? A boyfriend? Close buddies?"

"I've never heard of a bullying problem at Granite Ridge. The school keeps a sharp eye out for that, because the curriculum is art-focused and these are all creative children, the kind who might be, or might have been, bullied elsewhere. They have mental health services, ethics classes, supervised peer-to-peer suicide watch, that sort of thing. As for Mark's romantic life, I'd be surprised to hear he has one, though if he does, of either gender, more power to him. About his friends I know very little. I assume they're theater program students, or musicians." She answered my questions as though she were ticking off points on a bullet list.

"Musicians?" I asked, just to throw her.

She squint-eyed me as though she knew what I was up to. "Because Granite Ridge is small, they share music, dance, and drama classes with two of the other small art-focused private schools. Each semester they do a play and a musical as joint efforts. Mark had a starring role in the fall musical, and has another in the spring play."

Now I was the one who was thrown. "Wait," I said. "He's an actor? When you said art-focused I pictured him as a painter, a pianist, some solitary thing. I'd have thought Madison was the one who wanted the limelight."

"Not necessarily the limelight, as long as she can have the spotlight. But Mark's painfully shy. He's never been comfortable in his own skin. We sent him for acting lessons when he was small because we were told it would give him confidence and draw him out."

"And did it?"

"No. What he found was that on stage he could be someone else. He could dissolve himself, disappear. He loved it from day one. He's dedicated, almost single-minded. That's what he was doing, what he was 'thinking about,' when he ran away to Storm King. He was preparing for a role."

"Is he good?"

"I suppose. He can do Lear's mad scene with all the histrionics you might want. But as soon as the lights go up it's back to mumbling and averted eyes."

Lydia glanced at me and I knew what she was thinking. I play the piano; it means a lot to me, means so much that I go for a lesson every few weeks with a retired Juilliard prof named Max Bauer. But I won't play for anyone else. Including her. She's asked why, and I haven't been able to explain it. Mark's on-stage/off-stage personality change, though, was feeling familiar.

Okay, that was for later. Right now, "And your daughter?" I asked. "I guess she's also at home on the stage. That stunt during your inauguration—"

"That wasn't acting, though it sure as hell was histrionics, wasn't it?" That came with a dry eyebrow lift; but I felt, as I had earlier, that she was speaking with maternal pride.

That surprised me. "You're saying you enjoyed that press conference? It worked for you?"

"Actually, it did. I didn't see it live, of course. I was," a wry smile, "otherwise engaged. But I watched and re-watched it later. Did you see it?"

Lydia and I both nodded. The mayor smiled. "Impressive, wasn't she? The Timberland boots, the parka, the Ecuadorian knit hat. Fully inhabiting the persona, as fully as Mark might, on stage. The difference is, he would have lived it, while she just performed it. I'm sure she threw that hat into the trash the minute the cameras left. Her speech was cogent, too, I thought, if a little screechy. Her delivery could use work, but that would involve . . . work. But understand, that event got me an immediate flood of sympathy from every parent in New York. It also gave me the opportunity to talk about climate change, which is, in fact, one of my priorities. I've proposed planting fifty thousand new trees over the next four years. Five thousand in each borough's two lowest-income zip codes."

The zip codes where McCann had support but voter turnout was always low. I was impressed. Here was a woman who could make political lemonade out of pits and rind.

"All right. What else can you tell us that might help?"

"I can tell you Mark is a creative young man, and as I said, sensitive, but he is not particularly resourceful. His head's generally in the clouds."

"You're saying he's stoned?"

The mayor pulled back as though I'd dropped a dead fish on the table. "I'm certainly not saying that."

"Really?"

She took a breath, tapped her pen on her notepad. "I assume he smokes pot on occasion. He's not a prude. But the household staff's been briefed on what to look for, and his school's very proactive on that front. No one's reported any signs of an overuse of drugs or alcohol."

The staff's been briefed and no one's reported. Well, then.

"I'm sorry," I said. "But in my experience, when a kid—or an adult—takes off, it's often because they've gotten in too deep with someone. Usually a loan shark, which is unlikely for a fifteen-year-old, or a drug dealer. Someone they owe and can't pay."

The mayor's cheeks blazed crimson. "If this is the direction you're intending to pursue—"

"We're not 'intending' anything," Lydia said. "But you can understand why it would be irresponsible of us not to follow all lines of inquiry?"

"Well, you can drop that one," McCann said, though she seemed mollified. "Now, what else?"

I sent Lydia a quick raised-eyebrow thank you and asked McCann, "What's your relationship with him like?"

"My relationship with Mark? How does that matter?"

"Seriously? He's run away four times, two of them, including this time, from *your* home, and you don't think your relationship has anything to do with it?"

She frowned, and cast a glance at Lydia, who gave her a look I'd seen before. It said, *I know, and I agree, but there's nothing I can do.* It was generally, as in this instance, about me.

McCann sighed, tapping her pen into her hand. "I've adored Mark since the children were babies. I know it's supposed to be wrong to have a favorite, but I doubt if there's ever been a parent who didn't. I would do anything for either of my children, of course, but Madison, though she looks like her father, is very like me. That makes her harder to love." McCann's look dared me to respond with some inane platitude, some polite denial. I couldn't see a reason to.

"Mark's a sweet boy," she resumed, "one who's never been quite sure how the world works. Madison had it all figured out on the day they were born. When Mark was young he was a joy to spend time with. Now, of course, he's fifteen, so having his mother around, except perhaps in the audience, is embarrassing. And having his mother, the mayor, around is worse."

Lydia said, "Why are your children at different schools?"

McCann gave Lydia a measured look. "From their earliest childhood the two of them were at odds. We were told it was sometimes better for twins to be separated. Granite Ridge has quite a good theater program. St. Edward's, where Madison goes, focuses on engaging children who would otherwise tend not to be academically motivated. I'm sorry, but I don't see the point of these questions. We're getting far afield here."

"Just trying to get a picture of your son. Are Mark and Madison close now?"

The mayor looked at her gold pen for a moment before she answered. "Sometimes twins are preternaturally close. People expect that. I did, when my children were born. I've since learned that, at other times, a competitiveness develops early. Almost an antipathy. Especially with fraternal twins. My children are nothing like one another, and no, they are not particularly close."

"So you don't think she'd know where Mark could be?"

"I doubt it. She's told me she doesn't. They have few shared interests, no friends in common. They seem to have reached a truce where they don't bicker anymore—or rather, where Madison no longer baits Mark until he finally explodes—but I don't think they find one another particularly interesting."

"How did that work?" I asked. "Her baiting him?"

"As you probably know, girls develop earlier than boys. So she walked before he did, talked before he did. She was able to ask for what she wanted—or go and take it—while he was still frustrated, unable to express himself. He'd try to get up and follow her when she toddled around and she'd point and laugh when he fell. She'd take his toys. Often she showed no interest in something until he started to play with it. Then she'd demand it, snatch it away, start a fight over it. She used to sneak treats to the dog. She didn't have much use for that dog, but Mark loved him. Madison did it so the dog would like her better."

The mayor fell silent. *And you say this child is very like you*, I found myself thinking.

McCann sat up straighter, as though she'd heard me. "I'm sure my children's innate inclinations—hers to standing out, his to secrecy—were magnified by the nature of their interactions. I doubt very much if she'll be able to help find him."

"We'd still like to speak to her."

"Of course."

"How did your ex-husband react to Mark and Madison's early relationship?" I asked.

She frowned but she answered me. "Jeffrey barely noticed the hostility—or so he said—but whether or not he meant to, he encouraged it. He praised the children's every accomplishment, to reinforce their confidence and their willingness to try new things. I suppose he'd read that in a book someplace. Since Madison's every accomplishment was accompanied by her teasing Mark for not having reached her exalted heights, she took the wrong message and assumed that among the things she was doing well was making fun of Mark."

"And Mark took that message too."

She stared in silent anger. "I tried," she finally said, ice in her voice, "whenever I could, to correct that line of thinking."

I regarded her. "What does your gut tell you?"

"My gut?" She spoke the word as though I'd asked her what her coffee cup told her.

"You must have some idea what's going on. Why Mark left, where he'd go. Even just a feeling."

She stared straight at me. "My *gut* tells me to hire a professional. As I would in any other situation that called for one. A professional," she said, "who promises discretion."

I met her gaze, said nothing.

"And that brings up another thing," the mayor said. "I do *not* want Jeffrey Guilder involved in this."

"Mark's father? His son's missing and you don't think he has a right to know?"

"I'm sure he knows Mark's taken off. Madison will have told him. But that's happened before. I don't want him to know I'm hiring you and I don't want you going to him. Jeffrey doesn't give a tinker's damn about Mark except as a stick to beat me with. The children and I were never anything to Jeffrey but assets he could deploy to aid him in his relentless climb. If he knew I was worried about Mark it would make him drool. He'd put out statements, play the frantic dad, call a press conference to denounce me as an unfit, uncaring monster."

"Jeffrey Guilder on the moral high ground. That would be something to see."

"Please. High dudgeon is one of his most over-used modes. The opposition is pond scum, he'll proclaim from his mountaintop, and whatever Jeffrey's client has done is laughable compared to the depths of evil on the other side. Which evil, by the way, pushed the client into whatever action he felt forced to take. Or it can go the other way. He'll wink-wink nudge-nudge you, and before you know it you're agreeing with your old pal Jeffrey Guilder that the opposition has no sense of humor and Jeffrey's client has done nothing beyond commit a few peccadillos, and really, who among us hasn't?"

"That's the tack he's taking with Oscar Trask's divorce cleanup," Aubrey said. "Plus, the ex is a vampire, has already taken him to the cleaners, what do you want from the poor guy? Like that. Goes down well with male jurors. And women whose husbands don't have millions."

I wasn't sure why we needed to know that now. I had to assume Aubrey just wanted back in the conversation.

"Oscar's one of the most repellent clients Jeffrey's ever had," McCann responded. "Which is saying something. But you've seen Jeffrey do this kind of thing many times."

"I suppose," I said. "I don't follow his career all that closely. Though I'm surprised to hear he's a divorce lawyer now. I thought his specialty was corporate malfeasance."

"His specialty is anything his wealthy clients get up to. But no, not usually divorce. This was a special favor for Oscar. In return, besides his hefty fee, Jeffrey gets to go to ultra-exclusive parties on Oscar's yacht and at his overbuilt houses. With Oscar's A-list investors. To be on the A-list, too. To be one of Them." I could hear the uppercase letter. "Jeffrey doesn't come from money. In the way of a lot of people, he's bedazzled by it. Roosevelt Island, as I've said, was the last straw, but it was Jeffrey's inability to deal with my increasing political success—which he took very personally as a willful refusal on my part to be the wife he needed among the people he wanted to impress, to be the asset he could deploy—that destroyed our marriage."

"Word on the street at the time," I said, "was that you found his repellent clients a drag on your chances of increasing political success."

McCann's jaw tightened. "'Word on the street.' Another term for 'smear campaign.' A man whose marriage broke up as he climbed the political ladder wouldn't raise any eyebrows. But I find myself repeatedly called on to explain why I could no longer live with Jeffrey."

"I wasn't asking."

"No, you were accusing. Either that, or you were just pushing my buttons to see what would happen." She eyed me. "That's it, isn't it?"

She turned to Aubrey with a look I couldn't read, and then back to me. "You remind me of Herb Straley. You know him? President of the NYPD Detectives' Endowment Association. He does that, too. A push here, a poke there. We're in salary negotiations now, the City and the Detectives."

"I heard that song this morning. The whole city budget depends on the outcome of these negotiations, et cetera, et cetera, and so forth." I winked at Aubrey. She flushed, bit her lower lip.

The mayor threw a quick glance at Aubrey, then slapped her palms on the table. "You know what the outcome's going to be? I'm going to win. Each of these unions holds its members' interests first and foremost. As they should. I hold the City's. As *I* should. I'm going to maneuver them into whatever corner I have to, to make sure the City comes out on top. Look for their vulnerable points, exploit their weaknesses. They'll—Herb Straley will—be doing the same across the table. This table, sitting right there where you are. It's how the game is played." She leaned back again, moved her deliberate gaze from me to Lydia. "I don't give a good goddamn what you think of me. Keep this quiet, keep my ex-husband out of it, and find my son."

"We'll try," I said.

She gave me a stare so hard you could've walked across it. I waited for her to quote Yoda but after a moment she glanced at her watch again and turned to Aubrey.

"I have to get to the groundbreaking in High Bridge. Is the car ready?" Aubrey checked her phone and nodded. "Waiting for you."

Carole McCann waved a hand at me and Lydia. "Give them whatever they need." Folding her notepad, on which not a line had been written, she stood, said, "I expect to hear from you soon," and marched across the carpet to the door. She turned around. "As it happens, I like Herb Straley. Not that it matters. And Jeffrey Guilder was a prosecutor when I married him."

The Mayor of New York turned again and strode from the room.

# 3

Your boss doesn't like me," I said to Aubrey, as I watched Her Honor's wake tow the security people down the hall.

"Did you give her a reason to?"

"It wasn't my top priority."

"You know, I could almost believe you were going out of your way to piss her off just to make me look bad."

"If you were important enough to me, I would have." I turned back to her. "But I do know Herb Straley."

"What?"

"Just full disclosure. Before he was a desk jockey he was an actual detective. They called him Bulldog then, too. I ran across him once or twice."

"Why didn't you say something? Could be a conflict of interest."

"You want to hire somebody else, be my guest. Though most PIs in New York are former cops. It might be hard to find someone who doesn't know him."

She smiled. "You sound like you want to keep the job."

"I like to finish what I start. Not walk away from it. Or cheat on it."

"Ooh, ouch. Well, I'm going to tell Carole, just so she knows. If she wants anything changed I'll tell you."

"Whatever you say. Meanwhile, we'll need access to the townhouse. Photos of Mark. And I have a list of names I want contact info for. Plus, I want the numbers for the kids you called yesterday."

"I hope that list of names doesn't include Jeffrey."

"We have some places to start before we get to him. But if we need to talk to him, we will. Or you can fire us. We're looking for a missing kid. It's not our job to protect the mayor's public image."

"What if I said it was?"

"We'd quit."

Aubrey compressed her lips. "I don't think you have any idea how hard it is for a woman in politics." She looked to Lydia for some female solidarity. Lydia just smiled.

"According to you I have no idea about women at all," I said. "But don't worry, I'm not holding McCann to a higher standard than I do any other politician. In fact, my standards for politicians are pretty low and not a lot of people come up to them anyway." I tore out the page from my notebook and handed it to Aubrey. "We'll wait."

It took Aubrey a few minutes of rapid-fire thumb-dancing to send the info from her phone to Lydia's and mine. While she was doing that Lydia asked me, "So the ex. Is he really that awful?"

"You don't follow Real Sleazes of New York?"

"Reality TV?"

"Reality. Jeffrey Guilder's an audience favorite. Always ready with a quote, a sound bite, a smackdown. Like the mayor said, when you read in the paper about yacht races and billionaires' birthday parties, Guilder's at them. You read about wealthy White guys in trouble, Guilder's their lawyer."

"Oscar Trask," Lydia said. "That guy the mayor mentioned. I saw him on TV the other night, leaving the court house. That handsome man with him, that was Guilder?"

"If you can call a man with bright blue eyes, silver hair, and a permanent tan handsome."

It appeared she could, because she went on, "Why were they in court?"

Aubrey spoke without looking up. "Just fallout from Trask's divorce. Jeffrey wasn't his lawyer then but some things are still in litigation. And Jeffrey's not just the Music Man's lawyer. He's his pal. His friend. His butt hole buddy." She flicked a smile at me. "See? I can be coarse too."

"I never doubted it. Though for someone who's glued to the mayor's side you know a lot about her ex. And his pals."

"Trask used to be my client. Oh, look, something you didn't know."

"Yours is another career I don't follow all that closely. You met Trask through Guilder?"

"Totally the other way around." She kept scrolling through her phone and texting me numbers. "My PR firm handled Trask for a couple of years. All those press releases when some kid won a concerto competition, those photos of Trask with a bus he'd bought for some youth orchestra, where do you think they came from? Sometimes I even had to suggest the bus."

"I'm waiting for the punchline."

Bree sent a look, not to me, but to Lydia. "About three years ago a crisis developed. Trask's soon-to-be ex, probably to improve her bargaining position, was hinting she had dirt to spill. All of Trask's investors in Greenwood Holdings are A-listers and though he kept telling me the dirt wasn't all that dirty, he didn't want them clutching their pearls and fleeing in horror. He needed her and her rumors quashed. His lawyers took care of her with a big settlement and an NDA and I took care of Trask with a spit-shine."

"How?" asked Lydia. I wondered whether she was actually interested in the machinery of a PR firm, or really in just how low I'd stoop in a girlfriend.

Aubrey looked up, a little surprised, but perfectly willing to recount her victory. "Trask has one of those giant old mansions in Riverdale. He's a BFD up there, head of the Community Council, on every Board, acts like he's Mayor of the Fancy Bronx. Which is the only part of the Bronx he's ever seen, I'm sure. So I organized a charity event for him to sponsor. Black tie gala at Oscar's place, everyone who's anyone, be there or be no one, that kind of thing. Limited press passes, which of course makes the press beat down the doors. Ticket proceeds to pay for concerts in the city parks, given by the wunderkinds from his summer camp over in Greenwood Lake. The one percent brings music to the masses, doncha know. It wasn't anything new and different, just the old-fashioned culture wash. Wouldn't have been life-changing for anyone, especially me, except Carole came. Because everyone who was anyone, et cet. She wouldn't come within half a mile of Oscar now, because of Jeffrey, but then was different. She and I left the party to get some air on the terrace at the same time and got to talking. Turned out she was looking for staff for her run for mayor and I was about to roll up the PR firm and see what was next. We were mutually impressed. And here we are."

"So the Music Man brought you together," I said.

"Lovely, eh? And Jeffrey was also at the party. He rubbed up against Trask and purred, and that was the end of the other lawyers and the start of a beautiful friendship."

"Is that ethical, stealing another lawyer's client?" Lydia asked.

"Hello? This is Jeffrey Guilder we're talking about. It was also the end of Trask's contributions to Carole's campaign. Carole takes that very personally."

Lydia looked at me.

I shrugged. "I would, too."

"What about that nickname?" Lydia asked Aubrey. "Was it your idea to call Trask the Music Man?"

"God, no. You think I'd come up with something so cheesy? But people were already using it so I leaned into it."

"And why were they using it? Why is he called that?" Lydia asked.

"That's what he does with all that money," I told Lydia. "I mean, after the yacht and the houses. That summer camp for young prodigies, new stage curtains at the State Theater, new rehearsal space for the Met Opera. Gives scholarships, underwrites recitals. His name's plastered all over New York's classical music world. You never noticed that?"

"You never took me to the opera."

"Oh, really?" Aubrey said. "He used to take me." She slipped her phone into her Kate Spade bag. "There, I think I sent you everything."

"Including the friends' numbers?" I asked.

"Of course."

"Could your boss do that?"

"Do what?"

"Send me the numbers of her kids' friends."

"She doesn't need to. That's what she has me for."

"That's not the question. Could she? Does she have their numbers? Does she know their names?"

"Got it. You hate politicians. If I say no, she couldn't, are you going to quit the case?"

"I was just wondering. Now let's get out of here before Lydia and I get appointed to some damn committee."

Bree accompanied us through security and out of City Hall. Once at the top of the grand staircase she asked, "Where are you going first?"

"That would be telling. I'll call when we know something."

We left her gazing after us.

The first thing I did was try Mark's cell phone. I got his voicemail, identified myself, told him his mother was worried about him and I just wanted to make sure he was okay. I asked him to call. I was pretty sure he wouldn't. Then I called his shrink. I've never met a shrink who actually answered the phone; they call you back. Mark's was no different. I left a message.

Lydia waited until I was through with all that and we'd reached the bottom of the steps. Stopping to face me, she said, "Wow. If I didn't know better I'd think you were really a jerk."

"But since you do know better?"

"I know you're really a jerk. I mean, Aubrey I get. Your ex, plus she seems pretty cynical."

"Cynical bitch, I think you mean." I grinned. "You sure seemed interested in her working past."

"Don't think it's because she's your ex," Lydia huffed. "I just wanted to know how a PR firm cleans up someone's image, is all."

"Uh-huh."

"Stop smirking. Why did you guys break up?"

"You've met her and you ask that?"

"Well, then, how about this: Why did you start dating in the first place?"

"I hadn't met you yet."

"You're impossible. Tell me what you have against the mayor."

"She's a politician."

"You've worked for politicians before."

"Low-level. I didn't like them either."

"What about my cousin in Mississippi? He was running for governor. You liked him."

"He's related to you. And he lost."

"So you only dislike unrelated high-level politicians who win?"

"Not only, just most."

She didn't answer.

"Come on," I said. "For someone like McCann it's all about ambition. You're never doing the job you have, you're calculating your best route to the next one. When she was on the City Council she got a new park for her district."

"Isn't that what she's supposed to do? Serve her constituents?"

"That district already has a high ratio of parks to people. And a high ratio of constituents with country homes. They didn't need a new park but oddly, they got one, on a site where it protects their river views. Meanwhile uptown, where the parks actually get used, the benches are busted and the hoops have no nets. But her constituents lobbied for her to become City Council president and funded her mayoral run, because they could see she'd take care of them. And she will, because she'll want a second term. Or to run for governor, or senator. Or president."

"I see," Lydia said. "Also, she doesn't seem concerned about her missing son."

"Oh, crap. Are you going to tell me I have no idea how hard it is for a woman in politics?"

"No. I'm telling you it bothers you that Mayor McCann doesn't seem concerned about her missing son."

"It doesn't bother you?"

"Of course it does. What were you thinking about in there?"

"Thinking about?"

"When you looked mad enough to punch the mayor in the nose."

"When was that?"

She just kept her gaze on me, silently.

"My father."

"And your mother?"

I didn't answer that.

"And Gary," she said. That wasn't a question, and it was true. I didn't have much family, just my sister, her husband, their kids, and it had been years since we'd spoken. My nephew Gary, at fifteen, like the mayor's son, had run away from home. He'd been trying to save some lives. I'd gone after him. Things had ended well for some people, badly for others. And I'd disappeared for a while. When I was ready to come back into Lydia's life I'd been surprised she let me.

A nod, a quick touch of her hand on mine, and complete change in tone. "Where are we going first?"

On the subway on the way uptown Lydia brought up Mark's Instagram and TikTok on her phone. Both were plain vanilla: Mark with his mother, with some friends playing frisbee, Mark at a rehearsal, pictures of food, beach sunsets. "Yawn," said Lydia. "Though he is the mayor's son. He might be trying not to post anything that would embarrass her."

"That doesn't sound like any fifteen-year-old I ever met. Or was."

"Another thing," she said. "Are we really thinking he owes a drug dealer? Or, he *is* a drug dealer?"

"No," I said. "If he only had a couple hundred dollars then he's not selling, and if he had a couple hundred dollars and owed someone he was afraid enough of to run away from he'd have forked it over, at least as a down payment."

"He could've had a lot more sitting around that his mother didn't know about."

"Then why bother with the couple hundred from the bank account, and why run away?"

"All right," she said. "I'm semi-convinced."

"Semi-thank the lord."

"And another thing."

"Uh-oh."

"Herb Straley. The Detectives' Association head? You said you ran across him. Across him, or afoul of him?"

"Can I say, it wasn't my fault?"

"You can say whatever you want. I just want to know how much trouble I'm getting into."

"It was a long time ago. He probably doesn't even remember. I was really just dropping names."

She glanced over at me. "If your idea of how to impress Aubrey is to drop the names of people who don't like you, I can begin to see why you guys broke up."

"No," I said. "I was trying to impress you."

We emerged ten minutes later on the Upper East Side and made it about half a block before my phone rang. "Mark's shrink," I told Lydia. I stepped up against a building to get out of the way.

"Thanks for calling back, Dr. Bernstein," I said. "I called about Mark McCann."

"Yes, your message said. Is Mark all right?" Her voice was warm and, in my head, I saw her office: carpet, upholstered chairs, plants, sunlight.

"I don't know," I said. "He's left home."

"Left home?"

"Two nights ago. I'm a private investigator. His mother hired me to find him."

"Ah." A pause. I could feel her recalculating. "If you're asking me if I know where he is, no, I don't. If you're asking anything else, I'm sorry but I can't discuss a patient."

"I understand that. But a fifteen-year-old is missing."

"Are you sure he left home, and not that something happened to him?"

*Something happened.* The world's worst euphemism. "It looks that way. His sister says he talked about running away. Going someplace to think. Did he say anything to you?"

"Of course not. I'd have alerted the parents, because that would have represented an immediate danger." She paused. "I can tell you, within privacy guidelines, that he's done that before, and has always come home."

"Yes, I know."

"And," she added, "I can also tell you that it surprises me to hear he'd spoken about something that personal to his sister."

Dr. Bernstein wasn't much more help, and she wasn't much help to begin with. I hung up and said to Lydia, "See, I never saw the point of a shrink."

Lydia just rolled her eyes.

Although in New York the words "townhouse" and "brownstone" tend to be interchangeable, the divorce consolation prize on 67th Street, occupied by the mayor's half of the fractured McCann-Guilder family, was faced with actual brownstone. Developed in the late 1880s for rich people scrambling up-island ahead of the other kind of people, who were flooding daily out of ships' steerage decks and into downtown, some of these tree-shaded blocks had lost their air of exclusive toniness over the decades. Others had not. This one, with its curtained windows resting serenely beside front doors painted in serious colors—black, dark blue, forest green—radiated Gilded Age into the spring afternoon so strongly it might have been a perfume.

"Nice place," Lydia said as we contemplated the house from under a ginkgo tree across the street.

"I'll buy you one when my ship comes in."

"Your ship sank."

We jaywalked under the squinting eyes of a buzz-cut Black man in a gray suit. He sat in a NYPD security booth erected in what would otherwise be a parking spot in front of the mayor's house. When we approached he stepped outside the booth. "Help you?"

"Bill Smith and Lydia Chin." We showed him our IDs. There was absolutely no question that Aubrey had told the mayor's residence security detail to expect us, but the guy still acted as though we were the most highly suspect duo to come down the street since his shift had started. Maybe we were. It was a quiet block.

He handed our IDs back and spoke into the transceiver on his shoulder. It answered. While we waited I said, "You weren't on duty the night before last, were you?"

"No, I'm day. Why?"

I was saved from answering when the front door opened. In the doorway stood a White guy who, skin color aside, could have been the twin of the outside guy, down to the square shoulders, gray suit, and military haircut. Maybe they assigned them in pairs, like bookends, and the shift change would bring two tall skinny ones.

Behind Inside Guy stood a thin, middle-aged Black woman in a severe gray dress. "Thank you, Roger," she said. Roger Inside Guy stepped back as she stepped forward. "I'm Imani Overbey. I manage the household. Ms. Hamilton told me to expect you."

We introduced ourselves and shook her hand. Her slenderness was misleading; Imani Overbey had a powerful grip. She led us into a sitting room with brusque, angular furniture in pale blues and grays. Abstract paintings in the same palette hung on the walls.

Lydia and I sat side by side on a sharp sofa and Imani Overbey sat too, on the edge of a gaunt chair, her back so straight it made me wonder if, in the way dog owners come to resemble their dogs, a household manager might come to resemble the house.

"Please tell me how I can help you." Overbey's manner was business-like, no hint of a smile.

"So far," I said, "we've been told Mark 'ran away.'" I put verbal quotes on the phrase. "Do you have any reason to believe otherwise?"

"An abduction?" Overbey shook her head. "This would be a difficult house to break into but a simple one to leave. If he were taken against his will why would no one have heard anything? He only had to yell and the guard would have been alerted. And I'm sure they've told you the security system was rearmed. That seems like something Mark would do."

"In what way?"

She considered. "For exactly this reason. So we'd know he'd gone off by choice. Also, more practically, because if he hadn't rearmed it and closed the window again, after ten seconds the main panel would have chimed. It's in the front, where the guard stays."

"So he bought time."

"But don't the backyards here just butt up against the ones behind, though?" Lydia said, "There aren't any alleys. Why wasn't he trapped, if he went that way?"

"They do," Overbey said, "but there are occasional ways through. One house down, on the block behind, there's a narrow passageway between two buildings. I'll show you. The sidewalk gate has a panic bar on the inside."

"Mark would've known this?" I asked.

"He and Madison used to play with the children there when they were young."

"Maybe those kids have an idea where he might have gone."

"That family moved to France. Years ago."

I wondered if Mark had been sad when they left. "All right. Assuming he did run away, do you have any idea why?"

"No."

"How about where he might have gone?"

She shook her head.

"Friends, places he likes?"

"I'm the household manager," Overbey said firmly. "I have an office. I work nine to five and I don't live in, though I have a separate apartment on the grounds of the Easthampton house for the times the mayor's in residence there. I'm not a family member and I'm not a nanny."

"I see," I said, and I did.

At our request Imani Overbey showed us around the house. The ground floor was for formal entertaining: the sitting room we'd sat in, another larger living room that opened to the garden, a dining room. Everywhere, pale colors and pointed furniture. We saw the rear alarm panel and its proximity to the window Mark was presumed to have left from. "We're having a keyed lock installed here," Overbey said. I caught a look on her face that spoke of barn doors and horses. "And that garden, diagonally there? That's the house with the passageway."

"Where's the kitchen?" Lydia wanted to know.

"Below stairs."

Of course it was.

"And your office?"

"There also. Shall we go down?"

"Let's see the rest of the house first," I said.

On the second floor each family member had a bedroom. The third floor held the mayor's home office and an entertainment center, though I would've bet that the twins, being fifteen, spent most of their time behind their separate closed doors with Beats by Dre over their ears.

The first interruption in the cool, pale color scheme was Madison's room, where everything was deep pinks, neon greens, and airless. Blackout shades blocked the light from the windows as though the room's inhabitant worked the graveyard shift. A pink-and-black fuzzy leopard throw covered the bed and posters of rappers and rock stars, male and female, hung on the intense pink walls. The room was neat, but in the way of a hotel room, a place tidied up by someone who didn't live in it.

Apparently the hotel room analogy didn't stop there. "Was Madison here the night Mark disappeared?" I asked.

"No. The last time she spent the night here was the day before that. Madison spends most of her time at her father's house."

"Is that where she is now?"

"I don't keep the children's schedules." Overbey bristled, then relented. "At this hour she'll just be leaving school. She might come by here, but tonight I believe she's planning to be at her father's. Mr. Crewe will know."

"The chef?"

"He tries to keep track, so he can plan meals."

"Both the mayor and Aubrey say it's impossible that Mark went to his father's," I said.

"They're correct." Overbey gave a single, curt nod. "Those two do not get along. If Mark's run away to find a new, better life he will not have gone to his father."

"Is that why he ran away?"

"Is there another reason boys run away?"

"We're told Mark goes away to think."

"That may be," she said. "And why would he need to go away to do that, I wonder?"

I wondered too. "All right. But can you think of a reason he chose now, and not last week or next week?"

"No."

We left Madison's room and walked to a door down the hall. "This is Mark's room," said Overbey. A sign on the door read NO THANK YOU, but I supposed that wasn't relevant now.

"Oh God," Lydia muttered as Overbey let us in.

Having once been a fifteen-year-old boy myself, I didn't quite share Lydia's dismay, but I had to admit Mark's room was plumbing the depths of teenage housekeeping standards. Where most of the house was pale cools and Madison's room saturated hots, Mark's room was just dark. Midnight blue walls surrounded black furniture on a patterned midnight-and-navy rug, though it was hard to see any of this through the rubble of clothes and books. A computer monitor crouched on a desk amid papers and dirty cups and plates. Simu Liu as Shang-chi hung on one wall, Daniel Day Lewis young, in *Last of the Mohicans*, and older, in *Lincoln*, on another. Dark blue sheets swirled like a frozen whirlpool on the unmade bed. Here, as in Madison's room, the shades were down. Here, unlike in Madison's room, the air was a semi-solid wall of old coffee and older socks.

"Let me guess," I said. "He doesn't let the housekeeper in here."

"Of course he doesn't! You've seen the rest of the house. Mrs. Reyes would never leave a room like this."

In other words, don't diss my staff.

"We'll need to look around," I said.

"I thought you would. That's why nothing's been touched."

"We might be awhile."

"Understood." She made no move to leave.

I shrugged and turned to Lydia, to find her wearing nitrile gloves and holding out another pair. "Self-defense," she said.

I snapped them on, raised the shades, and we began the excavation. The first thing I unearthed, in the top desk drawer, was Mark's passport.

"I guess he's not planning on skipping the country," Lydia said.

"I wonder how much planning went into any of this."

Fifteen minutes later we'd found not much else, besides the desktop computer we couldn't get into and a stack of porn magazines that made Lydia blush.

"Gay or straight?" I asked her.

"Seriously?"

"It might help us find him if we know."

"Straight. Do all fifteen-year-olds—?"

"Not all," I said. "Certainly never your brothers."

She whacked me with a magazine.

"Stop that," Imani Overbey snapped. "Those magazines may be distasteful but they're Mark's things. I'd ask you to respect that."

"I'm sorry," Lydia said.

Before I could apologize also, a new voice interrupted.

"Hey! Who are you people? What are you doing in my brother's room? Mrs. Overbey, what's going on here?"

"It's all right, Madison," Overbey replied, her calm tones rimed with frost. "These are private detectives hired by your mother to find your brother."

"I'm sorry, what the fuck? I thought this was supposed to be a big fucking secret." A walking anime figure, all long limbs, shaggy ice-blond hair, and thick black shoes, stepped into the room.

"That's why it's us," I said. "And not the police."

"My God, such bullshit. Carole actually hired you to find that twerp? Like she cares. Anyway, he'll come back. He always does. He goes away to 'think' and then he comes back. Such a good boy, my brother."

If I hadn't known who she was, I'd never have taken this girl for Mark McCann's twin sister. Or, in fact, for fifteen. The badge on her blazer read St. Edward the Confessor Academy, the exclusive private school where Madison Guilder was a sophomore; but the height to which her green skirt was hiked and the depth to which her white blouse was open made the outfit seem more costume than uniform.

Scanning the room, she gave Lydia one glance and dismissed her. She turned to me and said, "Let's see your license."

"What?"

"Isn't that what I'm supposed to say? Otherwise how do I know you're not some douchebag reporters or something? You probably bribed Mrs. Overbey to let you in."

"Madison!" snapped Overbey. I got the feeling she said that a lot, in that same tone, to the same lack of effect.

"Oh, my goodness, I'm sorry, Mrs. Overbey." Madison put a hand to her mouth. "I don't know how that slipped out. Of course you would never. Now come on, big man. Show it to me."

"In New York State," I said, "a PI license is something for your wall, not your wallet. But here. My license number's on my business card. You can look me up."

She did; and down, too, as though she were trying to decide between two ice cream flavors and I was both. She took my card, flicked it with her thumb and laughed. "Bill Smith? Fuck, is that really the best you can do?"

"It was the best my parents could do."

"So lameness runs in your family."

"Where's your brother, Madison?"

She shrugged. "Fuck if I know. Or care."

"You don't have any suggestions?"

"I do," she smiled, "but they have nothing to do with finding Mark."

"Right now," I said, "finding Mark is all I'm interested in."

She laughed again. "Like I said, lame. Okay, good luck with that. I have things to do. Oscar's taking me to the opera."

She'd clearly dropped the name for a reason, so I bit. "Oscar Trask?"

"Oh, look at that, you've heard of him! That's because he's Daddy's star client, right?" She gave me some side-eye. "Though you're probably the kind of guy who believes all the bullshit trash his ex talks about him."

I gave Overbey a second to say "Madison!" but she stayed silent.

"The bullshit trash, you mean about the affairs and the emotional abuse?"

"Unhinged bitch. Emotional abuse. What even is that? If it was so bad why didn't she just leave him? Such total crap. Well, wait till Daddy gets through with her. But why am I even talking to you about Oscar? He's way out of your league, big fella."

With that she spun, sashayed down the hall to her own room, and shut the door behind her.

# 4

"L ike mother, like daughter," I said.

"What do you mean by that?" We'd all been watching Madison's exit; now Imani Overbey turned sharply back to me.

"Mayor McCann walked out on us, too."

Overbey allowed herself a small, brittle smile. "The comparison wouldn't please her."

"The mayor?"

"Madison."

"Not crazy about her mother?"

"She's her father's daughter."

"The mayor told us she enjoys Madison."

"That may well be true." Overbey didn't go on.

"Has she ever run away?" I asked.

"Madison?" Overbey turned her head to look down the hall again, this time at Madison's closed door. "Running away isn't the only way to leave."

Mark's room yielded nothing else. Lydia, to Overbey's obvious discomfort but without her objection, tried a few more times to get into Mark's computer.

"He's fifteen," she said finally, as though that were all the explanation needed for her failure. It probably was.

"I want to send Linus," I said. To Overbey: "We have an expert."

"Ms. McCann—"

"I'll clear it with McCann. Lydia, go ahead and give Linus a call. Then I want to take another run at Madison."

We'd used the services of Lydia's cousin Linus Wong before. He and his girlfriend-partner Trella D'Angelo ran a computer firm, Wong Security, out of his parents' garage in Queens. Their slogan: "Saving People Like You From People Like Us."

While Lydia called him, I called Aubrey.

"Found something already?"

"Your faith is touching. Mark's computer is here but we can't get into it. I want to send an expert."

"Who?" Straight business. Aubrey in professional mode. I realized I'd never really seen that.

"Linus Wong. From Wong Security. In Flushing."

"I'll need to check them out."

"Of course you will."

"Are they licensed?"

"To do what?"

"Whatever those people do."

Lydia, on her phone, gave me a thumbs-up.

"They're available," I told Aubrey. "Let me know when they're approved."

"If."

"When."

As we were leaving Mark's room Lydia took a phone call. "Um-hm. Okay. Thanks," was all I heard. She lowered the phone and told me quietly, "Joe Lenz. The autopsy on that girl, Amber Shun? Not complete yet, but so far no signs of a struggle, nothing to say it wasn't suicide." She put the phone away and said, "I'll call the parents later." That call wouldn't be fun.

Overbey led us to the other end of the hall where she knocked on Madison's door. It took two sets of knocks, the second much louder than the first, before the door was yanked open. A female rapper blasted from the nuclear-pink headphones clamped over Madison's ears. She pulled the headphones down and said, "Oh, God," drawing the words out as though she'd just been sentenced to stand on line at the DMV. "Back so soon? What do you want?"

"We want you to tell us about your brother," I said. "Anything you say might help."

"Or be taken down and used against me. My brother is a dipshit who thinks he's going to be the next Channing Tatum. Jerko."

From what little I'd seen, I'd have argued Mark's ambitions were more lofty, but I just said, "You don't agree?"

She shrugged. "Whatever. I have zero interest. Are you two sleeping together?"

That got a "Madison!" from Overbey.

"Oh, come on," said Madison. "Isn't it obvious? Though," she said to Lydia, "I think he's a little bit big for you."

"Most guys are," Lydia said with a smile. "I manage."

Madison laughed. "I bet you do. Okay, go ahead and grill me, if you want to waste your time." She flung the headphones onto the bed and stood before us, fingers primly laced and eyes wide in expectant innocence.

"Where's Mark?" I said.

"Whoa, hot stuff. You never heard of subtlety? Looking for clues, asking leading questions? What he likes, who his friends are, shit like that?"

"Okay," I said. "Who are his friends?"

"I have no fucking idea. Or what he likes, either, besides being a big giant hambone." She made huge eyes and wiggled her fingers at me. "He's lucky Carole built that room downstairs. My God, that fucking speech from *Angels in America*! You know he auditioned late, right? And he got that role anyhow? I mean, who the hell does he think he is, my punk-ass brother? If I'd heard him yelling that speech one more time I swear I'd've killed him."

"Did you?"

"Did I what? *Kill him?* Jesus Christ on a porno shoot, is that your interrogation technique?" She turned to Lydia. "Level up, sweetie. I don't even know you and I can tell you deserve better than this asshole."

"You might be right." Lydia looked over Madison's shoulder into the room. I followed her eyes. Evening clothes puddled the floor; lying flat on the bed was the winner, a burgundy floor-length gown, velvet with satin trim. "Sweet outfit. That what you're wearing tonight?"

"You need to see the shoes," Madison said. "Killer Jimmy Choos. Opera premiere."

"John Musto," I said, "*Penelope.*"

Madison's lips made an O. "It speaks! It knows opera! It shocks the civilized world!"

Lydia laughed.

"Your dad going too?" I asked.

A shadow skimmed across Madison's face, almost too fast to see. "Daddy hates opera. And anyway, he has work to do, like always. His loss. Oscar has a box. All kinds of people come sit with us. Oscar's clients, he invites them. You'd know their names but I'm not supposed to tell." She gave me a look of pity. "Oscar doesn't take just anybody to be his client, you know. Even if you're really rich. He has to decide if you're worth the effort."

"Oh, no. And I had my hopes up."

She rolled her eyes. "Too bad. If he takes you on he makes you lots of money. He's always right, too, you can tell because no one ever changes their mind and moves their money somewhere else. It's awesome." Her tone was smug, almost proprietary.

"Uh-huh," I said. "I'm sure."

"What the fuck, you don't believe me? Okay, I'll tell one. That detectives' union guy, that Carole's negotiating with? The Bulldog? He's Oscar's client. I sat with him last week. God, he's a riot! Maybe he'll come tonight. I could use a good laugh." She smirked at me, then said, "Another good laugh."

"Your mother likes him, too," I said.

"Oh, yeah, I bet she does. Who told you that?"

"She did."

"No shit. Well, if she likes him so much, maybe she should come to the opera. Oscar would invite her if I asked him to, even though Daddy wouldn't like it. Then she and Herb could do some off-the-record shit like they do at Camp David. But no-o-o, not Carole. Because she has a big old stick up her ass!" Madison winked at Overbey, who stood tight-lipped.

Lydia said, "Sounds to me like she's missing out. I'd go if I were her. I wonder if she has Jimmy Choos?" She gave Madison a sarcastic grin and got the same one in return. "But seriously, Madison," Lydia said. "About Mark. You said you don't know his friends. Does he have a girlfriend?"

"A girlfriend? As if. Who would date that loser?"

"Come on. Are you telling us you know as little about your brother as your mother does?"

"Carole doesn't know shit." Madison glanced away, at the dress on the bed. "About either of us."

"But you do. You said Mark had been talking about running away again, for a while now."

She whipped her gaze back to Lydia. "I said that? To who?"

"Whom," I said.

"Oh, Jesus Christ, what the fuck is your problem?"

"And the answer is, to your mother," I said, "but we heard it from Aubrey Hamilton."

"*That* ass-kissing airhead? What the hell does she know?"

"Bill used to date her," Lydia said. "He took her to the opera."

Madison's mouth fell open. "Are. You. Fucking. Kidding. Me." She looked me up and down some more. To Lydia, she said, "Seriously, sweetie—"

Lydia shrugged. "He's useful sometimes."

"I can't see how."

"But not always." Lydia turned to me. "Hey, why don't you go check out stuff downstairs? Talk to the chef? Things like that?"

"I don't—"

"I do." She turned her back on me, spoke to Madison. "Listen, I have a couple more things I need to ask you about. And I want to see the shoes. Silver, I bet."

Madison gave Lydia an approving look.

"Can I come in?" Lydia asked. "And can you put the music through a speaker instead of the headphones? I liked her last album better but this one's good, too."

Madison grinned like a wolf. "Then let's fucking play the last one." She moved aside for Lydia, threw me a sneer, and stepped inside. The door slammed shut.

"Well," I said to Overbey, as the walls began to throb. "Shall we go downstairs?"

Our steps coming down the stairs rousted a plainclothes cop who'd been manspreading on the living-room sofa, thumbing his phone. He dropped it back in his jacket pocket and came to his feet.

"Mr. Ahlgren," said Overbey.

"Mrs. Overbey." The guy nodded and looked me over. I did the same to him. No standard-issue suit for Mr. Ahlgren. Navy blazer, gray slacks. White shirt with French cuffs, silver cufflinks. Yellow tie. Shiny black wingtips.

"Bill Smith," I said, sticking out my hand. He shook it as though I'd dared him to.

"You need me, Mrs. Overbey?" Ahlgren said. To do what, protect her from me?

"No, everything's fine. Mr. Smith's a home security consultant," she said smoothly. "I'm showing him around the premises. Detective Ahlgren," she turned to me, "is Madison's weekday security detail."

Short blond hair, wide shoulders, big hands—everything about Ahlgren shouted High School Football Hero. That would have been about ten years ago, and I'd bet he'd headed straight to the NYPD the day after graduation. On second thought, no; he probably treated himself to a wild summer first. Lifeguard duty on a beach full of hot babes. But after that. And here, a decade later, he'd become That Guy, the one who knows how to game the system. The NYPD has lots of Those Guys. They take all the extra training courses, all the exams, get off the street early. Land themselves cushy gigs. Babysitting Madison had to be pretty soft duty, and came with overtime.

"Well, if you need me, I'm here. Nothing to do until the princess comes down." As we turned to round the staircase to the basement door he said, "Hey. Is it true the brother's missing?"

Since I was just a home security consultant, I didn't say anything. Overbey raised her eyebrows. "Is that what Madison told you?"

Ahlgren shrugged. "She says all kinds of things. I just can't imagine Danny Rodriguez losing track of him, is all. But," he added slyly, "here you are with a home security consultant."

"I'm expecting the plumber later," Overbey said. "Will you take that to mean Mark's in the bath?" She spun on her heel and stalked away.

I caught Ahlgren's eye and we traded whoa-don't-mess-with-her looks. Then I followed Overbey to the basement door.

"You shot him down," I said.

"Mr. Ahlgren can be impertinent." She paused with her hand on the knob. "Upstairs. You and your partner. Was that your good cop/bad cop routine?"

"We have many variations. Though I have to admit we often need to work harder at it than that."

"You," she looked me over, much as Madison had done, "could have worked until you were blue in the face and you'd have gotten nothing. Madison doesn't respond to pressure."

"What does she respond to?"

"In her own peculiar way, she wants approval. She likes to be patted on the head. Told she's doing the right thing."

"If that's it, she might want to stop being so relentlessly obnoxious."

"I hope," Overbey said, "you're not planning to try any of those good cop/bad cop variations on me."

"I have a feeling that would be useless."

"Worse." Overbey opened the basement door.

The scents of nutmeg and molasses swirled up and around us. Braided in with them, I heard the somber but swift notes of a Bach suite played on solo cello, as honeyed and dark as the aromas. Both grew stronger as we descended.

The door at the bottom of the stairs was propped half open. It led into a room of gleaming stainless steel appliances and cabinets. Copper pots and cast iron pans stood on shelves and hung from hooks. Under it all stretched a black-and-white mosaic tile floor, probably original to the house. To the right, through another glass-paneled door, I could see a wide pantry, lined with wooden cabinets and stocked shelves. This was a serious working kitchen. Large cocktail parties, family Thanksgivings, elegant and intimate dinners for two, all could be catered from here.

Right now, the action was at one of the ovens, where a lanky Black man in chef's whites was pulling out a tray of cookies.

"Mr. Crewe," said Overbey, raising her voice above the music.

The chef turned his head. "Mrs. Overbey." His tone was as coolly professional as hers, though I thought I heard in it a note of fond irony. He closed the oven, slid the cookie tray onto the stainless steel island, and removed his kitchen mitts. He looked at me, and at Overbey, waiting to hear who had invaded his realm, and why.

"Mr. Crewe, this is Bill Smith. He's a detective hired by Ms. McCann to look for Mark. He'd like to ask you some questions."

Crewe reached to a shelf, clicked the music off, and put out his hand. "Broderick Crewe." He was dark-skinned and tall, with the air of calm certitude chefs sometimes share with surgeons. Push that a little in either profession and you have a belligerent egotist, but I didn't see any signs that Crewe had fallen off that cliff.

"Good boy, Mark," said Crewe as we shook. His hands were solid and strong. "Happy to help."

Overbey seemed on the verge of speaking but her cell phone rang. She took it from her pocket and, looking at it, pursed her lips in distaste. "The plumber." Her glance moved between us.

Crewe said, "It's okay, Mrs. Overbey. I was going for a break anyway. I'll let you know if I need you."

"Thank you, Mr. Crewe," said Overbey. "I'll be in my office."

Crewe spatula'd two cookies onto a small plate. "New recipe. I need someone to tell me if they're any good."

Overbey took the plate with the not-well-disguised air of an aunt indulging a favorite nephew. Unlocking another glass-paneled door opposite the pantry, she took the plate inside and set it on a criminally neat desk. I saw her sit, straight-backed, and tap a number on her phone. I hoped, for the plumber's sake, he had good news for her. She reached and pushed the door shut.

Crewe turned to me. "She's something, huh? Ms. McCann may be the mayor of the city but Mrs. Overbey's the mayor of this household and don't you forget it. You smoke?"

When I nodded he strode across the pantry and through an outside door. I followed him into the backyard. Newly pruned rose canes stood against the enclosing brick walls; they'd be dazzling a month from now. In front of them a cloud of white hyacinths released perfume into the air. Afternoon sun lay on purple irises and pink tulips in pots on the wide stone steps. Those steps led up to a flagstone patio where a wrought iron table, painted a glossy black, held another pot of tulips. A breeze came up; the tulips shimmied. Broderick Crewe pulled out a chair there and settled onto it. He slipped a cigarette from a pack of Newports, stuck it between his lips, and held the pack out to me.

"Thanks, I have my own." I sat, took out my Kents and lighter, lit his cigarette, then mine.

"Call me Rick." The smoke he streamed blew away.

"Bill," I said. "Mrs. Overbey told you, we've been hired by Ms. McCann."

"We?"

"Me and my partner. She's upstairs with Madison. Right now we're just trying to get a read on Mark. Can I ask how long you've been with the family?"

"Going on ten years."

"Do you live in?"

"Good God, no. I'm in Brooklyn."

"'Good God,' why?"

"Too much. This is a job. I like it, lucky to have it, but live here? I have a wife and kid of my own. And," he smiled, "you live in, you have to think twice about quitting."

"You might quit without thinking twice?"

Crewe grunted. "I'm a chef. I think twice, three times, about everything. But Her Honor doesn't have to know that."

"You want her to think you'll walk out?"

"I want her to think she has to keep me happy." He took another draw. "How I met her, she was on the City Council. I was on my Community Board out there in Brooklyn, so I used to bring cookies and stuff to the meetings. One night a bunch of councilmembers came for some school policy discussion. Afterward Ms. McCann made a point of coming up to me, telling me how good my lemon tarts were. We talked a little, where I was working, where I'd trained. Few days later Ms. Hamilton calls to say Councilwoman McCann needs a party catered, am I interested? Went on from there. The next year I'm working here full time when the city gets set to repair some potholes in my neighborhood. Was supposed to be a bare-bones job. Patching, you know. But those streets, at the corners, they flooded every time it rained. Kids soaked up to their ankles on their way to school, people trying to cross in the middle of the block running out into traffic, wheelchairs with no place to go. What we needed was new grading. I told Ms. McCann about the flooding. How it made it hard for me to get in to work whenever it rained. How I thought sometimes it'd be easier to just go back to doing catering out of my home."

"Did the streets get regraded?"

"You know it." He grinned. "So. Mark. How can I help?"

A bird dashed out from a tree branch in the next yard. I said, "Tell me about the family."

A sly smile. "I'm thinking you don't mean mine."

"I'm sure yours is fascinating. But yes, this one."

He smoked and nodded. "Well, Ms. McCann's a good boss. Straightforward, direct. She'll tell me what people liked, what they didn't. Mostly leaves things up to me. When she wants a particular item or menu she's clear. Takes suggestions, generous budget. I have no complaints."

"And Mark? You said he's a good kid. You know him pretty well?"

"He hangs out with me when he needs a break. You know his rehearsal room's down here?"

"I'd like to see it."

"You need to ask Mrs. Overbey. But that's why you're here, right?" He tapped ash into a pressed-glass leaf. "Mark's different from everyone else in this family, in this house." Crewe waved his cigarette in a vague, encompassing arc. "It wears on him."

"Different. How so?"

He lifted an amused eyebrow. "Have you met the family?"

"The mayor and Madison. Not Jeffrey Guilder yet."

"The same, the three of them. Type A, goal-oriented. Driven. They know what they want and go for it. Not a lot of time spent smelling the roses."

"Not even these?" I gestured around us.

"Landscaper comes once a week. Weeds, trims, does the seasonal plantings. Cuts flowers for inside. Ms. McCann sometimes has cocktail parties back here. Small affairs for the big donors. Otherwise I have it pretty much to myself, on breaks or when I'm going through recipes, making ingredient lists. You know, the sit-down paperwork. Shame."

"Not even Mrs. Overbey?"

He smiled, shook his head. "We spend a lot of time together, Mrs. Overbey and I, but you still wouldn't know either of us has a first name. I told her my second day to call me Rick. She told *me* she thought things would go more smoothly if we stayed professional. All righty then. She's been here sixteen years. Up until the inauguration it was

'Ms. McCann,' then she switched to 'Madam Mayor.' I swear she'd call the kids 'Master Mark' and 'Miss Madison' if it didn't sound so damn silly."

"A woman who likes to keep her distance."

He shrugged. "Ask me, she's that way to protect a tender heart. She cares about the mayor, the kids. And I wouldn't bet against her intuition. But if she thought you knew that about her she'd have to kill you. And I think she could."

"So how is Mark different? Does he stop and smell the roses?"

"It's about all he does. Ms. McCann thinks he lives in his own world but I think she's reading him wrong. He lives completely in this one. She's the one who doesn't, she and Madison and Mr. Guilder. And Mrs. Overbey, for that matter. For them it's all about the future, the plan. What's coming, how to get ahead of it. Don't get me wrong, I like her."

"Mrs. Overbey? Or the mayor?" I asked.

"Both."

The breeze changed; the tulips accommodated it, started bending in a different direction.

"And Madison? Jeffrey Guilder?"

No response.

"Anything you can tell me about any of the family might help me find Mark," I said. "I'll keep where it came from to myself."

He met my eyes. Looking away again, he took another drag on his cigarette and said, "Well, now, Mr. Guilder, he never leaves the court-room, wherever he is. Anything not an argument, he'll make it one and then swoop in for the win. I mean, come on. You think there's too much salt, tell me there's too much salt, I'll use less. Don't ask why I use so much salt and then explain how my reasoning is wrong. It's tiresome."

"And Madison?"

He smiled. "Madison is—I think these days they say, a challenge."

"In my day it would have been 'a brat.'"

Crewe laughed. "Right, you said you'd met her."

"My partner's upstairs now, seeing what she can get out of her. I imagine she'll be down before long."

"With very little. Madison used to pick on Mark. After Mr. Guilder left she was told in no uncertain terms by Ms. McCann that that had to stop. So now she goes out of her way to ignore him. If she does know anything she might not admit it, so she doesn't spoil her image." He grinned. "Sometimes she asks me. Casually, you know? What's up with her loser brother. I fill her in if I can, even though she shrugs it off as soon as she asks, like she doesn't care. Good thing she's not the actor in the family."

"But they must not totally ignore each other, Madison and Mark. Madison told her mother Mark's been talking about running away for a week or two."

"Madison said that?" Crewe tapped his cigarette against the ashtray, looked past me at the roses. "Then I guess maybe. If she said so."

"Uh-huh. He never said anything to you?"

"Nope."

"And you guys talk a lot?"

He nodded. "When I started here, it took Mark a while to warm up to me. He was five, but the same kid he is now. So was Madison. I'll give them both that, they're consistent. Mark started hanging around with me because nobody else in this house, or in Mr. Guilder's house when it came to that, can tell Baldwin from Bach from a bagel. More to the point, they don't think it matters if they can. And they're right. It doesn't. But it matters to Mark that he can."

I had to smile. "It mattered to me, too. I was the only one in my house, except my grandma."

"Hmm. Does that make me Mark's grandma?"

"I don't know. But mine made damn good cookies. Mark's an actor, I've been told. But he's shy?"

Crewe threw me a look. "Shy?"

"His mother's word. She's wrong again?"

"I think so."

I thought about Madison saying, *Carole doesn't know shit. About either of us.*

"Wrong, how?"

"'Shy' implies a kind of fear. With Mark it isn't that."

"What is it?"

Crewe took a long, contemplative pull on his cigarette. "Well, on stage he disappears. It's someone else up there, it's the role. He likes that. Off stage he tries to disappear, too, but I think it's because he wants to observe. To study. That's easier if you're invisible." He gave a wicked grin. "He's a mimic. I'm sorry, he says 'impressionist.' Did you know that?"

"No."

"Does actors, comedians, singers, politicians. Does Her Honor, Mr. Guilder, and a mean Madison."

"Mean?"

"All that time she was picking on him, he was studying her." Crewe shrugged. "Impressionists are exaggerators. That's what makes people laugh. Mark's good because he gets inside people. You know this guy Oscar Trask? The Music Man, Mr. Guilder's client? You should see Mark do him."

"When I meet Mark, I'll ask," I said. "The mayor said Mark runs away to be alone, to think. Sound right to you?"

He looked across the garden, at the wall Mark had climbed. "Yes, it does."

I followed his gaze. "Looking back, did he give you a hint, any reason why, this time?"

Crewe shook his head. "If something was bothering him, more than, you know, just being fifteen and living in the world, he didn't tell me about it."

"School trouble? Girl trouble? Boy trouble?"

Crewe considered. "There was a girl. Back in the fall. Someone he was interested in, maybe even dating."

"A girl at school?"

"Not at his school. In one of the programs with the other schools."

"You know her name?"

"Sorry. No idea. Anyway, I think it ended after Christmas break. I didn't hear about her anymore after that. Not that I'd ever heard much."

"His mother didn't hear anything at all. Neither did his sister."

"Or maybe they did, but they didn't listen."

I watched the hyacinths glow in the sunlight. "What about his friends? Kids he might have talked to about what's on his mind?"

"That girl, maybe. But maybe not even her. He's not a kid who talks much, like I said."

"All right, then, let me ask this: Do you have any sense that he's in danger?"

Crewe looked sideways at me. "Any fifteen-year-old running around New York by himself could be. But if you're asking whether I think he was abducted, or ran away because someone was coming at him, no, I don't." After another moment: "You understand 'not in danger' isn't the same as 'not in trouble.'"

"Or, 'troubled.'" I gave it a few moments. "I need to ask: Could the trouble be drugs? More specifically, a drug dealer?"

He raised his eyebrows and at first said nothing. Then: "Mark owes money, you're thinking?"

"It's a reason to run. Or maybe it's not money, maybe he's using heavily, wants to stop, and went away to see if he could get his head on straight."

"Unofficial private rehab?"

"You don't sound surprised at the idea."

"Truth is, if that's what happened, I would be. But the rest of the truth is, nothing surprises me much. It's not the Mark I think I know but if it's true, then more fool me." Crewe stubbed out his cigarette and pushed away from the table. "I need to get back to work. Come try the cookies."

"Be right there," I said. "I have to make a call."

He picked up the ashtray and went back through the pantry door.

I tapped the phone.

"So soon?" Aubrey said when she picked up.

"There's a girlfriend. Or, there was. Seems to have ended. You know anything about it?"

"Really? God, no. Who said so?"

"Might be more of a crush. A girl in one of the joint programs with the other schools."

"You know which program?"

"No."

"Well," she said, "Carole obviously doesn't know. Let me check around."

"Good. Talk later."

I hung up and called the number she'd given me for Danny Rodriguez, Mark McCann's daytime bodyguard.

"I wasn't there," he said when I told him who I was and who I worked for. "By the time I got there in the morning the kid was long gone."

"I know. This isn't about anything you did wrong."

"Glad you feel that way."

"Not everyone does?"

"Felt a lot of side-eye, is all. Like I should've known the kid was thinking about taking off."

"He never said anything? Even something that didn't seem to mean anything at the time but looking back now?"

"Not a thing. You ever done protection work?"

"Yes."

"So you know. Sometimes the principal wants to be buddies, sometimes they want you to fade into the background. He was always polite, the kid, but you could tell he'd rather I wasn't there at all." A sly tone came into his voice as he said, "Not like his sister and the guys assigned to her."

"Oh?"

"You met her? She loves the idea she's important enough to need protection. Treats her guys like she's Beyoncé and they're her backup group."

"I'm not surprised. Look, one more thing. I understand Mark has a crush on a girl. Or, had, last fall. You have any idea who?"

"News to me. Someone from school?"

"Or one of the joint programs."

"You gotta understand, I'm generally outside the classroom, the rehearsal room, wherever. The theater, I'll be inside, because there's lots of ways in and out. Or if he hangs out with kids for coffee, I'll go sit at a table across the room. But at the school, a classroom with one door, Mark always asks if I can stay outside. So he can be just like any other kid. Always polite, like I said, but he knows what suits him."

I thanked Rodriguez, asked him to call me if he thought of anything, and went back inside, where I ran into Lydia coming through the staircase door.

"Hey," she said.

"Hey. Come meet Rick. Rick Crewe, this is Lydia Chin, my partner. Rick's the chef around here."

"Happy to meet you," Lydia said. "Did you bake whatever smells so great?"

"Sit down, both of you." Crewe grinned. "I'll get the milk."

Mrs. Overbey's office was empty and her plate was in one of the sinks. Crewe picked up a Post-it Note from beside the cookie sheet on the stainless steel counter. He laughed. It bore a large black checkmark.

While Crewe assembled vegetables for dinner Lydia and I ate oatmeal cookies, dark with molasses and thick with raisins. I asked Lydia what she'd learned from Madison.

"Nothing," she said. It sounded like a real "nothing," not a "nothing I want to talk about with a member of the household here." "Except some more complaints about her brother's uncoolness, and how she doesn't know his friends but she can guarantee they're as uncool as he is. And about her mother, because why not? And you."

"Me?"

"She told me I needed to ditch you fast because let's face it, I'm coming up on my use-by date. Which you, by the way, have long since passed. Though she doesn't see how there was ever a time when you were a bargain."

Crewe chuckled.

"Gee," I said. "And here I thought I was holding up pretty well."

"She offered to help me out. If I needed to meet people."

"You should probably take her up on it. Her mother's politico friends and her father's scummy clients. It's a hell of an offer."

"And she asked me why we were looking for Mark."

"Why we're looking? Um, because he's fifteen and he's missing?"

"She seemed to think there was more to it than that."

"Did she say what?"

"No, she wanted me to say."

I looked at Crewe. He shrugged.

"I'd be very interested to know what she thinks that is," I said.

"I pushed a little but she wouldn't tell me. She's on her way to her dad's, then dinner, then the opera, then back to her dad's for the night."

"Lah-di-dah. What was the music?"

"What music?"

"That she was listening to, that you said you liked the last album better."

"I have no idea. But there's always a last album, and it's usually better."

I polished off one final cookie. "Okay," I said. "I'm going to go hunt down Mrs. Overbey. I want to check out Mark's rehearsal room."

"Door's right there." Crewe pointed his paring knife. "Key," he said, directing the knife at a drawer, "is in there."

"I thought you said—"

"I didn't know you."

"And now you do?"

"How were the cookies?"

"Good as my grandma's."

"There you go."

Mark's rehearsal room yielded nothing except the unsurprising fact that a fifteen-year-old boy could make a mess in a nearly empty space. The carpeted floor was stained with old spills. Acoustic tile covered the walls and the ceiling, which also held two strips of fluorescents and three track lights. I guessed the tracks probably served as basic spots.

While we searched the room, I told Lydia about the possibility of a girlfriend.

"That would be an interesting complication," she said. "Maybe it's as simple as, she ditched him and he's gone away to lick his wounds."

"Rick Crewe said if there was anything going on it seemed to have been over by Christmas."

"Maybe he's a slow learner."

I lifted a highlighted script that reclined on a music stand. *Angels in America*; Mark was playing Louis. A dirty coffee mug stood on a folding table guarding an iPhone tripod that was probably there for a video set-up. No tech was in evidence, but the wall across from the table had a draped sheet of photographic backdrop paper, the better to record without distractions.

The table, and the chair behind it, were the room's only furniture. Besides the tripod and the cup, the table also held a music theory workbook, scattered pencils, and a desk lamp. The only thing I might not have expected, though it made sense, was a Masonite board in the corner, where a pair of tap shoes waited.

"He can tap dance?" Lydia asked.

"Politician's son."

Lydia looked at the *Angels in America* script. "Does Louis have a speech he screams, like Madison said?"

"Screams, no. But there's a lot going on. It's a tough, major role."

"See, I'd have known that if you took me to the theater."

"Or you took me."

She gave that the attention it deserved. Gesturing at the tripod, she said, "He makes videos."

"We should ask Linus to look on the laptop. In case he recorded more down here than monologues."

That was about it. We locked the room and returned the key to Crewe. "Thanks," I said. "We'd better go. Anything else you think of, you have my card."

We all turned as Madison slipped into the kitchen through the staircase door. "Oh God," she said when she saw me. "Are you bothering Mr. C? He has a lot to do, you know."

"Does that mean you're going to be home for chicken pot pie?" Rick Crewe asked.

"Oh, come on, Mr. C! You know I love that. Why are you making it when I won't be here?"

"If you told me when you wouldn't be here—"

"Yeah, yeah, yeah. Got popsicles?"

"You know I do. On the right, in the back."

Madison pulled open the freezer, rooted through, and found a purple popsicle. "Umm. You guys want one?" Lydia and I both shook our heads. Madison shrugged. Her eyes swept me. "Don't know what you're missing." Slipping back through the half-open door, she said, "Save me some of that stuff, Mr. C."

When she was gone I turned to Crewe. "Popsicles?"

"Sometimes she's still a kid. Mostly when she thinks no one's looking. I keep grape popsicles in there for her."

"Her brother's still a kid, too."

"Yes, he is," Crewe said. "And actually, I did think of something. Someone you could talk to, who might be able to help."

"Great. Who?"

"Spider-Man."

# 5

"D"id you know," Lydia asked me, "that the first Statue of Liberty mime on the New York streets was a Chinese immigrant circus acrobat in the 1980s? And so were the next half-dozen because he taught other Chinese immigrants how to do it?"

This was not the random comment it might have been at some other time. Reaching the top of the subway stairs in Times Square, Lydia and I had become a two-person spring flowing into a churning sea of tourists, hustlers, vendors, and costumed characters. Including the Statue of Liberty.

The Statue, its robes, crown, and face painted the green of oxidized copper, stood immobile, torch aloft, until someone slid a few bills into the box at its feet. Then it would smile and lean down to wrap its torch-bearing arm around a wide-eyed child—or half-drunk adult in a New York Fuckin' City T-shirt—while their picture together was snapped. Once that was over the Statue would solemnly unbend and resume its motionless pose, until the next bills fluttered down. I sometimes wondered if kids—or half-drunk adults—were disappointed when they took the ferry to Liberty Island and the real statue didn't do that.

The Statue of Liberty character was a boulder of calm in a swirling current of pop culture icons. Minnie Mouse, Goofy, Wonder Woman, Chewbacca, and Darth Vader were all there, as were Superman, Batman, Elmo, and our quarry: Spider-Man. None of them stood still. Under the ever-changing explosion of bright billboards rising into the afternoon sky, the characters looped through the crowd, swooping in on tourists they hoped to trap into photos. Their strategies included acrobatics and heroic poses; hand-claps and giggles (the Minnie Mouses were particularly partial to that approach); and if all else failed, a direct appeal to the weak link in the chain of "no, thank you": the children. Occasionally, verging on one-step-too-far techniques for which some of them had already been ticketed—more than once—they'd throw an arm around their sightseer prey and pull her or him into a photo-op clinch irresistible to other tourists. Cell phone cameras would snap away. Releasing the victim, the character would stick out a gloved hand or lift up a cash bucket to every picture-taker, and also to the victim. Ignoring them or waving them away were mistakes. So was throwing just a nickel or a dime in the bucket. Luckily, they were all masked so a little child couldn't see the moment Minnie Mouse stopped smiling.

"Okay," said Lydia, surveying the scene. "I see three Spider-Mans. Spider-Men? Based on what your buddy Rick said, that one looks too big and hefty. And that one's awfully skinny."

"Who are you, Goldilocks?"

"No, because that one over there doesn't look 'just right,' either. Not chunky enough."

"Rick Crewe never saw him. He was repeating Mark's description." I gazed at the lithe Spider-Man scrutinizing the crowd. "But at least that one's not holding some terrified child in his arms."

We hurried through the throng toward the empty-armed Spider-Man. It's hard to make a living squeezing tips out of tourists, but standing around produces no tips at all. We needed to reach him before he narrowed in on a new target.

Spider-Man had just taken a step forward, his pointed white eyes on a pre-teen girl standing with two adults and two younger kids, all eating ice cream cones. We flanked him, Lydia to his left and I on his right, each grabbing a padded elbow. He tried to wrench away. I reached into my pocket and took out a twenty-dollar bill.

Movement stopped.

"We need to talk," I said.

Spider-Man grasped for the cash but I stuffed it back in my pocket. I repeated, "We need to talk."

He pointed to his webby mouth.

"Yeah," I said, "right. If you can breathe through it I'm pretty sure you can talk through it. I'm looking for Emilio Vela."

The blue-and-red head shook back and forth.

"You're not him?"

More shaking.

"Then where do I find him?"

A shoulder shrug.

"I don't believe you," I said. "Everyone here knows how to find Emilio. Look, I'm not here to make trouble. I owe him money. I have it now. If I don't pay him off I'll just piss it away, and I sure as hell don't want him coming after me when I do that. Tell me how to find him and there's a little for you, too. Plus the twenty." I took the bill out again. "Where is he?"

If this was Emilio Vela he'd know that was baloney, but if it wasn't it might work. It didn't. This time I got both a head shake and a shoulder shrug.

"Really?" I said. "We have to do this?"

Spider-Man shrugged again, his huge white eyes fixed on me. I gave Lydia a tiny nod. She shot her hand out and yanked the mask off his head.

Her head.

Glossy black hair spilled down the blue-and-red back. That was nothing to the loud Spanish curses that spilled from the mouth of the young woman struggling to pull out of our grip. A passing family gaped in horrified fascination. The mother covered the little boy's ears and they double-timed on.

I waited until Spider-Person stopped for breath. Then I responded in Spanish, a remnant of the part of my misspent youth in the Philippines, where I'd learned to curse in three languages. I didn't curse her out, though. I told her that I understood everything she said, that I agreed with most of it, but that we still needed to talk to Emilio Vela.

"Hijos de puta!" She spat one more Spanish expletive at us, and then moved to English. "Cops! Let me go. I know my rights."

"We're not cops." I showed her my card. She sneered.

"Mierda. Eres ICE. I have papers. At home. Let me go. I go get them."

Any ICE agent who fell for that deserved to lose his quarry. I said, "No. Not cops, not ICE. We just have to ask Emilio a question."

She looked at me and it seemed she might be considering the request. She held out her hand. I put the twenty in it. She smirked. Then she raised her head and shouted, "Tortugas ninjas! Cops! Ayúdame! Tortugas ninjas!"

Ninja turtles? Seriously? But it seemed this was the *Hey, Rube!* of the Times Square world. The nearest characters, a Minnie Mouse and a Chewbacca, dropped what they were doing and marched toward us, taking up the shout to attract others. In moments we were surrounded by the entire Marvel, DC, and Disney universes. And no one looked happy.

"This is not happening," Lydia said under her breath.

"It might be," I said. "Be prepared."

I released my hold on Spider-Person at the same time Lydia did. The blue-and-red suit slipped away into the crowd. I made a stay-calm gesture toward the circle of creatures. "No somos tortugas ninjas," I said. "We're not cops."

"Quieren Emilio!" Spider-Person howled from a few rows back. "ICE!"

"Not ICE. Not any kind of cops. We just need to talk to him."

The Incredible Hulk took a step closer and said, "Go! Police is not welcome!" His accent was eastern European.

"We're not police," I said. "We're looking for a missing child and Emilio might be able to help us find him."

"Liar! Police is always liar!"

And just like that, The Incredible Hulk took a swing at me.

I forearm-blocked the punch and drove an uppercut into his belly. What was I thinking? It was like socking a Tempur-Pedic. He laughed and swung at my head. The same padding that made him hard to damage made him slow, though, so I had time to twist. I took the punch on my shoulder. Stepping back, I said, "I don't want to fight you."

"Police is always cowards, too!" He started toward me again, but as he reached to grab me he staggered. Lydia had kicked him in the back of the knee. I stuck my foot out, hooked his ankle, and crashed him down onto his well-padded ass.

A moment of stillness.

Followed by a full-scale free-for-all.

The circle of costumed characters, furious to see one of their own go down, charged in swinging. They seemed to be more brawlers than fighters and the costumes weren't designed for action. Mickey Mouse made a grab for Lydia but she wrenched away and Mickey's three-fingered glove slid off. A lumbering Elmo waded in, yanking off his shaggy red head. He pitched it at Lydia. She swatted it aside and it bowling-balled down the sidewalk. Superman flew at me—how real did he think he was?—but I ducked low and he smashed into Batman, toppling them both. They started pummeling each other.

Bystanders love a good brawl. Tourists and vendors had gathered and there was no question whose side they were on. I caught Lydia's eye, gestured that we should look for an escape route as shouts of "C'mon, Batman!" and "Go, Vader, go!" filled the air. Lydia nodded and gave Minnie Mouse a roundhouse kick. I flung an attacking Captain America aside with no harm to either of us, but doing it put me off balance. An enterprising Snow White shoved me hard and the next thing I knew I was flat on my back. Snow White loomed over me and mask or not I could swear she was sneering.

Captain America regained his footing and swung his shield high, ready to bring it down on my head. It didn't look very sturdy but it also didn't look like fun. I put my arms up to absorb the blow but it never came. Captain America jerked his head toward a new voice that bellowed above the noise.

"Tortugas ninjas!" A stocky man pushed through the churning mass. "Vienen! Cops are coming! Go! Disappear! Idiotas! Imbéciles!" He shoved the headless Elmo aside, shooed some others away. Looking at me on the ground, he shook his head, stuck out a hand to help me scramble up, and said, "Come with me."

# 6

Qué pasa?" Emilio Vela demanded. "Why the hell you did that?"

Lydia and I sat with him on folding chairs in a crowded storeroom. He'd led us away from the battlefield to an over-bright, overstuffed souvenir shop where no one seemed surprised to see Vela burst in the door and slalom through the racks of sweatshirts and the shelves of fake crystal to the back, followed by Lydia and me. In the brief time since Vela had appeared and told everyone to scram, Times Square had miraculously emptied of costumed characters. Although the arriving NYPD were no doubt right now hearing breathless tourist accounts of a multi-character melee—possibly already mushroomed into an intergalactic gang war—not a single cape or giant black shoe would be seen in the area for a couple of hours yet.

Which was what Emilio Vela was unhappy about.

"I'm sorry," I said. "We sure didn't mean it."

"Esta gente are just trying to make a living. They lose a whole night now, from you bobos."

"All we wanted—all we want—is to talk to you."

"Porqué?"

"You're the mayor around here."

Vela snorted. "Says who?"

"Everyone. You know what's going on. We saw how they all listened to you just now. Ellos se fueron."

He curled his lip at my Spanish.

"And they were protecting you," Lydia said. "They thought we were ICE."

"ICE." Vela snickered. "Ellos son as stupid as you. ICE agents siempre look like ICE agents. They wear big vests, say ICE! So everyone see they come to arrest you. You don't look like ICE. Not even like cops. Just idiotas."

"I don't disagree," I said. "But we need your help. We're trying to find Mark McCann."

"I don't know who that is."

I took out my cigarettes. "You mind?"

"You got one for me?"

I passed him the pack and my lighter. "You're not much of a liar," I said. "We know he comes here. To mime. To learn from you guys. We know he had to go through you and we know about the deal."

"Deal? Qué deal?" Vela asked that looking at the tip of his lit cigarette, as if he already knew it was more interesting than whatever answer I was going to give him.

"No one works here as a character without your say so." I repeated what we'd been told by Rick Crewe. "You assign territories and times. Mark's here to learn. He doesn't need the money. He turns over his tip bucket to you at the end of the day, and doubles whatever's in it."

Vela shrugged.

"He left home and I think he's in trouble," I said.

I saw a shadow flitter across Vela's face, before he shrugged again. "Yo no sé. Whoever that is, you looking, go look someplace else."

Lydia leaned forward. "I bet," she said, "that you don't keep it. What's in the bucket. I bet you distribute it to the other characters."

Vela turned to her silently. After a very long time, he looked at me again. He tipped his chair back and stuck his hands in his pockets. "Who are you?"

"Private investigators. We're working for Mark's family." I tried to hand him a card but he didn't take it, just peered at it. He did the same with Lydia's.

"Privados," he said. "In my country la policía hire privados to do the things even those pendejos are scared to touch."

"We just want to find Mark. If he's in trouble we want to help."

"How do I know?"

"If you don't know Mark, why do you care? Come on. He's a kid. You like him. I see it. Help us."

Another long stare. "You say you working for the family. The mami or the papi?"

"Mark's mother."

Vela drew thoughtfully on his cigarette. "La Alcaldesa. She tell you he come here?"

"No. I'm not sure she knows. Someone who works for her told us."

He looked past me, across the room. "You say to La Alcaldesa, I help you find the kid, she tell la policía to back off."

"I don't know—" I began.

"Entonces, I don't either."

"We'll tell her," Lydia said. "We can't promise what she'll do or what the police will do. But we'll tell her."

Pointing his cigarette at Lydia but looking at me, Vela said, "I think, ese, she is smarter than you." He laughed. "Sí, okay, es verdád, I like the kid. And you"—now the cigarette was aimed at me—"I watch you knock that cabrón Lusinski on his culo. That make me laugh."

Vela dropped his chair upright and took out his cell phone. He thumbed a text and waited for a response. When it came, he grunted. "He gonna be here soon."

"Lusinski?"

"Dios, no. Who want to talk to him? Ashok Sundari. Está un Goofy. Mark's friend."

Vela went to the front of the store and came back with two Cokes and, for Lydia, a club soda. Also for Lydia, a big bag of peanuts. Fighting always makes Lydia hungry.

"So," I said, just to keep the friendliness flowing, grudging as it was, "when Mark comes here he does Goofy?"

"Not just Goofy. One time, I let him do Spider-Man. He swing from the light pole, pretty good. He do Minnie Mouse, too, even make me laugh. He try to get Lusinski to teach him el Hulk, but esto coño tell him to get lost. So the kid, he sit and watch Lusinski all afternoon. Then he ask me, can he come next time Lusinski don't work and be el Hulk. So I tell Lusinski stay home the next day. The kid show up in a Hulk suit and Dios mío, after a while I got to tell him to stop because he scare todos los niños! That kid, whatever he do is mostly better que los otros. They do good enough for tourists. He do so good, you could believe him."

"How often has he been here since his mother took office?"

Vela shook his head. "Solo one time. Alone. He tell me he ditch his guardaespaldas. I tell him no, go home. We got enough trouble from la policía. La Alcaldesa say he need un cuidador, he come with the guy or he don't come. If something bad happen to him when he being Goofy, todos somos en la mierda. Since then he don't come."

Vela's phone beeped. He looked at the screen and from then on we sat in the dim room, drinking without conversation, Lydia cracking peanut shells, while Vela had two text exchanges and took a phone call in the ten minutes we waited. The call involved a lot of repetition of instructions and exasperated orders in broken English and obscene Spanish. Finally, he put down the phone and gulped his Coke.

"Maldito idiota! Un Batman, don't want to listen. Pués, tomorrow he don't work."

"You run a tight ship," I said.

"Estos cabrones," he said, as, now cigaretteless, he pointed the Coke can at me, "they come to great America, they got no papers. Maybe they un médico o el Presidente where they come from but here, how they gonna make a living? So they think, I get a costume, I be Superman, tourists take pictures, they throw money at me. Suddenly, we up to our culos in Superman. No one make a living. Somebody got to be in charge, ese. Somebody got to keep order." He looked at me, so I nodded. He grinned. "También, somebody got to take care of la policía. You think they want to break up la pelea you made today? We don't get paid, they don't get nothing. Pero el soborno only go so far. Sometime I take care of them, they come anyway, gotta fill their quota, some mierda like that. So you talk to la Alcaldesa." He said that with a look at Lydia. "Me, I come here years ago, was the first Spider-Man," he went on. "So I take over. Because someone got to."

Always true, I reflected. Someone got to. I didn't know if he expected an answer but it turned out I didn't have to make one. The door opened and a skinny South Asian man tiptoed into the room carrying a large duffel bag over his shoulder. He had big brown eyes and a thin black mustache. Taking in the three of us with a quick look, he spoke to Vela. "Emilio. You are wanting to see me? I have done something?" I could see why this loose-limbed, lanky man had chosen the role of Goofy.

"Hola, Ashok. No, no hay problema." I doubted that Ashok Sundari spoke Spanish but at Vela's casual tone his shoulders dropped away from his neck as though they no longer needed to protect it. He placed the duffel bag carefully on the floor. In the usual way of things, I guessed, a summons to the souvenir-shop sanctum was probably an occasion for deep reflection on one's character-life sins. "Ellos," Vela said, wielding the Coke can, "they look for Mark McCann. I tell them you can help."

Ashok Sundari frowned. He shifted from one foot to the other, squinted at me and at Lydia, and said nothing.

"Ashok," said Vela, "nobody got all day. The kid run away from home. His mami is worried." Sundari didn't meet Vela's eyes. Vela's face went red. "Coño! You know this already? You know where he is? El hijo de la Alcaldesa? Cabrón! Quieres ser deportado, y todos contigo? Jesucristo sálvame!"

As Vela let loose this barrage he rose from his chair. The words might have been unintelligible to Sundari but their ultimate meaning was clear. He stepped back, shoulders up by his ears again.

"Ashok," Vela said gently, "if la Alcaldesa, the mayor, if she find out one of you idiotas sabe donde está su hijo and don't tell, we all gonna be fucked. If that happen, you gonna be the fuckedest. Me entiendes?" A pause, with nothing from Sundari. Vela went nose-to-nose with him and said loud and slow, "Do you understand me, coño?"

Sundari nodded, his eyes huge.

"Bueno." Vela settled back into his chair. "What you know, you tell mi amiga aquí."

"Mi amiga" was Lydia; I hadn't earned "amigo" status, apparently. Ashok Sundari looked at Lydia. He swallowed. She said nothing, just smiled at him amiably.

"Yes," Sundari said, with an air of resignation. "I do know the young man. Many of us do." He threw a quick glance at Vela, but Vela's dark cloud of a frown wasn't nearly as welcoming as Lydia's bright encouraging smile. Back to her, then. "I am teaching him how to move properly. How to perform on the wire and the beam. I have been an acrobat, a circus performer, in Mumbai, you understand. I am able to leap from the back of one trotting elephant onto another, and thence to the ground. With a somersault."

"Ashok, no one give a shit—"

"Yes, yes, I am sorry. The boy. He has a good deal of talent, I think so. He is eager to learn. In India, the circus is dying. So I come to United States. I am continuing to practice my skills, so I can one day be a performer here. Cirque du Soleil! Big Apple Circus!"

Vela snarled.

Sundari tore his mind's eye from the sight of himself on the high wire in Madison Square Garden and hurried on. "I live in Queens with my aunt. In the backyard of her house I am putting a beam and a tightrope, also a trampoline. For practicing somersaults, you understand. This is where I am teaching Mark circus skills." He stopped, hands spread.

"Ashok?" said Vela, in a voice of disbelief. "Esto es todo? They looking for the kid, you got a trampoline?"

Sundari said, "No, no. That was to explain how it is Mark knows where my home is."

"Y qué?"

"This morning, he came there."

# 7

We sat impatiently as Ashok Sundari spoke to his aunt from Emilio Vela's office behind the souvenir shop. His first call had been to Mark's cell. I'd thought that might work—a call from the friend on whose doorstep he'd appeared had to be more appealing than one from some unknown PI—but Sundari only got voicemail, too. We gave Mark five minutes to call back but he didn't. So Sundari called his aunt.

"What's he speaking?" Lydia whispered to me.

"Hindi, I think."

"Is that one of your languages?"

I shook my head. I speak six, to varying degrees, and understand some pithy phrases in a few more, but none of them are languages of South Asia.

Moving the phone from his ear, Sundari said, "Mark is no longer at my home. I am sorry." He brought it close again, exchanged a few more sentences; then, face brightening, told us, "But he has said he will return."

"Where did he go?" I asked.

"My aunt does not know. But she will call when he comes back."

"Tell her to keep him there when he does. Come on."

Sundari, mouth open in alarm, gestured at the duffel bag. "I cannot go now. I must work. You understand."

"We'll cover it. How much do you make in an evening?"

Sundari hesitated, then said, "Three hundred dollars."

"Okay, fine. Let's go."

Sundari spoke into the phone. He hung up and pocketed it but didn't move.

I took out my wallet. Two hundred was all I had. Sundari shook his head. Vela just watched. Lydia added four more twenties, then showed Sundari that her wallet, too, was empty. He shrugged, nodded, and collected the cash. Stuffing it in his pocket he said, "Very well, come." He picked up the duffel bag.

Vela waited until we reached the door. Then he guffawed. "Mierda! If he make a hundred he have a very good night. Ashok, you maybe not tan tonto like I think. Adiós, todos. Buena suerte y don't come back. Y amiga"—to Lydia—"don't forget la Alcaldesa y la policía."

"I won't," she said. "Adiós. Amigo."

Sundari was disappointed when I pointed us to the subway. "Can we not take a taxi? After all, we are in a rush."

"So's everyone else," I said. "It's rush hour. A cab will take forever."

So, with the impression beginning to grow on me that Ashok Sundari, whatever else he might be, was also a hustler, we descended the stairs to the 7 train.

Among the Black, brown, and Asian faces in the subway car, mine was one of only two White ones. The other, you could barely see. It belonged to a man wearing a COVID mask—about a quarter of the people in the subway car had them, including Lydia—plus sunglasses and a baseball cap. He got on when we did. When he reached for the pole his shirt cuff slid up. Around his wrist I saw the entire Justice League of America standing shoulder to shoulder. Too bad the lottery was numbers and not words. Today I'd have played "superhero."

Because we got on near the start of the line we got seats, though I gave mine to a young woman one stop later; Sundari his to an old man the stop after that; and Lydia hers to a woman with a baby at the next stop. Soon the car was packed and Sundari's duffel bag was making enemies. When the train crossed into Queens the unloading started. By the last stop in Flushing it would be half empty, but we weren't going that far. At Jackson Heights we stepped out onto the elevated platform.

As soon as we stood in the open air the aromas of coriander, cumin, and roast meat from carts and restaurants below swirled up and around us, making my salami sandwich, and even Roderick Crewe's cookies, into pale and distant memories.

"Come," said Sundari. "We go this way."

We trotted down the north side stairs into the sea of scents. The sidewalk was about as crowded as the train car had been. Women in skirts and blouses, sweaters and jeans, or shalwar kameez—loose trousers and thigh-length embroidered tunics—and men in suits, or jeans and polo shirts, with the occasional fellow in a shalwar kameez too, shared the pavement with trinket tables, food carts, fruit-and-vegetable stands, and children in and out of strollers.

Even in the twilight the colors were exuberant. The sky by now had turned lilac and the lights were coming on. Roosevelt Avenue was lined with two-story buildings, with stores below and lawyers, driving schools, dentists, and doctors above. Every other awning-hung storefront seemed to be a restaurant. Pakistani, Indian, and Bangladeshi food competed with Colombian, Peruvian, Ecuadorian, and Tibetan to wrap their sights and smells around passersby and try to lure them inside.

"Do you feel hungry?" Ashok Sundari asked.

"No, I'm good."

"Me, too," said Lydia. For all I knew, in her case it was true.

Sundari smiled and nodded as though our answers pleased him. "Still," he said, "it would perhaps be wise to bring with us some little things. A few small snacks, you understand. In case we are required to wait some time for the boy."

"No," I said. "We're not stopping. We might miss him. In fact, call your aunt now and see if he's there."

Sundari did, and was sorry to report Mark was still in absentia and hadn't been heard from. He said, "So in that case, perhaps . . ." and gestured at a particularly inviting restaurant.

I shook my head. "Which way?"

Sundari sighed in resignation and pointed. We'd gone two blocks, been overtaken and then passed by the roar of a 7 train heading west, when Lydia stumbled. She twisted to right herself, straightened her jacket, and smiled at Sundari, who'd reached out a hand to help.

I'd reached out a hand, too, and leaned toward her. "What?" I said softly.

"Half a block back," she answered. "The guy from the train. With the Justice League tattoo, did you see it?"

Lydia doesn't trip over the sidewalk. Innate athleticism and decades of tae kwon do combine to make what had just happened a tactic I recognized: she'd seen something behind that she wanted a better look at.

"Okay," I said, not turning to look. "Ashok, I changed my mind. You and Lydia go ahead, buy some snacks. But in a place where you can leave by the back door. You know anyplace like that along here?"

Sundari, whose first reaction had been delight, now frowned. "A back door? No." He frowned some more, as though he feared his chance at snacks would vanish if he couldn't come up with a restaurant that met my weird criterion. Then he brightened. "Ah. The tea house on the corner has an entrance on this avenue and another on 68th Street. This is not a back door but it is—"

"That's fine. Come on."

"May I know why we are doing this?"

"Lydia will explain. Walk normally. Don't rush."

Ashok Sundari's gait was that of a rushing man trying to walk normally. I guessed it would have to do. When we got to the Benares Tea House he and Lydia went in while I stayed outside. I lit a cigarette and leaned on a mailbox, just a guy having a smoke, waiting for his friends, looking around, checking out the neighborhood.

Down the block Justice League stopped also. He peered into a clothing shop window. Maybe he was planning to buy his girlfriend a pair of gauzy cotton pants. More likely, he was able, in the reflection, to see me lounging at my mailbox.

I stubbed out my cigarette and took out my phone. I fiddled with it, then held it vertically, talking at it as though I were FaceTiming with someone. Two teenaged girls passed me, poked each other, and laughed. I kept talking. After a bit I lowered the phone, thumbed some buttons, and put it to my ear. I started back the way we'd come, heading right toward Justice League. My plan was to stay on the phony phone call, ignoring him, until I was practically crawling up his back. Then I'd tackle him.

It didn't work out that way.

I got where I needed to be, but as I pulled up even with him a group of hooting middle-school boys, celebrating their liberation from the day's classrooms, barreled down the sidewalk. They split a pair of stroller-pushing women and came stampeding right at me. In their defense, the ones in front were cracking up and looking back at their pursuers; in mine, I'm a big guy and though I've sometimes thought it would be useful to be invisible, I'm not.

I tried to sidestep. When they realized I was there, so did they. Same direction. Arms, elbows, knees, apologies flying. I untangled myself and lunged past them but by then Justice League was a block ahead, jostling his way down the sidewalk. I chased after him, angering old and young as people who'd already jumped with irritation from his path now found themselves leaping out of mine. At the corner he threw a trash can over. I was able to leap it but two pissed-off trinket vendors grabbed at me. One missed. One got my arm and I had to twist him off. By then Justice League had swung onto the subway stairs and taken them two at a time. I did the same, as far as the top landing. I stopped when I saw him vault the turnstile and shoulder into a pair of closing car doors.

Standing there panting as the train disappeared, I thought two things.

One, playing "superhero" in the lottery would've actually been a bad idea.

Two, we should have taken a cab.

# 8

I have not heard from the young man again." Maalini Sundari, a heavy, warm woman in an embroidered turquoise tunic and loose white trousers, smiled apologetically.

We stood around the second-floor kitchen in her house—an aluminum-sided two stories plus attic, residential upstairs, the office of Sundari Tax Preparer on the ground floor, on a block of similar structures in a neighborhood of them—while she transferred the riches from the Benares Tea House to platters on her bright patterned tablecloth.

Ashok Sundari and Lydia had gotten to the house just a few minutes before me, and were there with Ashok's aunt when I appeared at the door after my fruitless chase. Lydia had explained to Ashok once they were inside the café that we were being followed and I was following the follower. I watched him now as I gave them all a quick wrap-up, his wide eyes and jerky motions telling me he was spooked. Though fear hadn't prevented him, it seemed, from ordering a variety of dishes and condiments on Lydia's Visa card.

Pakora, both vegetable and paneer; the tender crepes and potato-and-spice filling of masala dosa; pulao with peas; the crisp curls of onion bhaji; and sweet syrupy gulab jamun. If this was a few small snacks, I was a Mumbaikar myself.

Ashok, looking abashed as I stared at the mounting collection of plates and bowls—a late entry out of the shopping bag was a container of mulligatawny soup—said, "My aunt works very hard. She is a tax accountant. At this time of year, she is very busy, you understand. Also, many people from the neighborhood are always coming to consult her. About problems we are having here. Always she is here to help. So when I go to a shop, people say, 'Oh, Mahila Mukhiya must try this, Mahila Mukhiya will like that. It would be wrong to insult them, I think so."

Lydia, grinning, asked, "Mahila Mukhiya?"

"Boss Lady, you understand."

The neighborhood Boss Lady waved away the praise with a small smile. While she lifted little containers of condiments and sauces from the bag I asked, "But Mark said he was coming back?"

"Yes." She nodded. "But not when."

"Or where he was going? Or why?"

Ashok and his aunt exchanged a glance.

"No," she said, without the smile. She took bright cloth napkins from a drawer.

I wandered to the back of the kitchen and looked out at the yard. It was smaller than the house, about twenty-five by thirty, and a corner of it was taken up by a prefab shed; but in that compact dusty space Ashok had indeed rigged up a balance beam, a trampoline, and two taut wires, one low, one high.

"What did Mark say about why he left home?" I asked, returning to the table. I lifted a paneer pakora, bit into it. The tempura-like crust was crispy and hot with pepper dust, and the cheese inside soft and smooth.

Maalini Sundari said, "He told me nothing."

Her nephew, avoiding everyone's eyes, pulled out a chair and sat himself at the table.

I looked at Lydia. Wiping my fingers, I took out my phone. "You know this guy?" I showed them the photo I'd taken of Justice League when I was poking buttons and faking FaceTime. The Sundaris both shook their heads, the nephew looking anxious, the aunt concerned.

"A mask, sunglasses, a hat," Maalini Sundari said, "there is almost no face to see."

"All right," I said. "Now look. A kid runs away from home. His politician mother's worried about him—or worried he'll embarrass her—so she hires us to find him. Important, but not a crisis, according to everyone. But now someone's so interested in what we're doing they pinned a tail on us. Obviously the mother's not the only one looking for the kid. I screwed up finding out who the guy was but I managed to chase him off. Now I'd like to find Mark before they pick us up again."

Ashok swallowed. "Why are you thinking the follower was looking for Mark? Perhaps he was hoping to speak with one of us."

Lydia sighed. "Ashok, he ran when Bill got near him," she said. "It's not us."

Ashok nodded miserably as the straws of hope he'd been clutching at blew away in the wind of obviousness. His aunt spoke to him in Hindi. He answered her. She spoke again.

Hindi's a beautiful language. Just watch any Bollywood movie. The dialogue in between the musical numbers is as melodic as the songs themselves.

But an argument's an argument, no matter how lilting the language.

Aunt and nephew went back and forth. He was dug in, tight and stubborn. She tried to persuade, to cajole.

"Does this help?" I broke in. "That guy following us, he had a gun."

The aunt's eyes widened.

"So do you," said Ashok. He turned to Lydia. "And you."

I was impressed; not everyone can tell when I'm carrying. There was definitely more to Ashok Sundari than at first appeared. "Yes," I said. "But we're the good guys."

He shook his head. "We do not know where the boy is."

The aunt regarded him for a few moments. "Ashok," she declared, "enough." She turned to me. "He was here. He said he was needing a place to stay, not for long, just for now. While he thought."

"Thought about what?"

"He did not say. But he was troubled. So of course we said he could stay." Another glance at her nephew. "He was here when Ashok called."

"From Times Square?" I stared at Ashok Sundari. He kept his mouth pressed defiantly shut and his gaze on the table.

"Ashok said you were there and were wanting him to lead you to the boy. He said that that Vela man was making him do it but I should tell the boy to leave."

"You're goddamn kidding me. This was all one big red herring?"

Ashok frowned around at the table. Maybe he was thinking he'd forgotten the herring.

"Ashok? You were wasting our time?"

Now he looked up. "I had to do what Emilio said. But equally I knew the boy did not want to be found. He is my friend and he was trusting us. I told my aunt to say to him, you were from his mother. Perhaps then he would want to speak to you. If he did not, then he should leave. But," he added, "we do not know where he has gone."

Maalini Sundari slapped her hand on the table. "Of course we do."

Sundari protested in Hindi.

His aunt leaned toward him and answered in English. "Ashok. The man following, he had a *gun*." She turned to me. "I would never let the boy leave without a place to go, after he came to us for help. I have sent him to a friend." She reached onto the counter for an address book stuffed with business cards and scraps of paper, thumbed through it, and on another scrap wrote out a name, address, and phone number. She handed it to me.

I read the address. "West 144th? In Manhattan? Harlem?"

"You are surprised I have a friend there."

"No," said Ashok darkly. "He is thinking you are sending him after another red herring."

Maalini Sundari smiled. "I am not. This lady and I, we met through the Grandparents' Guild. Older people to whom the tastes of home are important. We cook for one another, share meals and recipes. We have members, and so friends, all over the city."

Before we left—for Harlem—two things happened.

First, Maalini Sundari promised not to call her friend to say we were coming. She glared at her nephew as if to dare him to try to persuade her.

Second, Maalini Sundari said, "The boy, Mark. He is the son of the mayor."

"That's true," I said.

"Ashok and I are helping you find him."

That point was debatable, but I just nodded.

She went on, "Many people, like Ashok, go from here into Manhattan every day to work. Everyone always must allow extra time, because in Queens the trains are always running late. Is it possible you might speak to the mayor about this?"

"The trains?" I said. "The MTA is a separate agency."

"Yes, of course. And yet if the mayor particularly wants something to be done, perhaps the MTA might think it is important, also."

Maalini Sundari, I realized, had given way to Mahila Mukhiya.

"Well, but—" I started.

"We'll speak to her." Lydia overrode me. "There may be nothing the mayor can do. But we'll try."

"Thank you," the Boss Lady said.

All I could do was nod again.

# 9

I didn't want to make the same mistake as before so Maalini Sundari called a cousin who drove a black car. In New York when you say "black car" you don't necessarily mean a car that's black. You mean a for-hire but not for-hailing limo; though by "limo" you don't necessarily mean luxury. Maalini Sundari walked with us down the stairs to the front door as Ashok sat in stony silence at the table.

"If you hear from Mark, you'll let us know, right?" I said.

"Of course." Maalini Sundari smiled. "And thank you for the snacks."

The cousin's car drew up. It was actually black. I checked the street for any sign of a tail, but no one seemed interested in us. Lydia and I scuttled to the car and got in. Two pine-scented air fresheners and a tiny eight-armed Durga amulet swayed from the mirror. The cousin, a smiling, bearded man, punched the Harlem address into his GPS. He sent us a thumbs-up and pulled out from the curb.

Before we got to the corner my phone rang.

I checked the screen as I lifted the phone. "Hey, Bree."

"Where are you?"

"On the trail."

"Your techie's approved."

"Great. We'll send him right in."

"I'll meet him at the house. Security won't let him in alone. How'd you get along with the household?"

"The chef was so happy to know us he gave us cookies."

"Lucky you. He makes great cookies. Give me a report."

I was tempted to say, *molasses and raisins*, but I settled for, "Madison doesn't like me, Crewe does, Overbey's neutral. Madison took to Lydia, though."

"She's a nasty little thing, Madison, but she's not stupid."

"None of them seemed to have anything useful to say." What Crewe had had to say, and what it had led to, was something I wasn't prepared to share yet. "And someone else is looking for Mark besides us."

A pause. "Are you sure?"

"This guy." I texted her the photo.

"Who is he?" she asked.

"I thought you could tell me."

"How would I know? And how do you know he's looking for Mark?"

"He was following us, so unless he finds Lydia—or me—particularly delectable it's a fair bet he was hoping we'd lead him to the kid. We shook him. You have no idea who he is? Or who he's from?"

"No, but I really don't like it."

"Me either. I don't like that someone's looking and I don't like that they knew who and where we were, to pick us up."

"You're not thinking that came from here?"

"I don't know what I'm thinking. Go meet Linus and Trella. They'll be there within the hour."

"Where are you going?"

"To keep looking." I hung up.

Maalini Sundari's smiling cousin dropped us in front of a five-story yellow brick apartment building on West 144th Street and waved as he drove away. Lydia waved back. At the door, most of the buzzers had no names; one of the few that did, though, was the one we needed. H. Binney, it read, and we buzzed it. Twice. And got nothing. I was about to press some other buzzers to see if we could get into the building when I heard a "Yo."

I turned. A young boy, six or seven, reading a comic book on the stoop two doors down, called, "Y'all looking for Miz Binney?"

"That's right," I said.

"She in the park." He lifted his chin to point across the street. "Like always." His look was skeptical, as if he couldn't believe we actually didn't know that, so we must be up to something.

"Thank you," said Lydia.

"Ain't no thing." He nodded, I nodded, Lydia smiled, and Lydia and I headed across the street. After a moment, from the corner of my eye, I saw the kid follow.

Twilight was approaching, but on the park's two basketball courts physical, trash-talking games surged back and forth. The players on the far court were all young men, but each of the teams on the near court had a woman on it.

A form, shapeless in the dusk, sat on a bench with a view of the games and the rest of the park, too, the climbing equipment and the handball wall, the picnic tables and the other benches. As we neared it, the shape resolved into a thin old woman with her hair in a wiry gray bun. A tan jacket hung loose over her hunched shoulders.

"Ms. Harriet Binney?"

The woman looked up at me, one thin brown wrist crossed over the other in her lap. "Missus," she said firmly.

"I apologize, ma'am. May I?" I indicated the bench.

She kept the look going, then turned back to the game. "Free country."

I sat, and Lydia sat beside me, not Binney, so the woman wouldn't feel hemmed in.

"Maalini Sundari sent us here," I said. "We're looking for Mark McCann."

"Know her," Binney said, her eyes still on the game. "Don't know him."

"Ms. Sundari sent him here, too. To you." I also turned to the game.

"Guess so. But he ain't here."

"He left?"

"Never got here." Now she looked at me. "Sound like you from the South."

"Louisville."

"How long y'all been gone?"

"Since I was sixteen."

"Hmmph. I come up from Mobile in '72. Ain't never been back. You?"

"Once or twice."

Back to the game. After a time, "That boy. Y'all who been running after him?"

"Yes, ma'am. His mother asked us to find him."

She nodded to herself. "Maalini tell me he coming. Ask me could I look after him. But he ain't come."

Lydia leaned past me. "His mother's worried."

"His momma. She the mayor," Binney said.

"Yes."

A whoop erupted from one of the women on the court as the other made a great spin move into a layup. I watched as one of the boys high-fived her. The other team took the ball out and started up the court.

"Y'all see that boy there?" Binney nodded to the kid from the stoop. He was standing near the sideline, absorbed in the game. "Lamonte Mills. He ain't got no momma."

"I'm sorry," I said.

"That his sister. Little point guard there."

"She's good."

"They got another brother besides. They daddy trying to take care of 'em since they momma die. He got two jobs. Keeping 'em all in school. But he ain't home much."

I watched the sister's team fast-break down the court. It was beginning to get dark and I wondered how long these kids could keep playing in the glow of headlights and streetlights.

"Lamonte sister like playing ball. Lamonte, he like to read. They other brother, Kordell, he like chess. But ain't no after-school program round here where he could play chess at. So he be hanging out." She paused, but kept her eyes on the game, harder to follow now as the night came down. "Boys he hanging out with, they a bad crowd. Keep with them, they daddy gonna lose him. Shame. He trying so hard."

"I don't—" I began, but Lydia touched my hand.

"That school right there," Binney went on, nodding to a hulking shape at the end of the park, "be a good thing if they have a after-school program. For chess. Reading, maybe, too. Be a good thing for a lotta kids."

Now she turned to me. "The mayor office got they own money. Everyone know that. Slush fund, it called. Money she can give for projects, she decide to. Like after school, right here."

"We'll ask her," Lydia said, before I could speak. "We can't promise anything, but we'll ask her."

"Y'all tell that mayor it important. Keep Kordell, other children like him, keep them outta bad trouble. She worried about her son; Kordell daddy, he worried too."

"We'll try," I said.

Binney nodded. After a moment she said, "He call me."

"Who?" I wasn't sure we weren't still talking about Kordell's daddy.

Binney blinked at me. "Mark. The boy. He call to say he ain't coming. Don't want me to worry none, nor Maalini neither, case she call me to make sure he get here." She nodded. "Someone raise him good, teach him to do the right thing."

Locks the window after himself, calls his safe house so they won't worry. Maybe it was just good upbringing, as Binney said; though I couldn't help thinking he was feeling some ambivalence about his disappearing act. If he was, why?

"When was this?" I asked.

"Few hour ago. After he leave Maalini place."

"Did he say why? Or where he was going?"

"Why?" She stared in disbelief. "Didn't say why, but sure as shooting it because y'all chasing after him. That why Maalini push him out her place, ain't it? Because she know y'all's coming?"

"Yes, but Ms. Sundari didn't know us then. She didn't know we were the good guys. Now she sent us to you. Did Mark say where he was going?"

"Didn't say. And I don't know y'all neither."

If Harriet Binney didn't know where Mark had gone—or wouldn't say, though in fact I believed her—then this was another dead end. Damn it. A wasted day except for a few good cookies and some post-brawl bruises. "Okay," I said. "Thank you, Mrs. Binney. If you hear from Mark again, could you ask him to call me?" I handed her my card.

"Don't expect I will," she said. "But," she squinted up at me as I stood, "if all y'all's the good guys, I spose I can give y'all the number he call from."

Out of a pocket in her shapeless jacket she pulled the newest model iPhone. Two seconds of scrolling got her to where she wanted to be. She peered at my card, tapped on her screen, and a texted phone number appeared on mine.

"Mrs. Binney," I said, "thanks. Thanks very much."

I was about to call the number when Binney spoke again. "Another thing."

"Yes, ma'am?"

"When y'all talk to that lady mayor, about them after-school programs. This park here"—she waved a bony hand, at the games winding down, at the slides, the swings, the benches—"could use it some lights."

# 10

The first thing we did as we left the park was to check the number Binney had given us against Aubrey's list of Mark's friends. Not surprisingly, it wasn't there. Then I called it. Even less surprisingly, it went to voicemail. A kindly-sounding female robot suggested I leave a message after the tone. I did, stressing that Mark's mother was worried. If the kid was all that conscientious—or ambivalent—that might make a difference.

Then I pressed a number I had on speed-dial.

"Hey," Linus said, picking up on the first ring.

"Hey," I said. "You at the mayor's place?"

"Yeah. Kinda awesome. There's like a matched set of cops here. Tall skinny ones, navy blue suits and super-shiny shoes. One inside, one outside. Like they're twins."

"Uh-huh. Did you manage to get into the computer?"

"Dude," he said, with reproof, "eight minutes, fourteen seconds. When you find him, tell him he needs better passwords."

"I'll make it a priority. Anything yet?"

"Only just got here. Half an hour?"

"As soon as you can. Also, can you trace a phone?"

"Trace?"

"I want to know whose it is and where it is."

"Whose is easier. Where takes pinging towers and stuff. Or accessing the GPS. You know who the carrier is?"

"All I have is the number." I gave it to him.

"Okay, I got people at each carrier but I gotta talk to them one by one, you know? And we gotta . . . negotiate. Could take time."

"If you're negotiating about money, we'll pay." I paused. "If it looks like it'll take forever, tell me. I can have it done on the up-and-up, but I'd rather not for now."

"The kid's using it?" Kid. Linus was maybe five years older than Mark.

"Yes. And someone else is looking for him."

"Shit, really? Who?" He dropped his voice to a whisper. I wondered if Aubrey had just walked up on him.

"I don't know. Until I do, I want to keep things close."

"Gotcha. Well," his tones went back to normal, "we'll let you know."

"You do that. Thanks, Linus."

"Sure. And," whispering again, "can you get your friend to stop pacing? She's driving us nuts."

I called Bree.

"Stop pacing. You're driving my techies nuts."

"Your techies," now she was the one whispering, "are *children*."

"Who do you think knows how to do that stuff? You find our tail yet?"

"I asked around discreetly. No one knows him."

"Or admits it. All right. Give Linus and Trella whatever they need. Talk to you later."

"What are you doing now?"

"Actually," I said, "I don't know."

I hung up and Lydia said, "You don't know what?"

"Anything. You hungry?"

She grinned. "Starving. Can we go back to the Sundaris' and eat the snacks?"

"I doubt there's anything left. No, come on, there's an Ethiopian café near here that makes a shiro wot that'll knock your socks off."

Three steps down from the sidewalk, the Tsion Café took up the ground floor of a bow-fronted town house on St. Nicholas Ave. The buildings here had started their lives as elegantly appointed as the ones on the mayor's Upper East Side street. They'd been single-family homes with parquet floors and carved plaster moldings, high-ceilinged parlors and stone fireplaces. Over the years these houses had had a harder time of it, though, been divided up, disrespected, sometimes deserted; but when, as had happened here, someone took the trouble to try to bring one back to its original state, the building seemed happy to cooperate. The Tsion Café had exposed brick walls, shiny wood floors, a bar down one side and tables down the other. I asked for a back table and Lydia and I were shown through the swirling scents of berbere spices and clarified butter.

"I don't know this food," Lydia said. "You order." So I did.

While we waited and then while we ate, we worked the phones, each taking three of the six kids on Aubrey's list. "They don't call, they text," Lydia said. "Text first to tell them who you are and that you're going to call or they won't answer the phone."

I did what she said, wishing Aubrey hadn't called these kids already, because Lydia and I could've gone in with some kind of ruse that might have worked better than the truth. But each of them had been asked this morning if they'd seen Mark, and five of the six went to Granite Ridge so they'd know he hadn't shown up at school for two days. Anything we tried would be in that context. So, we used the truth.

Which got us nowhere. Each text got some variation on okay, so we'd made the calls, but the spicy chickpea stew, sautéed cabbage-and-potatoes, and spongy injera bread disappeared along with our hopes of finding Mark through his friends. "Well, it was unlikely anyway," Lydia said as I wiped injera across my plate for the last of the stew and she punched in the final number.

When the phone was answered, Lydia said what we'd each been saying: after telling the kid who she was, she told her Mark hadn't been home, his mother was worried, and she, Lydia, was just trying to find out if he was all right. Could the kid give Lydia any idea where he might be, or how to get in touch with him? At that point we'd been getting, "No idea," or, more elaborately, "Sorry, dude, no idea." Then we'd ask the kid to tell Mark, if they heard from him, that we weren't looking to take him back home if he didn't want to go. We just wanted to make sure he was okay, and could he please give us a call. We'd get, "Yeah, sure," or "No problem," in the signature half-hearted teenage way. I calculated the chances of any of this paying off at zero to nil.

I was only half listening, considering next steps while I waited for Lydia to say that second bit, when I heard, "Oh. Did he tell you that? . . . Well, I mean, that's how *I* was all through high school so—Oh, um-hm, I get it. Do you know. . . . What about the day before? . . . But you're pretty sure. . . . Thanks, really, and no, of course I won't. If you do hear from him. . . . Great. Thanks again, Astrid, really."

By the time she clicked off I'd sat up, ordered coffee for me and mint tea for her, and was ready. "Yes? Gold?"

"No, but something shiny. Astrid Bergson. She doesn't know where he is but she says he was upset at school the other day. Two days ago, the last time he was there."

"Upset? No one else told us that. Everyone said he seemed fine. I was beginning to think whatever happened came after school. Did he say anything to her?"

"She says he didn't, but she also reminded me he's an actor—and a good one, by her account—so seeming normal could easily have been a show. Until algebra. Then no one was looking at him—"

"But she was? Astrid?"

"She's a painter. She looks at people. It's what she does. In algebra, she says, Mark had either just gotten whatever news upset him, or he dropped the act. He was distracted. Staring out the window, not taking notes, almost didn't finish the pop quiz. She says he's never like that—he makes it a point to get the academic subjects out of the way so he can spend all his time working on his theater skills."

"Like Ashok's trampoline. Does she have any idea what was eating him?"

"No, or where he is now. It's not directly helpful, but it does narrow down the time of whatever happened."

"Sometime in the morning. After he left for school, and before algebra. When's algebra?"

"Eleven fifteen to noon."

I called Aubrey.

"Yes?" She had to shout to be heard over the rush of voices and the clink and clatter of food being served and eaten.

"Where are you?"

"At a devastatingly hot new restaurant. With my devastatingly hot date." I saw in my mind the smile she was giving that date across the table. "Is that why you called?"

"Your boss is paying me to track down her son, not you."

"And you have?" Her voice quickened.

"Not yet. I need to know where he was Tuesday morning."

"At school. That was the last day he went."

"I need it granularly. Minute by minute."

"It matters?"

"No, it's just an excuse to call and hear your cheerful voice before I go to bed."

"Alone?"

"No promises. Get back to me as soon as you can."

She dropped her voice. "If this is just some bullshit to ruin my evening—"

"Why would I bother? Though it's a nice bonus."

We were the last customers left in the Tsion Café. I'd finished my excellent thick coffee, Lydia was down to the end of her mint tea, and I had no next step to propose, when my phone rang.

"That was quick," I said, taking it from my pocket; but it wasn't Aubrey.

"Hey, dude," said Linus. "Hey, cuz, you there?" I could tell from the echo that he was on speaker. I put my phone on speaker, too, and set it on the table.

"Hey, guys," said Lydia. "I'm here."

"Hey, Woof," said Linus, "it's Bill and Cousin Lydia."

Linus's big yellow dog, Woof, gave a happy bark. That took care of the heys, and it meant Linus and Trella were back at the garage office in Queens. I asked, "Did you find that phone?"

"Not yet. I have people on it. The who isn't gonna happen, though. It's a burner."

"But the where?"

"Could still happen. And we have other stuff for you."

"Go ahead."

"Well, so, we're through with the laptop."

"They let you take it with you?"

"Didn't even ask. I cloned it onto a flash drive."

"Good thinking."

"Hey, it's what we do. So, it's kinda disorganized in there, but it looks like a lot of schoolwork, not much else. Essays on Lee Strasberg, the

Spanish Civil War, the difference between haiku and hokku. You guys ever hear of hokku? Me neither. It's—"

"Linus?"

"Oh. Yeah. So, algebra homework, some notes for stuff he's working on—"

"Working on?"

"Comedy skits, that kind of thing."

"Funny?"

"No. Someone else really needs to write his material."

"Okay. What else?"

"Rehearsal videos. We didn't watch them all, but you know, the same thing over and over, it looks like. I mean, not all the same, but different scenes, each one a bunch of times. In two of them he's with someone else. Once a guy, once a girl."

"Are they identified?"

"No. You want to see the videos? They're big so they'll take a while to download if I send them, but I could put them in a Dropbox."

I looked at Lydia and she nodded. "Yes, do it," I said. "And that's it?"

"Kinda. Except Trella found his Finsta and his FikFok."

Lydia and I exchanged glances across the table. "Sorry?" I said.

"The accounts you gave us," Trella said. "On Instagram and TikTok. We're guessing you got those from his mom?"

"That's right."

"Yeah, that's kind of who they're for. Parents all know their kids have accounts, so you don't try to tell them you don't. You just make two. As long as you keep adding content to the one they know about, they think they're following you, that they're up-to-date. It keeps them happy."

My grandfather used to say that age and rat cunning beats youth and skill any time. That may be true; but when it's youth that has the rat cunning, game over.

"Mark had second accounts?" I asked.

"Finsta, fake Instagram. FikFok—"

"Fake TikTok."

"Hey, check him out," said Linus. "He Toks the Tok and woks the wok."

"Okay," I said. "So what's in them? All the hot and juicy stuff he couldn't post where his parents would find it?"

"Not really," said Trella. "I mean, this stuff is different, more personal, but nothing that'll blow you away. And no recent posts since he's been gone. I'll send you the links."

"Great. Anything else? Hidden files on the computer?"

"Dude," said Linus, "gotta say, this is maybe the easiest—and dullest—deep dive I ever did. If this kid has secrets, he doesn't keep them here. Hang tight for incoming. Me and Trella gotta go meet some people at a club."

"Now?"

"You know it. The night's just getting started."

Once Linus and Trella had clicked off and gone to get their night started, I said to Lydia, "This Dropbox thing, you know what it means?"

"Of course. It's easier on the computer than on the phone, but I could access it now if you want."

"No. They're trying to close this place." I waved the waiter over and gave him my credit card. "Let's go home and you can do it in the morning. The kids in the scenes with Mark may be people we talked to already. I need to think about what to do next. Unless you have a bright idea?"

"Sleep."

"Not sure that will help."

"I am. Sleep helps everything."

# 11

By "let's go home" I had meant "together" and "to my place," but Lydia wanted to check in on her mother.

"Also," she said, "my computer's there, which means I can access Linus's Dropbox. Now if you had a computer—"

"I wouldn't be the rough-and-tumble tough guy you know and love. Anyway, that's why I keep you around."

"I thought you had other reasons for keeping me around."

"I did, but here you are, going home to your mother. So I have to console myself with your computer. It's pretty cold comfort."

She shook her head. "And the computer always speaks so highly of you."

"That's why I don't get one. They have poor taste."

When we got off the subway I walked her home. Our goodnight kiss was the opposite of cold comfort, but she went upstairs to her apartment just the same.

Which turned out to be lucky for her.

Downstairs from my place is Shorty's Bar. My uncle Dave had been an NYPD detective; his friend Lew had wanted to be a cop, too, but when he was coming up the NYPD had a height requirement he couldn't reach.

So he opened a watering hole, named it and himself after his stumbling block, and probably made more cops happy with his late hours and generous pours than he'd ever have even met on the Job.

I dropped in for a quiet drink. Because he'd known Dave, Shorty called me "kid"; rented me the upstairs apartment cheap in return for doing occasional maintenance around the place; and when I came in slid a Maker's Mark in front of me before I said anything.

Tonight, as he put down the glass, he asked, "How's it going?"

"Could be worse," I said.

"Don't say that. You know what happens."

I did. And it did.

I was a couple of sips in when the barstool to the right of me creaked under the weight of a bulldog-shaped body. The stool on my left side creaked too, but with less complaint. I looked at that one first. White guy, tall, thin, black hair, sharp features. Didn't know him. As opposed to the other one.

"Well," said a gravelly voice from my right, in exaggerated tones of wonder, "if it ain't Smitty." A smile about the same temperature as the ice in my drink spread between massive, pasty jowls.

I sipped, put the drink down. "It ain't." No one on earth has ever called me Smitty. But that's the trouble with drinking at a cop bar. Cops come in. Just plain cops, but also big shot cops. "What's new, Bulldog?"

"Not much. You? Dewar's, Shorty, no ice. Bozinski? Same?"

So the guy on my left was the Doberman. He nodded.

"Nothing much new here, either," I said.

"Oh, no, come on," Straley said. "You're a BFD. I heard you had a meeting with the mayor today."

Shorty, with a look at me, poured Straley's drink, and then Bozinski's.

I said, "I heard you had one yesterday."

Straley was briefly silent, staring at the bottles on the shelves behind the bar. He drank, then said, "You know, it's been tried before."

"Dewar's, without ice?"

"Jesus, don't you ever grow up?"

"Why mess with a winning formula?"

All the security at City Hall, including the mayor's own plainclothes detail, was NYPD, so it wasn't surprising that someone was reporting back to Herb Straley on McCann's every move. Anything might provide leverage for the contract negotiations. McCann for sure knew that, which was why she'd sent her security men out of earshot for our meeting.

Straley turned toward me. "Last time around, different mayor, same shit. Hired someone to find dirt on me. Didn't go well."

I stared. "Honest to God, Straley? You think that's what I'm doing? You think you're the only thing on McCann's mind right now?"

"If I'm not, I should be. Her tight little girl-jock butt is on the line. Hey, can I say that?"

"Say whatever you want. I'm not listening."

"She's smarter than the last asshole, I'll give her that. She knows what side cops are on, even ex-cops, so she hires a PI that was never a cop, to find my skeletons. Last guy hired a retired gold shield, you believe that shit? But he couldn't find no skeletons. Not a bone. Cause I got none. You could save yourself a lot of trouble, you just ask him. I'll give you his name if you want."

"Well, if I cared, I'd take you up on that. Even though since he was a cop investigating a cop maybe I wouldn't believe him. But, see, I *don't* care, because you're wrong. Hard as it may be to believe, that meeting wasn't about you."

"Oh, sure. What was it about, then?"

"Jesus, you think I'm that easy? Come on, show some respect."

His stool groaned again as he shifted his weight. I can't say I blamed it. "You know, Smitty," Straley said, leaning in closer, "a guy in your business could use a friend on the NYPD."

"Why, Bulldog," I said. "I didn't know you felt that way." I batted my eyes.

"Oh, fuck that shit." He pulled back a little, which had been my aim. "But it's got to be a two-way street. You scratch my back, I'll scratch yours."

"Right out there on the two-way street? For all the world to see?"

"You know, you're starting to piss me off. That's a really bad idea, in case you forgot. Now I asked you a simple question. I'd like a simple answer. Unless you and Her Honor have something to hide."

I met his eyes for a long few moments. Briefly, I wondered if his rabies shots were up to date. Or if mine were. Then I shrugged. "You win."

"Smart move. So?"

"I asked for that meeting."

"You? Why?"

I took a sip of my Maker's, set it on the bar. I faced Straley head on. "So I could tell the mayor how sick I am of the dog shit all over this city. Especially from bulldogs."

Straley flushed a color you'd have gotten if you cross-bred the pink tulips with the purple irises in the mayor's back yard. He took a hard swig of his Dewar's.

I turned back to the TV over the bar.

"No shit," Straley said. "And your partner? She sick of the dog shit in Chinatown? Then maybe they oughta stop eating puppy chow mein, what do you think?"

I squeezed my bourbon glass to keep my fist from his face.

"Oh, crap," he said with a grin. "That was un-woke, wasn't it? Now you're for sure gonna report my ass."

"The only thing I'm going to report your ass for is sitting where it wasn't invited." I turned to look at him again. "Of all the barstools in all the gin joints in all the world, you sit down on this one." He stared at me blankly. Sorry, Bogie. "Come on, Straley. You have something to say, say it and then consider getting lost." I was tired of him disrupting my quiet drink. Also, he was a bully. That was his resting state, but he didn't need to rest it next to me.

"All right, Smitty," he growled. "You don't want to play nice, it's your business. But remember this. Whatever you're doing, I don't give a shit, unless—"

"—I interfere with actual police work, in which case you'll pull my license, arrest me, and throw me in a pestilential prison with a life-long lock."

That last got me a stare and a muttered, "Jesus Christ." Not a Gilbert and Sullivan fan, either, I guessed. Straley threw back the rest of his drink and stood. "Just keep out of my business."

"Hey," I said. "You're the one who came over and sat next to me." But the Bulldog was gone, and the Doberman with him.

Shorty walked over. "What was that about?" he asked.

"I have no idea."

"You don't want to cross him."

"Jesus, Shorty, I crossed him so many years ago neither of us remembers the details. I'm still here."

"Then, he was just an asshole. Now he's an important asshole."

"If you give me another drink I'll be able to come up with a funny rejoinder to that."

"I doubt it," he said, reaching for the bottle. "And these days he's an important asshole in a rotten mood."

"The contract negotiations?"

"They need to go well. He's got a mutiny brewing." Shorty refilled my glass.

"In the DEA?"

"Yeah. A few years ago he talked them into putting the pension account into a hedge fund."

"Straley knows what a hedge fund is?"

"You shitting me? He can't even spell it. He just wanted to play in the big kids' sandbox. At first the returns were good and he was handing out cigars. When the market started tanking some of the hedge fund investors jumped ship. There got to be talk around the DEA about moving theirs someplace safer, too." He put the bottle on the bar in front of me, just in case.

"But Straley agreeing to do that would be too much like admitting he made a mistake," I said.

Shorty grunted. "He says only an idiot buys a new car because of a bump in the road."

"He made that up?" I raised my eyebrows at the metaphor and sipped my drink.

"Nah. Probably one of his Dog Pack. One who went to canine college. But Straley kept the money in, some of the other nervous investors stayed too, whole thing blew over. Now he sees himself as some kind of financial genius. Market's looking shaky again now but Straley's dug in."

"He can't be the only one making those decisions."

"He's not. Enough guys are upset about this—his attitude as much as their money—that he'd probably have been chucked out the window already except for the negotiations."

"No one wants to complain about the food and then have to be the cook?"

"You got it. As long as the talks are going on the other guys won't make waves. If Straley comes out with a nice fat package, he can probably count on getting re-elected."

"And if he doesn't there'll be a coup and he'll be just a regular asshole again. No more important asshole."

"Yeah. Which means he gives up the driver, the office, the big table in the boardroom, and the expense account. And he'll have to go back to doing actual work instead of just throwing his weight around."

"I seem to remember him throwing his weight around back in the day. Before the boardroom."

"Yeah. And so, if I was you, I'd steer clear for a while."

For a time after that I sipped, watched people come and go, checked out the basketball game playing silently over the bar. Knicks and Lakers, in LA. Both teams were long out of the playoff race so I only half paid attention. Something occurred to me.

"Hey, Shorty," I said, "you know Joe Lenz?"

"Haven't seen him in maybe a year, but yeah. He used to be down here, I think at the Seventh. They moved him uptown, not sure where."

"Straight?"

"As anybody, sure."

"Meaning?"

"He probably takes pencils home, pads his overtime. But he's a good cop. Why?"

"Wouldn't sweep anything under the rug? Or just shitcan something because he didn't want to bother?"

"Not the guy I knew. Why're you asking?"

"Lydia ran into him on a case. Just thought I'd check him out."

"Yeah, well, I was you, I'd forget about Lenz and worry about Straley."

# 12

I was almost done with the second drink when my phone rang. I considered not answering on the grounds that it was late, but given the hours I usually kept, those were shaky grounds. The number was unfamiliar. "Bill Smith," I said, keeping my voice calm and non-committal, in case this was Mark.

It wasn't. "Hey! Smith! You that jerk my wife hired to find my son? I want you over here now!"

"With whom am I having the pleasure?" I asked, although I'd guessed.

"Jeffrey Guilder, smartass. Fifteen minutes."

"Where?"

"If it didn't occur to that self-absorbed bitch to give you my particulars, she's an even worse idiot than I thought, and if you're so stupid you didn't think to ask for them, you're fired."

I was already wishing I worked for him so he could actually fire me. "Home or office?"

"Home."

"New York or Watermill?"

A tiny pause. "Jesus. Would I have said fifteen minutes if I were in Watermill?"

"Yes, you do seem like that kind of guy. Okay, leave the porch light on." I clicked off. "Sorry, Shorty," I said. "Finish this for me, will you? I've got to go."

The porch light was not on, because Jeffrey Guilder's New York home, a condo in a white brick high-rise, didn't have a porch. It did have terraces, one on the south facing 82nd Street and one overlooking Park Avenue. I saw that one through the windows of his aggressively stark living room when he yanked open the door. The doorframe held a discreet button, but though I'd seen it, I'd knocked.

"You're Smith?" He didn't need to ask; the doorman had told him I was coming up.

"Yes. You're Guilder?" I didn't need to ask, either. His silver hair and piercing blue eyes spent enough time filling up my TV screen when I watched the news.

"*Mr.* Guilder."

"*Mr.* Smith."

"Don't give me that bullshit. I come across dickheads like you every day. You're some asshole private eye my wife hired to pretend she's looking for my son."

"I come across dickheads like you, too. Most of them are lawyers. And I'm *the* asshole private eye your *ex*-wife hired to *find* your son."

His jaw tensed. "And it didn't occur to you to call me?"

"Why, is he here?" I made a show of trying to peer behind him as he stood in the doorway.

"Of course he's not here."

I spread my hands. "There you go, then. Actually, calling you did occur to me, but my client told me not to."

"And you were a good little boy and did what that narcissistic bitch said."

"That narcissistic bitch, the mother of your son, is paying me. You want to match my fee, I can be bought. Should I come in, or"—I raised my voice—"is this something you want your neighbors to hear so you can call them as witnesses in court later on?"

Guilder, teeth clenched, stepped aside. Once I was in he slammed the door behind me. I wondered how many of his neighbors over the years had considered trying to get him thrown out of the building, and despaired when they realized they were dealing not just with a lawyer, but with Jeffrey Guilder, and moved out themselves, instead.

In the living room the ivory carpet was thick, the furniture all angled chestnut leather, steel legs, and glass tabletops; the art on the walls was large slash-and-burn abstractions. The two long thin sofas didn't look comfortable, but Madison Guilder did, curled on one. So did Oscar Trask, sitting on the same sofa, at the other end.

"My daughter told me how you went plowing into her room," Guilder barked. "And my son's. You went through his things. You had no right and you'll stop now."

I looked at Madison. She wore the off-one-shoulder burgundy gown that had been draped on her bed last time I saw it. The silver shoes that I assumed were the killer Jimmy Choos lay haphazardly on the carpet where she'd kicked them off. Her smile was smug, though a lift of the eyebrows as she met my gaze had an invitation about it.

"Hello, Madison," I said. "Good to see you again." I crossed the room and held out my hand to Trask. "We haven't met. I'm Bill Smith."

Trask seemed amused. He didn't rise, but switched his martini glass to his left hand, offered his right, and gave me a smooth, cool shake. "Oscar Trask." That was another ID I didn't need. Head shaved clean, medium height, slow and confident in his movements, with a smiling, weathered face, Trask, whose day job was managing the money of the rich to make them richer, was a fixture of the New York cultural scene. Tonight he was dressed as I'd seen him in photos—and occasionally across the intermission lobby of concert halls over the years—in a tux I assumed was bespoke. Probably the elegant patent-leather shoes were, too. He was someone who was everywhere you'd find the anybodies who were somebody: at opening nights, building dedications, galas, and all the other Important Events. He loved the camera. The camera, I observed, also loved him; without a lens between us, the suit was still fine but the man looked a little shopworn.

"I didn't invite you here for a cocktail party," Guilder snapped.

"You didn't actually *invite* me here at all. What do you want?"

"I want you to stop harassing my daughter and leave my son alone."

"Okay, got it." I turned to the door.

"Goddammit!" he said.

"Yeah." I turned back. "Goddammit. Now listen. I didn't harass your daughter and if she says I did, she's bullshitting you. Which I suspect she does a lot."

Madison smiled and gave an unapologetic shrug.

"I talked to Madison in the presence of two women," I went on. "My partner and your ex-wife's household manager. So you can forget that line of country. About your son, he's missing. Gone. Not seen for two days, going on three now." Not quite accurate, according to the Sundaris, but why should Guilder learn things I hadn't told the client yet? "It's up to you whether that bothers you but it bothers your ex-wife. For what it's worth, it also bothers me."

"It's worth nothing. Mark's done this before. He's looking for atten-tion. When he doesn't get it he'll come back. If you keep chasing after him he'll keep leading you on. It's a game to him."

"Really? Because that doesn't sound like the kid I've been told about."

"By whom?"

"People who actually know him. It does sound like a great story for you to tell yourself about why he ran away from home—*your* home—a couple of times before this and you hardly even noticed."

Guilder took a step closer, and slightly to my side. If I were a witness on the stand my instinct would be to turn toward him, which would mean turning my back on the jury. Just before he spoke I bet myself he was going to lower his voice.

"How much to get you to stop?"

I won my bet. Now, because he'd established dominance, I was supposed to want to mirror him and drop my voice, too. That would mean the jurors would have to strain to hear me. Which would make them annoyed. At me.

Stepping back so I was once again facing him squarely, I asked a little loudly, "Why?"

From the corner of my eye I caught Trask smiling, winking at Madison as he sipped his martini. He was watching us as though this were a well-played scene in an opera buffa. I couldn't help agreeing, and though I'm an opera fan, I prefer tragic to funny every time.

"What the hell do you care why?" Guilder demanded, raising his voice to match mine.

"Is it because he doesn't need to be found? Because you know where he is? Maybe you're even helping him stay lost."

"Are you crazy? Of course I'm not."

I frowned as though I were thinking hard. "No, I withdraw that. Mark doesn't like you enough to go along with that kind of shit." Madison gave that big, round eyes and a perfect little "O" mouth. I ignored her and went on. "It would've been a good plan if you could've pulled it off, though, wouldn't it? So maybe, even though you didn't engineer Mark's vanishing act, you decided to use it. You just need to make sure he stays gone. Because worrying about Mark could distract your ex just enough that she'd screw up these contract negotiations, the ones with the NYPD detectives that so much rides on. Her first major challenge as mayor, and she's up against Herb Straley? She needs to be on her game. If Straley gets the upper hand that could be a big problem for her."

"I don't give a shit what's a problem for her and if she's so goddamned worried about Mark let her call the actual cops instead of some jerk who thinks he's Sam fucking Spade."

"And calling the actual cops could be an even bigger problem for her, public-relations wise. How can she run New York when she can't even keep track of her own kids, you know, all that. As a matter of fact, it's an interesting question, considering how you feel about her, why you haven't already called them yourself. Talk about pulling the rug out from under her negotiations."

"I haven't called them because if Mark knows he's being looked for it'll just feed his ego and cause him to prolong this game. Which is why you need to stop, also. And," he looked me in the eye, "though this may be difficult for a man like you to believe, I actually love this city."

"Even though your ex-wife is running it?"

"You have a dangerously naïve idea of politics if you think the mayor actually runs anything."

"She's running the salary negotiations right now."

"And I'd like these negotiations to conclude soon, with a settlement that's a win-win for all parties." His chin lifted; he was about to pull rank on me. "I happen to know Herb Straley. He's a reasonable guy and if Carole worked with him instead of treating him like the spawn of Satan they could move this shit along."

"You're right, it's hard for me to believe. And I know Herb Straley too. In fact, I was just having a drink with him when you called."

Madison, from her end of the sofa, laughed out loud. "Ooh la la! It knows important people."

"Shut up, Madison," Guilder said. To me: "Do not even *try* that bullshit on me. For one thing I don't care if you were drinking with God himself. For another, that's just about as likely as you drinking with Herb."

"Drinking with God herself would have been more fun than drinking with Herb, which was almost as much fun as being here with you. And I couldn't help noticing that you said you loved this city but you didn't mention loving your son."

"You know," Trask broke in, and Guilder and I both whipped around to face him, "Smith, is it? Smith, you should have been a lawyer." I realized that, though I'd been seeing photos of Trask for years, except for giving me his name just now, I'd never heard him speak. His tenor voice was rich, amused, and oddly seductive.

After just these few minutes, I already understood that to be part of Guilder's circle you'd have to prove yourself, and then keep proving yourself. He didn't want you, didn't need you. To a certain kind of person—and no doubt to a certain kind of juror, and no doubt he knew just how to pick those jurors—that made him irresistible.

Trask was different. He seemed to grant you immediate citizenship in his exclusive kingdom. You and he, and a select few others, against the world. Oscar Trask would have your back; he was trusting you to have his. Unless and until you disappointed him. Showed yourself unworthy. Then you'd be exiled to the barren badlands, the gates of El Dorado would be shut against you, and it would be completely your fault. You'd been given a chance. You'd failed.

"Or are you?" Trask went on. "Do you have a law degree? Because you can run in meaningless but confounding circles almost as well as Jeffrey."

Madison, having been told to shut up, acted as though she were sti-fling a giggle, which of course drew attention to it.

"I can't speak for Jeffrey," said Trask, "but I'd be amazed to find he knows where young Mark is and it's frankly ridiculous to even have thought that he was hiding him. Mark is a teenager. Teenage rebellion is tiresome but inevitable, especially in boys." A smile at Madison. "Jeffrey's forbearance in not calling the police is remarkable, but as much as he might be worried, and also be tempted to embarrass the boy's mother—we are none of us perfect," he said with an indulgent smile at Guilder, "I would think his love for the boy is evidenced by the fact that he *hasn't* called them. Ignoring childish nonsense like this is the best thing to do." Once again, he winked at Madison, who, once again, giggled. I wondered if she'd been drinking. She had no martini glass, but at the opera, the intermission bar would have been open. "Turn off the spotlight," Trask said, "and he'll tire of the game and come home with his tail between his legs." He sipped his drink. "Now be a good man and go away. I have a long drive home—not that I'm doing the driving, of course," he lifted his glass in a salute, "and I'd like to enjoy my cocktail in peace. I'd invite you to stay for a martini but I think Jeffrey would have a seizure." Trask gestured to a full glass on a side table, with a silver shaker next to it. "Poor Jeffrey hasn't even started his, and I make a very good martini. Perhaps you'll take a rain check? I'd be delighted to buy you a drink some other time."

I looked from Trask to Guilder. The king had spoken benevolently from on high but in this scene the battle was between the knights.

Guilder took his cue. "How much? To get you to stop?"

"Well," I rubbed my chin in thought like the stage clown I was, "I did say earlier that I could be bought. That was before I knew you, though. To do this job I'm getting a pretty good fee. To not do it?" I looked him up and down. "Sorry, you can't afford it. I'll see myself out."

S. J. ROZAN

I strode across the room, out the door, and, so that my exit wouldn't turn anticlimactic while I stood around waiting for the elevator, I pushed through the fire door. It was eleven flights to the lobby, but never let it be said I have no commitment to my role.

Madison's giggling fit followed me down until the door above me shut.

# 13

I considered calling Lydia to get her take on all that, but by now it was close to midnight and she'd said that thing about sleep helping everything so I assumed she was trying it.

I went home and, after another Blanton's, did the same myself.

The phone woke me, Lydia's ringtone. I grabbed it. "What's up?"

"I'm not sure."

"Why? What happened?" I saw sunlight outlining my window shades. I fell back on the bed, relaxed a little; something might be up, but this wasn't a middle-of-the-night emergency call.

"Last night I went through Mark's social media that Trella sent," she said. "Then I went to bed. I didn't do the rehearsal videos until this morning. The boy in a scene from *Angels in America* with Mark is one of the kids we talked to, who said he didn't know anything. But the girl—I watched about three seconds of it, and then I had to stop. Bill, it's Amber Shun."

"Amber—"

"The suicide. The case I turned down."

I grabbed a cigarette, struck a match. "Shit," I said. "You're sure?"
"Yes."

I drew in smoke and my head cleared a little. "Okay. I need coffee. Can you meet me at the Square? Twenty minutes?"

The Square Diner is neither square—it's long, low, curve-roofed and essentially triangular—nor on a square. Its name echoes a park called Finn Square, which it faces, and which is also triangular. Non-rectilinear areas like this are the result of the rational grid set down by the planners of New York City meeting the meandering cow paths of the various original villages the city devoured as it grew. All the boroughs have these spaces because they all absorbed much older towns. The attempts at rationality in Manhattan were more heavy-handed than in other places, though, which makes their failures more evident.

I was making no attempt at rationality myself, only at waking up after a damp walk to the diner through a hostile, spitting rain. I was in a back booth halfway through a mug of black coffee when Lydia pushed through the door. She wasn't alone.

"Hi," she said, sliding in opposite me.

Dropping into the booth beside her, also with a "Hi," was Detective Chris Chiang of the Fifth Precinct. Lydia's yellow slicker, and Chris's black one, were both shiny with rain.

"Hi," I said. "You guys want coffee?"

Chris, yes; Lydia wanted tea. The waiter went off to deal with it.

"Good to see you, Chris, and why are you here?"

Chris is a big guy, about two inches shorter and ten years younger than I am. "Good to see you, too," he said. "I'm here because Lydia and I share a, um, let's say, discomfort, at how the guys uptown handled the

Amber Shun suicide. I don't have any new evidence and I sure don't have the seniority to challenge a guy like Joe Lenz, but when Lydia called me this morning I wasn't surprised."

"I'm always surprised when she calls me," I said. "You must have a more healthy male ego."

"Than yours?" Lydia said.

"Don't scoff."

"Hard not to. I called Chris," Lydia said, "because we have a problem now, and I'm not sure where to go with it."

"We do," I agreed, "and neither am I." The waiter came along with two steaming mugs. I looked from Lydia to Chris. "How much—"

"All of it," said Lydia. "I told Chris who our client is and why it's us, not the NYPD."

"But if the Shun suicide is Lenz's case—"

Chris picked up his coffee and said, "I'm off duty. Just having coffee with friends."

I nodded. "So unless the Amber Shun investigation is reopened, what you know will stay between us?"

"No. First, it's not technically closed yet. The tox report isn't in. So 'reopening' isn't the issue. But even if Lenz closes the case, if I come across anything he might need to know I can't sit on it."

"All right, understood." The waiter returned with the coffee pot, refilled my mug. "Meanwhile we now know our runaway, the son of the mayor, knew a girl who killed herself."

"Probably," said Chris.

"Definitely knew her, probably killed herself," I corrected my own words, "the day before he ran away. I suppose that might not—"

I was interrupted in the middle of my non-starter of a supposition by the ringing of Chris's phone. A true cop, he slipped out of the booth and went outside to take the call.

Lydia and I looked at each other. "In view of this—even without it—I need to tell you what else happened last night," I said.

"Last night? After I went home?"

"I headed home, too. But it didn't last."

Before I could start my story, Chris pushed back through the door and dropped onto the bench beside Lydia. "Okay, things just got worse," he said. "When Bing Lee sent Amber's folks to me I called a buddy at the ME's lab, in Queens."

"I thought the NYPD had a strict no-favors policy about that kind of stuff," I said.

"Yeah." Chris grinned. "But at the Academy I took a couple of extra forensics courses. Because I'm a science genius. Lydia knows."

Lydia rolled her eyes.

"The guy who was my instructor, Eddie Chao, he runs that part of the lab now. The toxicology part. He was willing to look into something for his prize student. His prize student," he amended, "and a bottle of Moutai."

"He needed that to pickle specimens in?" Lydia said.

"Hey, whatever works," Chris answered. "I wouldn't touch it either, but you know, the old guys. . . . Anyway, he's the boss, he can do what he wants. That was him. The tox tests aren't complete but it looks like Amber Shun may have had diazepam in her system. Valium, or something like it. Not enough to kill her, but enough to slow her down."

I drank more coffee and wished you could still smoke in restaurants in New York. "All right," I said. "Okay. That may not move the needle for Lenz, but it does for me. Slow her down. Make her sleepy. Easy to handle."

"Easy to kill." Chris looked at me over his mug. "The report will be going to Lenz at the end of the day. I can pretend I don't know anything about it until then, or about this," he gestured at us with his mug, "but even if he decides it's meaningless because she could have easily taken the diazepam herself, I'm going to have to tell him a boy she knew has disappeared. And even if he decides *that's* meaningless, I can guarantee his bosses won't once they know who the boy is."

No, they wouldn't. Especially in the middle of domino-effect salary negotiations. I could just see it: a five-borough, all-hands search. Full press briefings, Mark's picture handed out. Tactical Command trailer, coordination with the police departments of surrounding counties. And states. Possible abduction, the mayor's son.

Possible fleeing homicide suspect.

And either could be the truth.

Or the truth could be something else, and Carole McCann's political future could get swept up in this current and wrecked on these rocks, not to be pieced back together, even after the truth came out.

"You guys," Chris said. "I can't shield a suspect."

"Or ignore a witness," I said. "I know. But right now, you're just having coffee with friends."

"No, I'm leaving." He stood. "And my friends"—he looked at us—"will either find the kid they're looking for today, or I'll have to call Lenz. I'm a cop, you guys."

"Yeah," I said, "I get it."

"Thanks, Chris," Lydia said.

"Before you go," I said. "One thing. I don't suppose there's any chance you could get a look at Amber Shun's phone?"

"No chance in hell. A peek at the tox report is one thing. Pawing through another detective's physical evidence is another."

"Okay," I said. "Thanks." Chris waved, but didn't look back, as he pushed out the door.

"He's taking a chance," I said to Lydia, after the door had shut.

"So are you." Her look was straight on. "What we know about Mark and Amber might be material to her death. Withholding it could be an issue. You don't like the mayor. Why aren't we just turning this over to the NYPD and washing our hands of it?"

"Is that what you want to do?"

She shook her head. "It's your case. We do it your way. It's just, if I'm risking my license I want to know why."

"You don't have to, you know. I could—"

"Oh, stuff it. Just tell me why."

I smiled behind my coffee. "Well, for one thing, McCann's the client. I don't like her, you're right. Though having met her ex, I admit I'm warming to her."

"You met her ex?"

"That's the story I need to tell you. Part of it. I had a busy night. But whether or not I like the client, we took the case. We—I—can't just throw her overboard."

"We."

I nodded. "For another, the Mark we've heard about . . . He just doesn't sound like the kind of kid who'd kill."

"No, to me either. Okay, I buy your reasoning. You have a next step?"

I considered. "I think we need to know more about Amber Shun. And just how close she and Mark were."

"Okay." Lydia nodded, took out her phone, and made a call, speaking in Chinese. When she put the phone away she said, "We have time for you to tell me what happened last night. Maybe make a few calls. At nine we're meeting Amber Shun's parents at my office."

# 14

I ordered eggs and bacon to pay the rent on the booth at the Square, though neither the waiter nor the counterman seemed to expect us to hurry back out into the rain. Lydia didn't want anything, just nursed her tea while I brought her up to date on last night's two exciting events: Herb Straley going out of his way to tell me to stay out of his way, and Jeffery Guilder summoning me to, and dismissing me from, his apartment.

"I don't know about 'dismissing,'" she said. "Seems to me you made a pretty melodramatic exit."

"I was inspired by all these theater people we keep coming across," I said, as the waiter put down my food and refilled my coffee cup again. "If I knew Ashok Sundari better I might have used a trampoline. But I wasn't dismissed by Guilder. It was the guy who really counts. Trask."

"Maybe he just didn't want to drink alone. Though it's true Guilder sounds like he doesn't want his son found."

"I was thinking about that. What he really doesn't want, it seems to me, is his son to be *looked for*. Especially by people working for his ex."

"Which could imply, as you said, that Guilder knows where he is. That he's hiding him."

"Except Mark's not hidden, in that sense. He's on the run, he's moving around. I can't believe he's either being directed by Guilder or reporting to him. No one's said they have that kind of relationship."

"The opposite, from everything we've heard."

"Right. I think Guilder's mostly a control freak and since we're not working for him he wants us to go away."

"Us? No one's told me to go away."

"And really, why would they?"

"And Straley? He actually thinks the mayor hired us to find dirt on him? Seems a little self-absorbed."

"Self-absorbed paranoia can be a survival mechanism in public life. Apparently the last mayor did."

"Did what? Hired someone to dig into him?" She reached for a piece of my toast. I'd ordered rye because she likes it and I knew she was going to do that.

"Just another reason to hate politics," I said.

"I'm beginning to agree. Did they find anything, the last mayor's people?"

"No, and Straley says there's nothing to find. But there's another angle, too. He seems to be figuring, if it wasn't about him, maybe the mayor has a problem he can leverage."

"That's why he leaned on you? He's that eager to find out?"

"Please remember he first offered the warm hand of friendship. Shorty says Straley's beset with enemies and has to come out of these talks with a fat package for his members or he'll be voted off the island."

"I think if it's a quid pro quo it's not actually friendship."

"No? And just when I was beginning to think I'd won him over. Anyway, he got flummoxed when I started talking about dog shit. Finish my toast and show me the video."

"You might have separated those sentences better," she said, taking the last bite. She wiped her fingers, tapped her phone's screen, then put the phone on the table between us. She hit "play" on the video. We both leaned closer.

The music began, and I recognized it: "Somewhere," from *West Side Story*. I also recognized the place: Mark's basement rehearsal studio. Mark McCann and a small, long-haired Asian girl held hands and gazed into each other's eyes for the opening bars. His entrance was first and he came in right on cue, without taking his eyes from hers. She joined him a few lines later. His voice, though still that of a teenager, was the better one, rich and expressive; she hit all her notes, but the sound was more breathy, less full. The effect, though, was touching in its artlessness.

Until she forgot a line. She stopped and giggled. He stopped too, picked up his phone and clicked the music off. She apologized. He smiled and said it didn't matter. He gave her the line. She thanked him. He asked if she was ready, she said yes, he smiled again, tapped the phone and turned the music back on, and all that time, until he resumed his position in front of the camera and took her hand as the music started, he never looked her in the eye.

Then they began again, holding hands, gazing deeply, with the same intensity as before.

"God," Lydia said. The video continued and they went through the song again, this time flawlessly. "To see this, knowing she's dead . . ." She tapped her phone and the music stopped. I waited, watching out the window as the rain pounded the sidewalk.

"But," Lydia drew a breath, gathered herself, "that's our Mark, isn't it? On stage, he disappears. Off stage, he wishes he could."

I turned back to her. "Do you want to take the Amber Shun case?"

She put her hands around her mug, as if for warmth, though it was empty. "I want to know what happened. If that girl"—she gestured to her phone—"killed herself, I want to know why. And," she added, "if that boy had anything to do with it . . ."

I said, "Okay. Then let's get on it. Where they were, that was his studio, right?"

"Yes, I think so."

"Is there a way to be sure? And to know when it was?"

She took up the phone, clicked, swiped. "When was six months ago. End of October. Maybe they were going to audition for the spring show?"

"He's doing *Angels in America*."

Lydia shrugged. "I guess he didn't make it. Or maybe he wasn't really going for it, he was just helping her out. And the where," some more tapping and swiping, "yes, GPS says it was the 67th Street house."

I took out my phone, too, and for a few minutes Lydia and I did what pretty much everyone did these days: sat at a table together, talking to other people.

My call was to Rick Crewe.

"Hey," he said. "Did you find Emilio Vela? I'd ask if you found Mark but I think I'd know by now."

"We talked to Vela. He got us closer to Mark but Mark outmaneuvered us."

A chuckle. "That's Mark. He'll be found when he wants to be found."

"Yeah, maybe. But there's a problem. More than one. Mark ever mention a girl named Amber Shun? Ever bring her home, maybe down to the studio?"

"I don't think I've heard that name. He doesn't bring many kids down here. Who is she?"

"Hold on, I'll send you a photo." Which I did. "Could she be the girl he was interested in, up until Christmas?"

"I guess she could. He didn't say much about that girl. Never told me who she was. Like it could be unlucky, break the spell or something.

But there was one time, back in the fall. I was out in the garden working on a dinner party menu. The kitchen was hot so I left the door open. I saw Mark and a girl leaving the studio. I waved but they didn't see me. Madison was down there rummaging in the freezer for a popsicle. They talked for as short as Mark could make it and hightailed it upstairs."

"And the girl Mark was with—it was this girl?"

"Might be. Or I might be racial profiling. I think that girl was Asian but I may only think that now because you showed me this. She had long dark hair, I know that. I just caught a glimpse. Does she say she knows Mark, this girl?"

"This girl," I said, "killed herself a few days ago."

"Oh my God. Why?"

"We don't know. But it was—"

"Right before Mark disappeared. I get it."

"If you—"

"Yeah, I will."

Lydia's call was to Astrid Bergson, the one friend of Mark's who'd noticed he'd been upset the day he disappeared.

It went better than mine.

Lydia was still speaking to Astrid as I started my next call. She put her hand on mine to stop me. "Thanks, Astrid," she said. "Yes, I will. And you'll call me if—great, thanks."

She clicked off. "Astrid says Mark and Amber discovered each other in the middle of October. They each needed a duet partner for tryouts for the spring musical, the combined one with the other schools. They're doing *West Side Story*. Mark and Amber auditioned for Tony and Maria."

"She made it, he didn't?"

"No. They both did. They had chemistry, Astrid said. On stage and off."

"He made it, but didn't take it. Hmm."

"Maybe the *Angels in America* role is better?"

"It's a meaty one. But so's Tony. And at that age, to play a doomed lover opposite your girlfriend . . ."

I waved the waiter over for one last coffee refill and called Bree.

"Amber Shun," I said.

"Which is who?"

"Mark's girlfriend."

"He really had one?"

"I need to speak to the mayor."

"You need to wait on line."

"Her son—"

"Ten o'clock. She'll talk to you then."

"For God's sake." I almost told her Amber Shun was dead, but there was something I needed first, and I wanted to be sure it was unrevised. "You were going to get me a breakdown of Mark's morning on Tuesday."

"I have it. You want it now?"

"I wanted it yesterday."

"Okay, I just sent it. Call at ten."

She clicked off. I almost called back so I could be the one to hang up.

"The mayor's not available?" asked Lydia.

"Aubrey's not making her available. Until ten."

"Doing her job, guarding the gates?"

"Like a dragon. She did seem to genuinely not know who Amber Shun was. And surprised to hear the word 'girlfriend.'"

I signaled for the check, then opened the file Aubrey had sent. It had Mark's schedule down to the minute, thanks to the miracle of high school programming: his classes, his breaks. "Mark had ten minutes between World History and Algebra," I told Lydia. "Enough time to hear bad news."

I paid the check, including a big tip, and Lydia and I headed out into the rain. We walked west to her Canal Street office to talk to the bereaved parents of Amber Shun.

# 15

The Shuns were a faded, frail couple. I wondered if that had always been true, or if robustness had been drained from them by the death of their daughter. Mr. Shun, in gray slacks, a striped shirt, and a blue cardigan, helped his thinner, shorter wife, in patterned blouse and shapeless skirt, to one of Lydia's guest chairs. He himself dropped into the other like a capsized sailor who'd made it to shore with the last of his strength.

Lydia sat behind her desk and I sat to the side of it, on a chair I'd borrowed from the travel agents who were Lydia's landladies. The bad news and the good news about this former storeroom were the same: its one window opened on the lightwell between this building and the next. That made the paper-piled place claustrophobic, but together with the lack of a nameplate on Lydia's buzzer it also made it possible for clients to come to her without their need for help sizzling along the Chinatown grapevine. Also, as Lydia had pointed out more than once, I was in no position to comment on her office in any case, mine being the back booth of Shorty's bar.

"Mr. and Mrs. Shun, thank you for coming," Lydia said. "Is it all right if we speak in English, for my partner?"

Mr. Shun looked at me and nodded. I thanked him.

"What have you learn? About daughter?" He seemed unsure where to direct his question: to the elder, bigger, White man, or the younger, smaller, Chinese woman. His wife, though, had focused a blade-sharp stare at Lydia, ignoring me entirely. Mr. Shun, after a few seconds' hesitation, followed her lead.

"I need to ask you," Lydia said, "was she seeing anyone?"

"Seeing?"

"Going out with. Dating."

"Dating? Boyfriend? No." Mr. Shun shook his head emphatically. "An-An don't dating. Have no time for boyfriend. Too much studying, plus too young. How she keep grades for scholarship, she have boyfriend? Study, practice singing. Homework, concerts. Want to do well, at school, at singing. No, don't dating."

Mrs. Shun waited until her husband's oration was through. Then she said, "Yes."

Wide-eyed, Mr. Shun snarled something at her in Chinese. She snapped back. The fight was on.

Lydia gave it a few back-and-forths before she stepped in. She spoke in calm, measured Chinese. Both Shuns fell silent and turned to her.

"Thank you," she said. "I'd like to go back to English? Shun Taitai, you say An-An was dating a boy, and you knew about it. But you kept it a secret?"

"How I can tell him?" Mrs. Shun jutted her chin at her husband. "You hear him. Must studying! No time for dating!" She shook her head. "I young girl once. First discover boy, wonderful. An-An, same. Plus, this America. Girl don't hide in village, wait for matchmaker to say to father, 'Here, I find boy.' Boy, girl, same school, all day. An-An beautiful girl."

She turned to her husband and laid a gentle hand on his. "Of course she dating."

"You don't tell me." He sounded hurt.

"Because you saying stop!"

"Have no time for dating!"

She gave a sad smile. "Girl, boy, always time for each other. When you young, I young, we have time."

He grunted.

"Last fall," Mrs. Shun said, "An-An meet boy she like. So young, not serious." She squeezed her husband's hand. "But he make her happy. Boy happy, too." Turning to look at her husband, she said, "How can happy be bad?"

He squeezed her hand, too.

Lydia looked from one to the other. "Shun Taitai? Were they still dating?"

Mrs. Shun blinked at Lydia, as though she'd forgotten she and her husband weren't alone. "Still? You mean . . ."

"Yes. Recently."

A long breath. "No. I think no. I think, no more dating, after school Christmas break."

"Why?"

"An-An don't say. Just, sad. No, sad not right." She spoke in Chinese to Lydia.

"Upset," said Lydia. "She was upset?"

"Yes, upset." Mrs. Shun nodded. "Sad, go away. Upset, keep bothering."

"But you don't know why?"

"She don't tell. Just, stay in room, work hard." Mrs. Shun paused. "Don't tell, but I think, boy say, no more dating."

"You think he broke up with her?"

"Broke up, yes. He broke up."

Lydia took out her phone, swiped to a still of the "Somewhere" duet. She turned it to face the Shuns. "Is this the boy?"

Mr. Shun leaned forward with fierce curiosity. Mrs. Shun inspected the phone's screen, then said, "I don't know. Never meet, or see picture."

"Who this boy?" Mr. Shun demanded. "This boy date An-An? This boy kill her?"

"It's still possible, Mr. Shun," I spoke for the first time, "that your daughter took her own life. We'd like to look into it, though, with your permission."

He looked from me to Lydia. "You taking case?"

"Yes," she said.

He sat back. "Good. Good."

Lydia asked the Shuns a few more questions: Amber's friends, her social media accounts.

"Friends from school, don't know. Old friends, can tell you." Mrs. Shun took out her phone, an early-model Samsung, and copied down some names and numbers.

"And her social media?"

Both Shuns frowned. Lydia spoke again in Chinese.

"Ah. Don't have those," said Mr. Shun. "We give her phone, but tell her not for wasting time. For we calling her, she calling us, school send announcements. Those things. No tweeting, no selfie." He glanced at his wife to make sure he was right this time. She nodded.

Lydia looked at me; we'd talk to Linus later. Before she could ask another question, her phone rang. I expected her to let it go to voicemail but she checked the screen and said, "Excuse me," to the Shuns. "Hi," she said, putting the phone to her ear. "I'm in a meeting. Can I call you back? . . . Oh. Well, yeah, I guess we would . . . Really? How do you know? . . . Oh. Yeah. Thanks, Chris."

She clicked off and said to the Shuns, "Do you have An-An's phone?"

They both looked puzzled. "No, don't have," Mr. Shun said, again checking with his wife. "An-An always have."

"She didn't leave it home?"

"Why? Never leave home. How can calling? Police must have."

"Yes, of course. Thank you."

We ushered the Shuns from the office after negotiating a small retainer, which they counted out in twenty-dollar bills. It was enough to make them feel like they weren't a charity case but not enough to pay for our time. That was fine because Carole McCann was already paying for our time.

"That call from Chris, that was about Amber's phone?" I asked Lydia as soon as they were gone.

She nodded. "He said just because he couldn't go through the evidence locker doesn't mean he couldn't get a look at the manifest. That's on the NYPD system. They didn't find a phone."

"Do they have her purse?"

"Her backpack. It was by the body. But everything that would be in a purse is in it. Wallet, keys, makeup. Schoolbooks. So where's the phone?"

She took out her own phone and tapped a number. "Hi, Detective, it's Lydia Chin. . . . Yeah, isn't it? I'm soaked. I just have a question, I'm asking for the parents, you know? Amber Shun's phone. . . . Yes, sure. Of course. . . . No, they'd just like to have it. . . . No, they know that. . . . Okay, well, thank you." She clicked off. "Joe Lenz says he's looking for it. He also says kids lose their phones all the time."

"No," I said. "People like me lose our phones all the time. Kids live on theirs. They drop them, they break them, they drip ice cream all over them, but they don't lose them. If it's gone someone has it."

"It might not tell us anything, even if we find it."

"But knowing who has it will."

# 16

My phone must have gotten excited by all the phone talk, because right then, it rang. I took it out, checked the screen, and answered. "Bree."

"Ready for the mayor?"

"Bring 'er on."

Lydia rolled her eyes. Bree blew out a tiny exasperated breath, and then, "Carole, are you on? I have Bill Smith for you."

"And Lydia Chin," I said. "I'm putting my phone on speaker."

"I'm here," said McCann. "Aubrey, stay on. Mr. Smith, your report?"

"Your son had a girlfriend," I said into the air in Lydia's office. "Her name was Amber Shun. She went to Macauley Prep."

A pause. "All right, I'm surprised. But why do you say it in the past tense? My son—"

"No," I said. "The girl. Actually, there are two reasons. One, we think the relationship ended around Christmas. Two, I'm sorry, but there's no easy way to say this. The girl is dead."

"Oh my God," McCann said slowly. I felt for her. Her head was probably filling with gut-twisting scenarios involving Mark; others, equally terrifying, involving her own future; and also, with guilt for paying any attention to the latter when the former were looming.

"Do I have any hope," McCann said, "that this was a natural or entirely accidental death, and what you're telling me is that Mark may have run away to process it, but nothing else?"

"Again, I'm sorry, but no. That may be why he ran away, but the girl's death was suicide. At least, the ME says it was."

She paused. "That's bad enough. But I'm hearing that you think it's worse."

"It could be. I'm just not sure."

Aubrey broke in. "Is the girl's death being investigated?"

"The NYPD is treating it as a straight-up suicide. She was a scholarship student, an academic high-achiever, and a musician, and they're thinking the pressure got to be too much."

"Did she leave a note?"

"No."

"Does anyone else know about the connection between them?"

"A lot of people do," I said. "But what you're really asking is, do the police know. I don't know if they do. We haven't told them. I'm hoping to find Mark first."

"First before what?" asked the mayor.

"That," I said, "is a damn good question."

With the rain washing down the lightwell window, Lydia and I, phone calls over, tried to fill in the picture. Both McCann and Aubrey had denied knowing anything about Amber Shun. I'd sent the video, told them to call me back as soon as they'd watched it. To my surprise they had.

"You never saw her? Either of you?" I said.

"No." That was Aubrey.

"No," said McCann. "Poor child. And Mark seems to have had it bad."

"Unless that was just acting."

"It might have been acting. But Mark's a method actor. He gets deep inside his roles. When he was cast as Perchik in *Fiddler on the Roof* he started reading Karl Marx. And for the run of rehearsals and the play he went to synagogue. If he was supposed to be so completely in love with this girl for this role, it's not outside the bounds of possibility that he really did fall in love. But you say they broke up around Christmas?"

"Yes. We don't know what happened."

"Well," she said, "I suggest you find out."

"We did actually think of that," I said. "That's one of the reasons we're calling you. In case you had any insight."

"As I say, I never met the girl, or heard her name."

"Okay. There's also something else you need to know. Jeffrey Guilder called me last night."

"I told you to keep him out of it," she snapped.

"Let me repeat—Jeffrey Guilder *called me* last night. He demanded I come to his place and when I got there he ordered me to stop looking for Mark."

"How did he know who you were and what you were doing?"

"I can't say for sure. But Madison was there enjoying a post-opera snack with him and Oscar Trask."

"For God's sake." The mayor hissed a breath in. "Damn him. All right, unless you have something else?"

"I guess we don't. Do you?"

"One thing. Give Aubrey the girl's parents' details. As the mother of one of her friends I'd like to send a sympathy note."

The mayor left the call. I did as she asked, relaying the info to Bree. "I have to admit I'm surprised," I said. "That she'd bother to do that."

"She's not an icicle," Bree said. "You have an attitude problem."

"I always have had."

After that Lydia and I went back to work. Lydia, on her phone, went through what Linus and Trella had called Mark's Finsta and FikFok.

"Are those real words?" I asked.

"Are Instagram and TikTok real words to begin with?"

I conceded the point. "Trella said nothing on them was hot stuff," I said.

"She's right." She kept scrolling. "But she also didn't know what to look for. Bill, she's here."

I leaned to look at Lydia's phone. Swiping slowly through the Finsta account, she showed me photos of Amber Shun: in clowning groups of kids; in a few selfies with Mark; and alone, both posed and candid. The group photos were the earliest, and faded out in favor of the selfies and portraits as we went through the months from October to January.

After which, Mark made many fewer posts, and none of Amber Shun.

In the FikFok, Amber didn't appear. The posts on that platform were brief videos, all of Mark solo, but in an astonishing variety of personas, all without costumes. Goofy, The Incredible Hulk, Minnie Mouse; Louis from *Angels in America*, Tony from *West Side Story*; other roles, and celebrity impressions, some I could identify and some I couldn't; and people I could have sworn were Ashok Sundari, Emilio Vela, Rick Crewe. Mrs. Overbey. Jeffrey Guilder. Aubrey—the tossing of the hair was perfect. Oscar Trask. And his mother, the mayor.

"Wow," said Lydia. "He's good."

"He sure is." Something struck me. "Who watches these?"

Lydia took the phone back and tapped the screen. "These, no one," she said. "The FikFok is a private account. That means only people he approves can follow him. He hasn't approved anyone." More tapping. "The Finsta has a very small group of followers. Those kids we called, plus a couple of other names."

"Amber?"

"Yes, she's here. So she did have social media accounts."

"You can tell that?"

"You can't like or follow or anything if you're not on the platform."

"I'll take your word for it."

"But," she said, "she's still here. That's weird."

"It is?"

"Whatever happened between them, she never unfollowed and he never blocked her. But after January she doesn't comment or like anymore. Interesting."

"Or is it? Maybe they just didn't want to bother."

"Blocking? Unfollowing? It's a couple of clicks. Come on, when you break up with someone the first thing you do is run around collecting and throwing out everything they ever gave you. Their letters, their gifts, their old sweatshirt. You unfollow them on every platform, take them out of your phone contacts and delete their email. Even if the breakup's one-sided, one of you does that."

"That sounds like the voice of experience."

"You did something like that with Aubrey, I'll bet. And I guarantee she did it with you."

"What? She threw out my Yankees sweatshirt?"

"Two seconds to unfollow an account. To block someone. They weren't seeing each other anymore but neither of them did that? It's weird."

"I'll take your word for it. So what do we think it means?"

"It means," she said slowly, "they weren't together, but neither of them was done."

Lydia plugged in the kettle and made green tea. I went out onto Canal Street and had a smoke. When I came back into the office Lydia said, "I just talked to three of Amber's friends from her mom's list. They all say the same thing. She was really happy at her new school until around

Christmas break. Then she started to seem stressed. All she'd say about it was that the work was hard and she had to study. They didn't see her much after that. They were all really upset to hear about what happened and they can't explain it."

"Did she say anything about seeing a boy?"

"I asked, but they all said no. But their moms know her mom and you know what the Chinatown grapevine is like. It was probably smart of her, if she and Mark were a thing, not to talk about it." She tapped a pencil on her desk. "You think I can call Linus this early?"

"It's not actually early anymore. Even for me."

"You weren't out clubbing last night."

"How do you know? Maybe I felt the need to drown my loneliness in the madding crowd."

"I think that's a mixed metaphor." She picked up her phone and texted.

A few minutes later Lydia's phone sang "Bad Boys."

"Linus," she said. "Let me put you on speaker."

"Just don't turn on the lights."

"Late night?"

"And whisper. Oh, God, thank you."

"I didn't whisper yet."

"No, Trella gave me coffee. This is really important, right? Because I know you wouldn't call me at the break of dawn if it wasn't really important."

"It's half past ten."

"That's what I said." We heard him slurping.

"Yes, it's really important. I have another phone for you to find."

"We didn't find your first two yet."

"This one may be easier." She gave him Amber Shun's number. "We know who it belongs to. I want to know where it is, or where it was last time it was on. I want to know who it called and who called it."

"You don't ask for much, do you, cuz?"

"Only because you guys are so great."

"Uh-huh, right. Bye." He cut the call.

I said, "He sounds like I used to, in the mornings."

"Um, sometimes you still do." Lydia put the phone away and stared at the ceiling. "You know who we need to speak to?"

I looked up at the ceiling, too, and damn if it didn't work. "That friend of Mark's, who knew he was distracted."

"Astrid Bergson, and bingo." Lydia texted Astrid Bergson, got an answer, finished her tea, and we headed uptown.

# 17

On the subway to the Upper West Side Lydia asked me, "Working for the Shuns—is that double-dipping?"

"I think it's the opposite. Or maybe we're letting Peter pay Paul's bills?"

"Seriously, Bill. We just took a case that might be a conflict of interest with the case we already have. Didn't we?"

"It depends on a couple of different definitions. Oh, don't give me that look. Definitions aside, if Mark McCann had anything to do with Amber Shun's death, we wouldn't keep it to ourselves anyway, right? Whether we had the Shun case or not. Protecting the client only goes so far."

"You and I know that. But it could look compromising."

"I'm already compromised in the eyes of the law, of man, and of God. You're the one with a reputation to protect."

"No," she sighed. "It's too late for that. I'm your partner."

Astrid Bergson had directed us to the Crossbar, a café with a soccer vibe. Iron puddles reflected the gray sky, but the rain had stopped when we came up out of the subway on West Eighty-sixth Street. We found Astrid sitting with a freckled Black girl with a great fluffy halo of hair.

They both had earbuds in and sketchbooks on their laps. Wall-mounted TV screens silently carried games from halfway around the world, or from half a year back; the café menus included instructions on how to Bluetooth your way into the broadcast for sound. The baristas wore referees' stripes and a whiteboard stood between two pastry cases, carrying the latest scores from FIFA matches and the local kids' leagues.

"Astrid?" said Lydia, as we approached the table.

Both girls took out their earbuds.

"I'm Lydia Chin. This is my partner, Bill Smith."

Astrid Bergson's strong handshake was in keeping with her height, obvious even when she was seated, and the bright smile I recognized from her Instagram profile. She wore her blonde hair in a single braid down her back. "Good to meet you," she said. "This is Olivia. We're sort of cutting school." Astrid grinned while Olivia shook our hands. Her handshake was softer than Astrid's, more gentle.

"Sort of?" Lydia asked, as I brought over two chairs from another table so we wouldn't loom over the girls.

"We're supposed to be in the painting studio, but it's an honor system. Sometimes kids come here instead. Coffee's good and it's a great place to sketch."

"Could we see?" Lydia gestured to the sketchbook.

"Sure." Astrid handed the book over without any disclaimers, about the roughness of the sketches or anything else; and also, it seemed to me, with interest but no deep investment in what we thought of them. As though our opinions would tell her more about us than about the value of her work. Olivia, on the other hand, closed her book with a shy smile.

Astrid's work was very good. Clearly, as I'd thought when I'd heard Mark McCann sing, the artist was young, with technical lessons yet to be learned; but the immediacy of her subjects' emotions, their jubilation, pride, despair, disgust, and nail-biting anxiety, was all there on the page, in many subtle variations.

"You've really caught them," I said.

"It's what I'm interested in. People. What's really going on inside them and how you can . . . expose it with just pencil marks on a page."

"Most people don't observe this closely."

A pleased shrug. "But it's kind of made me snoopy," she said. "People sometimes get annoyed that I'm staring at them. I'm actually only looking at how their eyes echo—or contradict—their shoulders, how deep their forehead wrinkles are, stuff like that. I really don't care anything about *them*. You explain that to someone, though, and it makes it worse." Another grin. Then it faded. "Anyway, you want to talk about Mark." To Olivia she said, "They're looking for Mark McCann. You know him, right?" Back to us: "Olivia's a first-year."

Olivia shrugged. "Not really. I kind of know his sister. From that workshop." Her voice was soft.

"The video one?"

Olivia nodded. She glanced at me and Lydia and realized she was going to have to explain something to adults. "I'm in video production. Behind the camera. We did a weekend tech workshop and we needed people on the soundstage. You know, for blocking, camera angles, lighting, sound. . . . Some of the theater program kids volunteered and some outside kids, too, if their schools let them do it for makeup credits."

"Mark and Madison?" I asked.

"Not Mark. He was busy." Olivia's face lit in a sly grin. "I think that's partly why Madison did it. She likes to be in front of the camera but she doesn't hang around with him."

"So I understand. But Astrid, you know him. What can you tell us?"

"Well, so, what I was saying before, about how snoopy I am?" Astrid said. "That's how I knew he was upset. He was way distracted in algebra, even during the quiz. Somebody else, I might have thought he was trying to find the answer out the window, you know, staring while he thought, but that's not how Mark works."

"And Amber Shun," Lydia said. "We need to know about her, too. About them as a couple. You seem to be the only one of Mark's friends who knew about them."

"Well, they kept it on the down-low because I don't think she was supposed to date. Also, she didn't go to our school, she was one of the theater-combine kids, so they weren't together all that often. But, come on. The way they looked at each other? Especially Mark, who never actually looks at anybody straight on, he only looks to study them?" She tilted her head. "I guess, kind of like me."

"So what happened?" Lydia said. "They were together, everything was fine, and then after Christmas he dumped her. Why? Do you know?"

"*He* dumped *her*? Who told you that?"

"Her mother thinks so."

"Absolutely not. She's the one who broke it off with him."

"How do you know?"

"One, they stopped talking but he couldn't keep his eyes off her whenever she came to Granite Ridge for a class or a rehearsal. And two, she kept the role. Maria. He left the show." She looked from my blank stare to Lydia's. "It's obvious. He couldn't stand pretending to be in love with someone he really was in love with, while she was just pretending."

# 18

I had a few more questions for Astrid Bergson but didn't get to ask them. Her phone buzzed with a text. She glanced at it and put her hand to her mouth. Olivia's buzzed at the same time and her reaction was widened eyes. Astrid's thumbs flashed on her phone in reply. So did Olivia's on hers.

"A problem?" I said.

"Oh my God. One of the kids was shot this morning."

"*What?*"

Astrid glanced up at me. "Not Mark. Jacob Dolo. On Staten Island, that's where he lives. He's in surgery now." She went back to her phone, sent another text, then stood, grabbing up her sketch pad and shoulder bag. Olivia was already standing. "There's an assembly. We need to get back."

"We'll come with you. I want to talk to the principal."

Lydia and I stood too and we all fast-walked the two blocks to Granite Ridge Prep.

"Jacob Dolo," Lydia said to me, low, as we kept a few paces behind Olivia and Astrid. "Isn't he—"

"Yes. One of Mark's friends, from Aubrey's list." Jacob Dolo, like the others, had told me he had no idea where Mark was. Whether that had been true when he said it, whether it was true now, and whether this even had anything to do with Mark were questions to be answered. "Astrid," I said, catching up to the girls, "tell me about him. Jacob. He's a friend of Mark's, right?"

She nodded. "He's in my program, Visual Arts. He's mainly a sculptor. Found objects, welding and torch-cutting, plastics. Lately, 3D printing." She spoke without self-consciousness, an artist characterizing another artist by his media. "He and Mark got to be friends when they were working on *Sunday in the Park with George* last year."

"Jacob was in the show?"

She flashed a surprised smile. "Oh, no, no. We do the sets and props. Visual Arts does. Jacob 3D printed some very cool stuff for that show. Mark was really into it."

A flag outside a West Eighty-fourth Street double-width building told us we'd reached Granite Ridge Preparatory Academy. The windows and the big wooden door were trimmed with limestone, the Gothic arches at their heads announcing the seriousness of the scholastic purposes within. Astrid spoke to the uniformed security guard in the foyer. "They need to see Dr. Philippa, Mike," she said. Turning to us: "We'd better go."

"Of course. Go ahead."

I could hear the standard high school bedlam of sneakers slapping, voices calling, and lockers slamming when Astrid yanked open the inner set of glass doors and the girls went charging up the entry steps. Overlaying all that was a crackle of uncertainty, an anxious electric charge. I gave my card to the guard and he called Dr. Annis Philippa, Granite Ridge's principal. "We're working for Carole McCann," I told him.

If the mayor's name impressed him, he didn't show it, but then I imagined, working at Granite Ridge, he heard boldface names dropped around him every day. When he hung up he said, "Dr. Philippa can see you in half an hour. She's about to hold an assembly now."

"Can we attend?"

That didn't require a call. "No. School family only at this one. You can wait here."

I wasn't happy. I wanted to know not just what had happened to Jacob Dolo, but also what the principal was going to tell the students about what had happened. I wanted to see how she intended to tamp down whatever rumors were sizzling through the electricity in the air and what those rumors were. I wanted to watch the students as they reacted. I wanted to know if any of the kids were going to connect Mark's absence with Jacob's shooting. What I sure as hell didn't want was to sit here in the foyer doing nothing until the assembly was over.

Mike, though, had his eye on us in a way that said security was his name and security was his game. He also, I was sure, had a button under his desk that sent a silent alarm to the local precinct. So Lydia and I took seats on a wooden bench worn smooth by generations of people waiting for things.

I took my phone out.

"Are you going to call Aubrey?" Lydia asked.

"I think I'd better. I wish I knew more, though. This might not—"

"—have anything to do with Mark. And pigs might fly. But okay."

Aubrey didn't pick up. Just as well. I left a message—"Something new. Call me."—and we settled in to wait. I wondered how many sweeps of the old-fashioned clock's second hand I could watch before I exploded. I'd gotten to three when Lydia's phone blared out "Bad Boys."

"Linus," she said to me, and then, to the phone, "Hi. Yes. Should I put you on speaker . . . ? Oh. Okay, that's it . . . ? Oh. Why? Really . . . Okay, I will. Thanks. Talk later." She clicked off. "Linus says Amber Shun has no fake social media accounts Trella can find. Social media is her department and besides she seems to bounce back from a super late night faster than he does. She went through all the Instagrams and TikToks she could identify of Amber's classmates. She even tried Facebook."

"Why 'even'?"

"Gen Z doesn't use Facebook. It's for old folks."

"Oh."

"Anyway, Amber's name checked a bunch of times, but with the accounts we know."

"And that means?"

"The kids were using the same accounts I found. Nothing hidden. Whatever secrets Amber had, they're not on social media."

That was that. I glanced again at the wall clock. The second hand was still sweeping. I watched for a while.

This time the phone that saved me from exploding was my own. The number was blocked. Maybe the mayor. Or Aubrey, calling from the mayor's phone. In case it wasn't someone I knew and disliked, though, I just said, "Bill Smith."

"Yeah." The voice was young, male, and a little tentative. "Um, this is Mark McCann. I hear you're looking for me."

# 19

W e don't even know it's really him," Lydia said. Once I'd hung up from Mark's call, we'd bolted from Granite Ridge, and were standing on Broadway trying to wave down a cab.

"That's true."

"Or that he'll still be there when we get there."

"Also true."

"This could just be something to get us to go all the way out to Clifton for no reason. A distraction."

"Again, true."

"Although," she said, "it isn't like we have any bright ideas to be distracted from."

But when the voice that said it was Mark told me where he was and that he'd stay there until we arrived neither of us had for one moment considered not going.

We got in a cab and raced down the West Side Highway, jumping out at the Staten Island Ferry Terminal in Battery Park. There would've been no point in driving into Brooklyn and over the Verrazzano-Narrows Bridge; getting to Staten Island that way would have taken forever. On the other hand, the ferries ran every twenty minutes, and we caught one just as it was loading.

Usually I enjoy that trip, salt air and the Brooklyn or Jersey skylines, depending on which side you choose, and nothing to do until you get where you're going. But on this trip, I couldn't sit still, and I felt Lydia beside me, leaning on the rail, just as tense.

We were at the front of the ferry when it docked and the first people off when the deck hand unhooked the chain. That and a sprint through an annoyed crowd put us at the head of the line for a cab.

Staten Island, like Rome, is a place of seven hills. They form a spine northeast to southwest on the northern half of the island. Clifton probably used to encompass a couple of them but now the neighborhood had shrunk to where it lay on gently sloping streets on the inland side of what Staten Islanders call the Eastern Shore. In under seven minutes we were on Targee Street pushing through the door into Esther's African Food Café.

An automatic smile from the woman up front as the door opened changed to a frown when we registered to her. I had the sense that though she'd been expecting us, she wasn't happy we were there.

"Go to the back," she said, with a cold nod in the direction of the restaurant's rear.

We thanked her and walked through the half-full café. The crowd was exclusively Black. On a TV over the steam table a glamorous young Black woman interviewed people at a just-opened seaside resort in Monrovia. The luxurious foliage around it was unfamiliar to me. So were most of the steam table dishes. I recognized the fufu bread and jollof rice. I couldn't identify anything else but, the Square's eggs and bacon notwithstanding,

I'd have sat right down and tried it all, so great were the spicy, meaty smells swirling in the air. But we were on a mission.

At the back a curtain of heavy plastic strips separated the café proper from the kitchen. We parted them and saw, on the right, a stainless-steel counter, a trio of big sinks, and a large stovetop with bubbling pots, and, off to the left, a desk covered with invoices, brochures, and piles of miscellaneous paperwork. The two people sitting at the desk over coffee cups looked up as we entered.

One was a large, bald-headed Black man in a business suit.

The other was, indeed, Mark McCann.

"Well," I said. "Good to finally meet you."

Mark wore jeans, Nikes, a too-big yellow hoodie that said "Esther's African Food Café," and a worried look. His dark hair was uncombed and I had the idea that if he'd been old enough to grow a beard he'd have been unshaven. A Patagonia backpack lay at his feet.

"Bill Smith," I said to both of them. "This is Lydia Chin." I shook hands with Mark, who took my hand in a firm grip but barely glanced at me. He gave Lydia the same treatment. I turned to the other man.

That man's hand was giant and callused. We shook and he said, "I am Joseph Tamba." His voice was as deep as his wide chest implied. "Chef David," he called, "please ask that young lady to bring our guests some chairs."

The chef nodded and spoke to a young cook chopping vegetables. She wiped her hands and hurried into the dining room.

Tamba turned back to us. "You might have heard, my nephew was shot this morning."

"Jacob Dolo?"

"Yes. My sister is with him right now. Jacob is out of surgery and they say he'll be all right, praise God." Tamba fixed a stern look on Mark. "Jacob is a good boy, and very talented. My sister and brother-in-law send him to Granite Ridge Academy at great expense. Great sacrifice. Jacob has never been involved in any of the trouble we have had here in this neighborhood. Nevertheless, this morning when he was shot, we all assumed it was a gang situation. Perhaps he had been mistaken for another boy."

The young cook reappeared carrying two folding chairs. I took them from her and set them up for Lydia and me. We sat, Tamba nodded his thanks, and the cook went back to her vegetables.

"Mark was with Jacob when the shot was fired." Tamba's bass voice softened. "Mark may have saved his life. He could have run away but he stayed and stemmed the bleeding with his clothing until the ambulance arrived."

I glanced at Mark and saw dark streaks on his jeans, the kind of thing that could happen if you'd been pressing a cloth, say your own sweatshirt, to a bleeding wound, and later wiped your hands on your pants.

"Soon after the ambulance came my brother-in-law Thomas and I also arrived. Mark had called Thomas, who called me. Yes, Mark may have saved Jacob's life. But according to him, he also put it in danger."

"I wanted to leave," Mark said. "You made me stay."

"Of course I made you stay! You tell me my nephew has been shot because someone was shooting at *you* and then you expect me to allow you to just wander away so they can shoot at you again?" Tamba turned to me. "How do the young ever grow old?"

"I don't know," I said. "But you and I did, so it must be possible. Mark? That shot was meant for you?"

Mark shrugged.

"Why?"

Another shrug.

"Mark—"

"I think it was just supposed to scare me," Mark said to the floor. "Not really . . . not really, you know, hit me."

"Why do you say that?"

"We were moving. You know, walking. But stopping, and talking, and then walking again. Me and Jacob. We'd stopped and then Jacob stepped out ahead of me right then. If he didn't the bullet would've hit the wall. It was, like, three feet in front of me."

His logic didn't convince me. Trying to hit a target on a public street while keeping your own escape options open isn't all that easy. And who knew how good a shot this guy was in the first place? But I had a feeling Mark's theory might be helping ease his guilt so I didn't argue.

"All right. Why did you call me?"

Nothing.

"Who gave you my number?"

The start of more nothing, but a roar from Tamba. "Mark!" The chef and the young cook looked up.

Mark swallowed. Scrutinizing the kitchen tiles, he said, "The phone I called Mrs. Binney from. You left a message." He lifted a black, no-frills, pre-paid cell phone, the kind you get at Best Buy.

After another few seconds, when it became clear nothing more was coming from Mark, Tamba said, "I told Mark he must call the police. He said he couldn't. I told him to call his parents. He said he wouldn't." After a measured silence Tamba went on, "I understand when a man distrusts the authorities. And when a boy has . . . reservations about his parents. Yet one boy is in the hospital and the one who claims the bullet was meant for him, the son of the mayor of New York City, is prepared to go off on his own. Do you see my dilemma? I was going to call the police myself. Mark said no, there were other responsible adults he could call."

"Thanks for the endorsement," I said to Mark. "But now what? If you won't tell us what's going on there's not much Lydia and I can be responsible about."

By now when Mark spoke I half expected the floor tiles to answer back. "I won't go home."

"You don't have to. You're old enough to make that decision. I was, when I ran away." Mark glanced up for a second. Then, away again. "But if someone's shooting at you we need to know why," I said. "Otherwise what did you expect us to do when we got here?"

"I was just . . . I needed time to think. Mr. Tamba was about to call the police."

"So you called us to buy time? And what did your thinking produce?" Mark shook his head.

"Mark," Lydia said, her voice quiet, "as Bill said, you're old enough to make your own decisions. But that doesn't mean you have to carry everything on your own. Your mother hired us because she's worried."

Tamba's eyebrows went up.

"We're private investigators working for Mark's mother," I said to him. "Mark didn't tell you that? He didn't say who we were?"

"Mark is very good at saying very little."

"All right." I stood. "Let's go." Checking on my phone, I wrote Aubrey's number on one of my business cards and gave it to Joseph Tamba. "Mark? I mean you."

Now Mark looked right at me. "Where?"

"We're taking you off Mr. Tamba's hands. He has enough to worry about. Mr. Tamba, if you'll call that number you can get us verified."

"Whose number is that?" Mark asked, panicked.

"Aubrey Hamilton's."

"No. She'll tell my mother."

"Tell her what? That we found you? That you're okay? That'll be a big relief."

"I—"

But Tamba was already on his cell phone. "Good morning, Ms. Hamilton. Joseph Tamba calling. Yes, I'm fine, thank you. And yourself? That's good to hear, very good. Yes, the African Center is doing very

well, thank you for asking. I'm sure you know how much we appreciate
Her Honor's support of the Liberian and greater African community here
on Staten Island. We hope we can look forward to that same support in
the future. Our asylum-seeker community is particularly counting on her
sponsorship. Excellent. Now, the reason I am calling. I have before me
a gentleman named Bill Smith and a young woman called Lydia Chin.
Mr. Smith suggested I call to ask you if they can be trusted. Well, I'm
not sure. Only that he gave your name. I see. Quite so. Very well, I'm glad
to hear it. Yes, of course."

Tamba handed me his iPhone.

"Hello, Bree," I said.

"What the hell is going on? Trusted to do what?"

"I don't know. I—"

"Don't give me that BS. A kid at Mark's school was shot this
morning."

"News travels fast."

"The school called the parents. To quell rumors. Also, any parents
who want to collect their kids early, they can come get them. Of course,
Carole doesn't have to worry about that, because her kid's not in school,
is he? Does this call from Joseph Tamba have anything to do with that?"

"With the shooting, yes. The kid is Tamba's nephew."

"Oh my God."

"They say he'll be okay."

"Thank God for that. And Mark?"

"What about him?"

"Joseph Tamba's nephew gets shot and Joseph calls me to ask if you
can be trusted—and God help me, I told him you could—and you say
it's not about Mark?"

"I didn't say that. But I don't know. There are other people here.
Someone wanted me verified before we went any further." Lydia could

only hear my side of the conversation; still she rolled her eyes at my slippery phraseology.

"Who else?"

"Do I have to keep saying I don't know?" That was beyond slippery, but so what?

"Mark and the kid who was shot—are they friends?"

"He was on the list you gave me, yes. Let me figure out what's going on here. I'll talk to you later."

I ended the call and gave Tamba back his phone. "You knew her already," I said.

He smiled. "The mayor made a stop here when she was campaigning. She had dinner from my steam tables. Some of our newest Liberian and greater African community members are recent arrivals but a good many of us were born here to immigrant parents. We vote, Mr. Smith. Ms. McCann is one of very few politicians who has ever courted us. We were honored to have her here. And we will be delighted to have her help for our newest community members, as Ms. Hamilton has just assured me we will." He stood. "Now, I would like to get to the hospital to see my nephew. You will take charge of this young man?"

I looked at Mark.

"You didn't tell her you found me," he said, meeting my eyes.

"You didn't want me to. Let's go."

# 20

We didn't quite go. Lydia called a Lyft and we waited in the back of Esther's African Food Café. (Tamba, as he left: "Esther is my wife. The charming lady at the front.")

"So," I said to Mark as I sat again. "Who shot at you?"

Mark, back to looking at no one, shook his head.

"Why?"

"I don't know."

"Then how do you know you were the target? Maybe Jacob has enemies, too. Joseph Tamba said there's a gang problem here."

"Jacob's not in a gang."

"So it was a mistake. Or maybe he is and you don't know it."

"He's not! And if it was a gang thing here, the shooter would've been Black."

Ah. "All right, Mark. So you saw him. A White guy. Who was it?"

"I don't know. He was wearing one of those ski masks. I only saw his hand, that's how I knew he was White."

"Could you describe anything about him?"

A headshake. "Not as tall as you, not real short. Not fat."

"Wearing—?"

"Dark jacket. Maybe a pea coat? And dark pants. I don't know."

"Anything else about him?"

No answer.

"Okay," I said. "Why did you come out here?"

"Here, where?"

"For God's sake. Staten Island."

"I thought Jacob could help me."

"You wanted him to hide you?"

He shook his head.

"But you've been here since last night, am I right?"

A nod.

"So he did hide you."

"I guess."

"Mark—"

Lydia put her hand on my arm. "Mark," she said, "we want to help. We really do. This has something to do with Amber Shun, doesn't it?"

Mark, still staring at the floor, seemed to shrink into himself. I got the feeling he would've shut his eyes and put his hands over his ears, if he could have done it with a fifteen-year-old's dignity intact.

"I'm sorry," Lydia said. "But we have to talk about her. Whatever's going on, she's at the center, isn't she?"

He stayed silent. I opened my mouth but Lydia shot me a look. "Mark?" she said, almost whispering.

After an interminable time, he said, "That was my fault, too."

"What was your fault?"

"Amber."

"Her suicide?"

"Yes."

"Your fault, how?"

"I can't tell you."

"How do you know it was? Maybe—"

"Stop it! It was my fault, I can't tell you why, and leave me alone!"

"We can't," I said.

"Why not? Why can't you? Just go away!" He sounded like a sad little boy.

"Mark. Your mother hired us to find you. You didn't want Tamba to call the police but for God's sake, his nephew was shot. Your friend. I guarantee the police are investigating already. They'll be looking for you as a witness. Even if Tamba lies for you, they'll come after you eventually. We can take you away, hide you, but not forever. Amber's dead and Jacob was damn lucky and if you tell us what's going on we may be able to help but if you don't we have no choice but to take you back home."

"I won't go."

"Sorry, but you will. What you do after that is your own damn business but I—"

"The car," said Lydia, looking at the map on her phone. "It's here."

We left the kitchen, Mark sullen but not objecting. Gripping onto Mark's arm, I smiled at the charming Esther Tamba at the front, was gratified to see her smile back. Probably that was just out of relief at getting rid of the giant worry that was Mark, but I'll take my smiles as they come. I waited until Lydia had scouted the street and given the all-clear before I hustled Mark to the waiting sedan. I was prepared for him to try to pull away, but he didn't. Staying on Staten Island where a gunman was looking for him must have seemed the lesser of whatever evils we had in mind.

He seemed relieved, and tentatively intrigued, when the address I gave the Lyft driver wasn't his. I didn't actually have anything in mind, evil or otherwise, beyond getting Mark to a place where we could persuade him to talk to us. So I used my own address on Laight Street. The driver tapped it into her GPS and pulled away from the curb.

As we rolled toward the Verrazzano Bridge, Lydia glanced over at me. Did I want her to continue along the gentle lines she'd started in the café kitchen? I shook my head. I had a strong feeling that would only make Mark dig in deeper. Her questions, any questions, gave him something to fight against.

Watching the bridge's cables slide rhythmically by, I tried to come up with a way to unlock a fifteen-year-old boy. This kid was scared, he was stressed, he was in over his head on something and he knew it, but he wouldn't say one word.

What had worked on me at that age?

Nothing. My father's threats, my mother's pleas, his fists, her tears—nothing could make me give up a secret I was determined to keep.

What were those secrets about, then? Why was I so determined?

Almost always, I was protecting someone else.

The friend who'd thrown the rock through the church window. My sister and the boy she'd snuck off to see. The source of the three bottles of cheap rum four of us had polished off.

So who was Mark protecting?

Amber? Or her memory? Did he know something that would paint a darker picture of Amber Shun than the one people saw now? One that would break her parents' hearts even further? And would he keep that up now that another of his friends had been shot?

His mother? Was something going on that could damage her? Bree had called Carole McCann "principled" and I'd gotten the feeling she believed it, but if Mark had stumbled across something corrupt, Bree might have been out of that loop.

His father? God knew Guilder could easily have been up to his butt in any number of cesspools. Mark didn't like his father, but if it came right down to protecting him or selling him out, which would he choose?

Or was it someone else? One of the other kids, or maybe someone we hadn't even met yet?

I was still thinking along those lines, and probably making Mark nervous by my silence, as we exited the bridge and headed north on the Gowanus Expressway. After ten hypnotic minutes of the whoosh of tires and the enigmatic murmur of the driver's almost sub-sonic radio, I was startled by the ringing of my phone. I checked the screen; the number was one I'd programmed in the day before.

"Ashok," I said. "What's up?"

Beside me in the car, Mark glanced over.

"Mr. Smith. This is Ashok Sundari. A gentleman here would like to speak to you."

"Who?" I said, but before that question was answered a new voice began.

"Smith? Don't put this call on speaker. Bring the kid. Or I'm going to kill both these nice people here."

I held up a hand to keep Mark and Lydia silent. "Who the hell is this?"

"Not your problem. I just want to speak to the kid. I won't hurt him."

"Would it surprise you to know I think that's bullshit?" Especially from a man who'd just offered to kill two people. "But first, let's make sure we're talking about the same kid."

"The mayor's kid, asshole. Mark McCann."

"Okay, that's what I thought. Too bad. I don't know where he is."

"You're lying."

"I was hired to bring him home. If I knew where he was, wouldn't I have done that?"

I felt Mark tense as he realized I was talking about him.

"I don't want to hear this crap," said the guy on the phone.

"And I don't want to hear yours but it looks like we're stuck with each other. I have a bead on the kid. Let me follow it up and I'll get back to you."

"I should shoot these people just for you thinking I'm dumb enough to fall for that. Where are you?"

"On the Gowanus heading north."

"That's probably crap, too, but if it was true you could be here in twenty minutes."

"It's true that's where I am but you're a hell of an optimist."

"You better hope there's no traffic. Twenty minutes."

"Then what?"

"If you get here, we go together to 'follow up.' If you don't, I shoot these people, find the kid myself, and then hunt you down for fucking with me. Your cute partner, too. Hey, she with you?"

I might have denied it and ditched both Lydia and Mark before I went to the Sundaris', but trying to leave Lydia babysitting Mark while I faced down a gunman was not going to fly. Plus having Lydia beside me in any kind of showdown always weights the odds heavily in my favor. "Yes, she's here."

"Bring her with you. I don't want her trying to kung fu me from behind or any of that shit. Oh, and if I smell a cop, or see a gun, everyone dies. You walk in here with your hands empty and visible. How's that for a deal?"

"Stinks, but it's a start. We'll come there, we'll negotiate. Except when we get there, if either of those people has been hurt—"

"Yeah, yeah, yeah. The faster you get here, the more likely they are to keep breathing."

He cut the call.

I leaned forward, told the driver we'd had a change of plans, gave her a new address, a couple of blocks from the Sundaris' place. She shrugged and tapped it into her GPS.

"And the faster, the better," I told her. "If we miss the curtain there's no late seating."

# 21

"O kay," I said quietly in the back seat, as we merged from the Gowanus onto the Belt. "Here's the deal. Someone's at Ashok Sundari's place. He says he has a gun and he's holding Ashok and his aunt. Whether it's the same guy who was following us, whether it's the same guy who shot Jacob, I don't know. He says he's going to kill them, the Sundaris, unless I lead him to you." I looked at Mark. "You're a dangerous guy to know."

"That's not funny." Mark was ashen.

"Damn right it's not. If we had time I'd lock you up someplace, but we're barely going to make it as it is. So you're coming with us and when we get there you're going to stay in this car and be invisible. Because if I were doing what he's doing I'd have a spotter on the outside. I don't know what the hell you got yourself into but I don't doubt that someone wants you dead. You get that?"

He swallowed. "What are you going to do?"

"Lydia and I are going to go clean up your mess."

"How?"

"Damn good question. I told him—you have any idea who he is, by the way?"

Mark shook his head.

"Yeah, I thought not. I told him I think I might know where you are. He said to come there and we'd go together to find you. I'm pretty sure he doesn't have any intention of doing that, though. He'll want me to tell him what I know. Then he'll want to leave me and Lydia there with Ashok and his aunt while he hunts you down."

"Leave you there." He forced the word out: "Dead?"

"I have to assume that's what he's thinking. If I'm wrong I'll apologize later."

"And Ashok and Aunty Maalini?"

"Them too."

"But—"

"Yeah," I said. "But. You get now what serious shit this is?" At the look on his face I relented. "Lydia's the secret weapon," I said. "We work together pretty well. We'll find some way to distract him. Then we'll take him down."

Mark was unconvinced. "Distract him how?"

"Who the hell knows? But we will. And then, Mark, then we'll come back and get you and you're going to tell us what's going on. Non-negotiable. If you're not here when we get back, we're going to call Madam Mayor and resign from this case. I'm not chasing after you anymore. I'd walk away right now if it weren't for the Sundaris—just walk away and leave you to take your chances in the big, bad world."

The panic in his eyes when I said that made him look like a little boy. He turned to Lydia. She had no more intention of calling his mother, or letting him take his chances, than I did. But I felt that the point needed to be made and underlined, and apparently, she agreed. All she gave him was a shrug.

At the Roosevelt Avenue location I'd given the Lyft driver, Lydia and I got out of the car. I explained to the driver that we had something to take care of and the kid was going to stay behind and do his homework until we got back. She explained to me that as long as we were paying her for her waiting time she didn't give a damn what we did. "But he can't be smoking in my car. Vaping, neither."

"Hear that?" I asked Mark.

He nodded dumbly.

"Finish that algebra." I squeezed his shoulder. "We won't be long."

We walked down the block, past the trinket sellers and the food carts. "So," Lydia said. "What you told Mark. Is that really the plan? Because it kind of sucks, you know."

"You have anything better?"

"Hey. Your case, your job to make the plan."

"If I don't show up he'll shoot those people."

"Rear entrance? Fire escape?"

"Single-family two-story, commercial on the ground floor." Which means, in New York real estate speak—something every New Yorker is fluent in—that rear doors can legally be kept locked and fire escapes are not required.

"All right," Lydia said. "Whatever you come up with—"

"You'll hold my beer. I know. Have I told you lately that I love you?"

"That sounds too much like a goodbye. Take it back."

"Okay, I take it back. Not only don't I love you, I don't even like you."

"I never liked you either and neither does my mother."

"That's why I don't like you," I said. "You tell lies."

We'd reached the Sundaris' tax-business-and-home. I rang the bell. We got buzzed in and started up the wooden stairs.

Before we reached the top landing, the apartment door creaked open a few inches, pulled by an unseen hand inside. "Get in here," a voice snarled.

"What the hell do you think we came for?" I answered. I pushed the door wide open, and from the hallway, swept a fast glance around the kitchen. No one was in sight except the Sundaris, seated on kitchen chairs, Ashok looking ill, his aunt angry and thin-lipped. The guy with the voice must be behind the door. I took a long stride in, hands up and empty like he'd said. I spun around to face him. Lydia slipped in after me and moved fast across the room. First thing: separate, make it hard for him to keep an eye on us both.

The door slammed shut and we saw a guy in a black ski mask, a suppressor-fitted pistol in his nitrile-gloved hand. He used it to wave me over beside Lydia. I went, slowly, and she moved also, keeping as much distance between us as possible. Now Ski Mask was on one side of the table and we were on the other, with the Sundaris.

"You guys all right?" I asked Ashok.

"Shut the fuck up!" Ski Mask barked as Ashok nodded. "You're not here to talk to them. Talk to me. You carrying?"

"Yes."

"Her too?"

"She can talk, you know. And yes."

"Both of you, take them out with two fingers, slide them over here. You first."

He held his gun straight out at Maalini Sundari as I did what he said, slowly, sending my Colt skimming across the floor. Lydia did it too, with her .22.

"Very good. Where's the kid?"

"I don't know," I said. "I was told to go to the Bronx. Someone said he's staying with friends up there."

"The Bronx? Where?"

"Riverdale."

"Figures," he sneered. "But it's a big place, Riverdale. All those mansions. *Where?*"

"I don't know. I'm supposed to call when I get close."

"Call who?"

"Again, I don't know. My contact."

"This is bullshit."

"As far as I'm concerned this is all bullshit."

Even under the mask I could see his brow furrow, probably because what I'd said was meaningless. The point was to keep talking, keep *him* talking, until I figured out what to do. Even if he believed me and decided he needed me, I couldn't see him just walking out and leaving the Sundaris—or Lydia—alive. Lydia would be ready for whatever I did; I just had to figure out what that was going to be.

"His number," Ski Mask said.

"What?" I'd heard him perfectly well.

"Your contact's goddamn number. So I can call him myself, asshole."

Again, I swept my gaze around the kitchen, the table and chairs, pots and pans.

"Won't work. He won't answer a strange number and he knows my voice."

Nothing presented itself but this: Turn the table over. He'd shoot for sure, but it would be wild. We'd have to get to him in time to stop a second shot. Not great, but it seemed like the only plan.

"Then you call him, and tell him you're *inconvenienced*." The wool-circled lips smiled. "Say you're sending a trusted associate. And you know," he waved the gun casually at the four of us, "be convincing."

I gave Lydia a tiny nod and grabbed the table's edge.

Before I could heft it, a better distraction burst into view.

Goofy.

Scrabbling sounds at the window made us all whip our heads that way. A giant Goofy head popped up, big white Goofy gloves beating at the glass before head and gloves dropped down and a second later shot up again.

I flipped the table. Ski Mask, fixated on the window, didn't catch the movement. The table whacked his thigh, made him stagger. I banged my shin as I leapt across it to knock him down.

He still held the gun and as I thought he would, he fired. The suppressed pistol made a mild sound, like a sneeze. The teapot that got hit made a bigger noise. Ceramic shards rained down. I hoped the Sundaris hadn't been overly fond of that pot.

Pinning him as he squirmed, I bent his gun arm back and tried to yank the pistol away. I noted with interest but no surprise the Justice League of America circling his wrist. I wrenched the arm hard and was reaching for the mask when he got his left hand loose and socked me in the side of the head. My grip slackened. I was still seeing stars as he shoved me off and leapt to his feet.

He slip-slid as he headed for the door. A tinkling crash and another shower of ceramic shards announced the demise of more pottery. I looked around as he staggered. Maalini Sundari had thrown a bowl at his head.

Lydia dove at Ski Mask and jerked the gun from his grip. He shoved her away and took off, slamming the door behind him. Lydia threw the gun down, yanked at the door. It had locked behind Ski Mask. She fumbled with the bolt, pulled the door wide, and dashed down the stairs.

I lurched to my feet, galloped down after them. By the time I burst out the front door neither of them could be seen.

Running back up, I pushed past the Sundaris on the landing and crossed the kitchen to peer out the window.

No one in the backyard. The shed door was open, though. The discarded head of Goofy lay on the concrete, wearing a vacant grin, white-gloved hands beside it. The trampoline now stood close against the wall of the house instead of in the center of the yard.

Ashok came to stand beside me. Looking down, he said, "Mark?" His voice held a note of pride.

"If he comes back," I said, sure that he wouldn't, "keep him here and call me. I want to thank him. Then I'm going to kill him."

# 22

I picked up my gun and Lydia's, slipping mine back into my shoulder rig and Lydia's compact pistol into my pocket. I picked up Ski Mask's gun using plastic bags as makeshift gloves, slid the magazine out, and put gun and suppressor in another plastic bag. I shoved those things in my pockets.

"You have any idea who that guy was?" I asked the Sundaris.

"None," said Maalini, while Ashok shook his head.

"How did he get in?"

"He rang the bell, saying he needed tax advice. When I opened the door, he pushed in holding the gun." Maalini looked at her nephew. "I always thought Ashok had the exciting life, in the circus. I am a tax accountant."

I called Lydia. No answer. Either she was still chasing Ski Mask, she'd caught him, or she'd lost him. She was damn quick, but he had a lead, so the odds were even. I was about to head out to see if I could help when my phone buzzed with a text from her: Vanished. You still up there?

I texted Yes and a minute later she came through the front door. "I chased him three blocks to the subway," she said, trotting up the stairs.

"I ran up after him but a train came in and by the time I got to the plat-form it was empty."

"Sounds familiar." I handed her back her gun. "Which direction?"

"Deeper into Queens."

"And Mark?"

"Told the Lyft driver he was going to vape and got out of the car. She said how was she supposed to know she was babysitting? We didn't tell her to keep him locked up. I gave her a nice tip in cash and told her to go."

"You have any idea if there was a second guy?"

"I have to think there wasn't. If there was he'd have been watching the back, and he'd have seen Mark come do the Goofy thing. That was Mark, right? Not actually Goofy?"

"They may be the same." I called Mark's cell. That call wouldn't do any good unless he turned the phone on, but you never knew. "That was great," I said to his voicemail. "You saved our butts. That doesn't mean I won't cut yours loose like I said I would. You'd better let me know where you are, soon." Next I called the phone number he'd left with Mrs. Binney, the burner phone. The kindly-sounding female robot was still on duty. I left the same message. "I'd bet on Mark to go back into Manhattan. I think we can figure he's safe for a while," I said.

Lydia stuck the gun in her belt clip. "What now?"

Maalini asked, "Shall we call the police?"

"If we call them," Ashok said slowly, "we will reveal that Mark has run away."

"Your friend Mark," Maalini said, "has cost me a bowl, my best teapot, and a giant fright."

Both Sundaris looked at Lydia and me.

"I'm not sure what the police can do," I said. "None of us saw the guy's face and we have no fingerprints. The tattoo tells us he's the same guy as before, but we don't know who that guy is."

"You have his gun." Ashok sounded reluctant but dutiful. "Would there not be fingerprints on that?"

"Unlikely. He was wearing gloves. But maybe. We can trace it and get it printed unofficially."

"Really?" Ashok's eyes lit with interest. "How?"

"We do not need to know that, Ashok," said Maalini severely. "Mr. Smith, Ms. Chin, do you think this man will come back?"

Lydia said. "It's possible. Is there somewhere else you can stay for a while?"

Maalini blew out a sharp, irritated breath. "With my sister. In Flushing. I'll call her." She eyed me, then Lydia, then her nephew. "It is a good thing tax season has just ended."

After her sister, Maalini called her cousin, the same cheerful fellow who'd taken Lydia and me to Harlem last evening. We stayed until she and Ashok and their suitcases, including a satchel with Goofy's body parts, were loaded into the car and away.

We didn't wait idly, though.

As the Sundaris packed, Lydia called Chris Chiang. She put him on speaker and said, "I have a gun."

"Is this a holdup? Because it would work better if you were actually here."

"Didn't you once tell me a lot of criminals are really stupid?"

"Is that why you're calling? To say you've gone over to the dark side and it cost you IQ points?"

"No. I have a gun and I want you to tell me whose it is."

"Oh shit."

"A Beretta M9A3." She gave him the serial number from the barrel. "I—"

"Do I want to know?"

"No. It might have prints. Bill can get them pulled but—"

"But you'll need me to run them for you. Shit. Please, please tell me you also have the kid."

"Had him. Lost him."

"Lost him? What do you—"

"Long story. He's not a killer, Chris."

"Dumber words were never spoken."

"But there's a tattoo."

"The kid has a tattoo?"

"No, the gun guy does. The Justice League of America on his right wrist."

"You want me to identify a gun and a guy."

"I do."

"You're really pushing it."

"Bing Lee will be happy. The mayor will be happy."

"And I'll be working security at Target. This is it, Lydia. No more favors. And the end of the day. You have the kid by then or I call Joe Lenz."

"I know. Thanks, Chris." She hung up before he could respond.

Then she called Linus. Nothing yet, he said, he'd let us know.

"Is there anywhere," I asked both Sundaris, as Maalini checked for the third time to make sure the stove was off, "*anywhere*, that you can think of where Mark might have gone?"

Maalini shook her head, and gave Ashok a look that, when he said he couldn't think of anyplace, made me believe him.

Down on the sidewalk we watched the Sundaris drive away in the cousin's black car. "Crap," I said.

"I can't argue."

"I need to call Bree. Maalini and Ashok don't have to report this to the police but the mayor—the mother—has to know."

As I took out my phone to do that, though, it rang. An unfamiliar number. Unlikely it was Mark, but possible. I gave it a neutral, "Bill Smith."

"Mr. Smith, this is Imani Overbey. I'd like to speak with you."

I glanced at Lydia. "Sure," I said.

"Not on the phone. There's a small playground on First Avenue and Sixty-seventh Street. I'd like you to meet me there."

"We're in Queens," I said. "Half an hour?" Assuming the trains were running well, which Maalini had said they so often weren't.

"That will be fine."

We took the subway into Manhattan. It ran perfectly well, as it had yesterday when we'd come out here; but then, two rides were a small sample.

New Yorkers on the subway are pretty blasé about what they overhear. Still, in this case, I thought texting was the better part of valor. Guy with gun demanding Mark's whereabouts, I texted Aubrey. Threatened some people. Lost him. Same guy as before, masked, same tattoo on right wrist.

She answered fast. No one knows him. Any ideas?

Time for the cops, I said.

But she said, Hold off. Can you call?

I wouldn't be texting. On subway. Will call from street.

"She doesn't want the cops?" Lydia asked.

"She said, 'hold off.' She didn't say no."

"Optimist."

I called as soon as we'd climbed the subway stairs. "Hold off why?" I said.

"The negotiations are at a delicate point. The Doberman's out today and the Bulldog himself is doing most of the talking. He's digging in, it's what he does. It would be a disaster if—"

"Bree? I don't care. I'm thinking it would be a disaster if this guy found Mark."

"Come on, Bill. What good can the police do?"

THE MAYORS OF NEW YORK

"They can throw a wider net than I can."

"For Mark? He'll slip out, you know he will. For the guy? How? We have a masked face and a tattoo."

"That tattoo might be enough to identify him. The Justice League of America around the wrist."

She paused; I could practically see her chewing her lip. "All right, let's do this. I'll get the tattoo checked out. If he's in the NYPD system we'll find a reason to get him picked up without mentioning Mark. Then we'll go from there."

"We'll go from there." Another rotten euphemism, this one meaning: "I'm going to resist doing what you want as long as I possibly can."

"Yeah," I said, "great. You'll tell the mayor, though."

"Tell her—"

"That someone threatened to kill some people unless I turned Mark over, and that someone—maybe the same guy, maybe not—shot at him! Dammit, Bree. This—"

"Unless you turned him over? You mean you found him?"

I stopped. "That's what you heard? My inconsistent grammar? When there's a guy, possibly two, with guns looking for a fifteen-year-old kid?"

"I—"

"I have a meeting. I'll talk to you later."

I couldn't deny saying that gave me a perverse little thrill.

Lydia had gotten the gist listening to my side of the conversation but I filled her in as we walked to the park.

"I wonder how much of that is coming from her, and how much is the mayor," she said.

"How much of what?"

"I just mean, if the mayor knew what was going on, would she really still want to keep the cops out of it?"

"And if we think the answer to that is no, does that mean that for the good of McCann's political career, Bree's not going to tell her what's going on?"

"And if we think the answer to that is yes, should we tell her what's going on ourselves?"

We entered through the park gate. I spotted Imani Overbey, wearing a Burberry trench coat, carrying a black handbag, and standing near the track. No one was running. Maybe she was watching an imaginary race. "Let's see what Overbey has to say. Then," I couldn't help adding, "we'll go from there."

Overbey spotted us as we approached. "Mr. Smith. Ms. Chin. You're very prompt."

"The MTA," I said. "Greatest transit system in the world. What can we do for you?"

Surprisingly, she smiled. "You sound like Ms. McCann." The smile faded. "I called because there's something I think you need to know."

"Please. If it might help. Shall we sit?"

Overbey shook her head. "I prefer to stand, if you don't mind."

"Whatever you like."

She looked to Lydia, then back to me. "Mr. Crewe tells me you spoke to him earlier."

"That's true."

"He said you asked him about a girl. A possible friend of Mark's, a young woman who took her own life recently."

"That's correct. Amber Shun. Do you know her?"

"No. If Mark knew her, if he ever brought her to the house, I'm unaware of it."

"Then—"

"The reason I called you," she said, "is that she wasn't the only one." Overbey turned to the track again. An older woman in gray sweats was now jogging around it.

"Not the only one what?"

"Not the only suicide attempt. Though the other, thank goodness, was unsuccessful."

Lydia and I exchanged a look.

"You don't mean, Amber Shun tried once before?"

"No, I don't. A different girl. Last summer. School was out and she was at camp, but it was a girl from the school."

"Mark's school? Granite Ridge?" I asked.

"Yes."

"Was she a friend of Mark's?"

"Whether she and Mark were friends I couldn't say. But it's a small school. They certainly all know one another. Her name is Lauren Spence. She no longer attends Granite Ridge." Overbey shook her head.

"And so, you're saying maybe this suicide hit Mark hard because of Lauren Spence's attempt, and he really did go away to think?" Lydia asked. "That sounds like Mark, but—"

"No. I'm not saying that. I don't know what was in Mark's head when he left. As I told you, it's not my job to keep an eye on the children. My obligation is to Ms. McCann. I try to do my work and keep my own counsel. Still." She turned to the track again, where the gray-haired woman was taking another slow, steady lap. "Still. I don't think it would be a mistake if you were to speak to the parents of Lauren Spence."

# 23

I mani Overbey had nothing further to tell us. I asked about contact information; she said both of Spence's parents were attorneys, in different firms. She didn't know the firms' names but she said drily, "You're investigators. I'm sure you can find that out." She left us in the park and went back to her office in the mayor's house.

Lydia called Linus. "Another set of social media accounts to check. A girl named Lauren Spence. As soon as you can. Thanks." She hung up, but then said, "Should I have asked him to find the parents?"

"There are probably faster ways." I called Aubrey.

This time she answered right away. "I don't have anything on your tattoo man yet. I don't think he's in the system."

"I'm not calling about that. Lauren Spence. Familiar?"

Silence. Then, "Last summer. She was a class ahead of Mark at Granite Ridge. She—took a huge handful of pills, if I'm right. She was lucky to pull through."

"And when I told you Amber Shun had killed herself you didn't think to mention her?"

"No. Why would I? Are you saying the two are related? How can they be? Suicide isn't a serial crime."

"Although it can be contagious. That's not the point, though. It didn't jump out at you, a second suicide attempt in that group of kids?"

"I'm not sure what you mean by 'that group.' The Shun girl—"

"Amber."

"She was in a different school."

"She'd been spending a lot of time in rehearsals at Granite Ridge lately. With Mark. But fine, never mind. Now tell me about Lauren Spence."

"Lauren Spence? I don't remember ever meeting her. If Mark knows her—that's what you're asking, right?—I don't know."

"Can you get me her parents' contact info?"

"Her parents took her out of Granite Ridge over the summer, after she recovered."

"Did they take her off the planet, or can you get me the info?"

"Jesus. You—"

"You hired me. What did you think I was going to do? Call me back." I hung up.

"She's no help?" Lydia asked.

"She's a pain in the butt."

"What's her problem?"

"I'm not sure. The mayor's future is her future, but I have a feeling there's something else going on."

"She dislikes you as much as you dislike her?"

"Not possible. But even if true, why hire me and then drag her feet when I ask for help doing what she hired me for?" I lit a cigarette. "I have a thought."

"Oh good."

"God, you too? If Mark knew these girls, maybe Madison did too."

"Does. One's still alive."

"My grammar's getting bad grades all over the place. I think we should talk to her."

Lydia thought for a few moments. "I agree. But."

"But?"

"Not 'we.' You find Lauren Spence's parents. Leave Madison to me."

"Alone? Don't you think we'd be better off good-cop-bad-copping her?"

"Oh, we're going to." Lydia tapped numbers on her phone, put it to her ear. "Hi, Madison? It's Lydia Chin. . . . Yeah, no, not yet, but check it out, we did hear from him . . . Basically, he said he's fine and we need to knock it off. . . . Yeah. No, Bill will keep looking, because that Aubrey Hamilton person says to. . . . Uh-huh, well, see, that's sort of why I'm calling. Um, this is a little weird. . . . Well, I've had it. With Bill, with this partnership. If anyone ever asks you, it's a bad idea to date your partner. . . . Yeah, probably a lot of people could've told me. But I guess I was hoping—anyway, this is it. I'm going out on my own. . . . Yeah, thanks. But the thing is, the kind of cases he's been bringing in—well, this is the first time in years I've met people like you. He only knows lowlifes. . . . Yes, I guess it does figure. So why I'm calling, I'm going to need, you know, contacts. Clients. Not his kind, the kind I want to work with going forward. And you offered. . . . Yes, right. If it's okay I'd like to talk. . . . Oh, I didn't mean to. . . . Well, that would be really great. Thanks so much! I'll see you there."

Lydia slipped her phone away.

I said, "You've had it? Lowlifes? It figures?"

She smiled. "See, you can be the bad cop without even being there. And I'm having coffee with Madison Guilder in half an hour."

"I'm calling my lawyer." And I did.

"Kirschenbaum."

"Hey, Leo. Bill Smith."

"Shit. What now?" I could hear the echo; he had me on speaker.

"Just a question."

"Yeah, I know—how fast can I get you out? Where are you?"

"Sixty-seventh Street."

"The Nineteenth Precinct? You pissed off the Silk Stocking boys?" He sighed. "Okay, give me the details."

I pictured Leo, jacket off, tie askew, curly black hair in desperate need of a cut swirling around the bald spot that colonized more of his big, round skull every time I saw him. He'd be in his avalanche of an office, blunt pencil ready to take notes on the back of someone's Parole Violation Appeal form.

"I haven't seen a cop all day," I said. "I'm in the park."

"Then what the hell are you calling me for? To say Happy Pesach? You're late. If it's Happy Shavous, you're early."

"I'm looking for a lawyer."

"What? I'm fired? And just when your damn bills are all paid up."

"Two, actually. A married couple named Spence. Though I'm not sure what name the wife practices under, now that I think about it. Separate firms."

"In New York?"

"I think so."

"What kind of law?"

"I have no idea."

"No idea, you think so, you're not sure. Vintage Smith. Okay, hold on."

I did, listening to the click of computer keys. Leo's disheveled, distracted persona wasn't exactly a sham; he'd been that way as long as I'd known him, and to hear him—and his wife—tell it, all his life. It was great cover, though, for a lightning-fast mind and an encyclopedic understanding of the law. He was a legend around the criminal bar: the formidable sad sack all the other lawyers went to for advice, the attorney's attorney, the back-room mayor.

"Okay," he said. "There are eighteen Spences practicing law in New York State, eleven in New York City. But luckily for you, only two of them are married to each other. Drew Spence, Trusts and Estates at Braverman Cummings. I'm sending the contact info. And his bashful bride, Andrea Savoy-Spence, in-house at Bloomingdale's."

"Whoa. Sounds fancy."

"In-house? Way easier than private practice. Or did you mean Bloomingdale's? She's been there since fall. Before that she was at Alcott and Alcott. Also in Trusts and freaking Estates. In-house at anywhere would be less time-consuming, not to say soul-devouring, than T and E at A and A."

"You're just jealous because she gets the Bloomingdale's employee discount. How do you keep up your sartorial splendor, paying retail? Listen, do you know either of them?"

"Me? I have clients like you. I don't get invited to meet and greet the elite."

"Their loss."

"No, probably mine, but too late now. Let me get back to the paying customers. Who are, god knows, few enough. Call me next time you're in the shit." He hung up.

Lydia had taken on Overbey's job of watching the gray-haired woman jog around the track. I didn't know what lap the woman was on but she showed no signs of stopping. I wondered if she'd been a marathoner in her youth. Hell, she could be a marathoner still.

"Get something?" Lydia asked.

"You're going to be sorry you decided we should split up. I'm on my way to talk to an in-house attorney at Bloomingdale's. If she likes me she might let me share her employee discount."

"If she likes you." Lydia looked me up and down. "I'm not worried. See you later."

# 24

Lydia headed uptown, and I down, both on the Upper East Side. Not home turf for either of us.

As I walked, I reflected: Lauren Spence's mother had been in Trusts and freaking Estates at a big-deal firm until last fall, when she'd moved on to a new, less stressful job.

A change a person might make if, say, her daughter had attempted suicide in the summer.

The walk from the park to Bloomingdale's took me ten minutes. Normally, if I'm going to see a professional in her office, I'll call to make sure she's there. Often I'll BS who I am and what I want, so she doesn't actually know I'm coming, but no point in wasting my time if she's out. In this case I didn't call. My experience with in-house counsel, limited though it might be, was that they generally could be found in-house.

From across Third Avenue I watched the well-heeled and well-dressed stream in and out of the big glass-and-bronze doors under the Art Deco Bloomingdale's sign. Not that people who worked in the corporate offices would be going to their desks this way. Typists and mailroom clerks, IT nerds and secretaries—folks who probably had to wait for post-season sales to get any use out of their employee discounts—would have another, less grand, way in.

In salary terms, in-house counsel would be a different thing; still, while they were probably paid well enough to outfit themselves from the designer floors, they would not stroll through them on the way to work. I joined the throng of classy people ambling in, and asked the security guard just inside where to find the corporate office entrance. He was happy to tell me, because otherwise he'd be stuck following me around waiting for me to pilfer something.

I went in the narrow side door on Sixtieth Street. Another security guard, this one behind a desk, sent me to the seventh floor. Frosted glass doors opened off the elevator lobby to reveal a smiling young woman whose ruby lips and tiny white Bluetooth earpiece elegantly set off her deep brown skin. She asked how she could help me.

"I'm here to see Ms. Savoy-Spence," I said. "My name is Bill Smith." I keep cards of various persuasions in my wallet. I gave her one that claimed I was an accountant.

"Is she expecting you?"

"No, but I won't keep her long. I'm doing an audit. It's about Alcott and Alcott."

When she dubiously repeated, "Alcott and Alcott?" I just smiled.

She suggested I take a seat and waited until I did. Then she tapped a key on her desk pad, spoke softly into the air, nodded, tapped another key, and spoke more loudly, this time to me. "Ms. Savoy-Spence says to give her a minute."

I did. I planned to give her five and then get pushy, but after three a pale woman about my age, a gently highlighted brunette—you could make a fortune on the hairdressing contract for this case—opened the inner door, held it for me. She asked if I was Mr. Smith and I admitted to it. She nodded me through. Wordlessly she led me down a carpeted corridor to an office with a view of the Roosevelt Island tram cars sliding back and forth over the East River. When we were inside, she closed the door behind us and turned to face me.

"I'm Andrea Savoy-Spence. Mary said you want to talk about Alcott and Alcott?"

"Bill Smith. I'm a private investigator."

Her blue eyes flashed. Annoyance, I thought, and maybe also alarm. "Mary said you were an accountant."

"That's what I told her. I also told her it was about your old firm, because I figured that would get me in to see you, but that's not true either. It's just I didn't think the whole office needed to know your business. I'm here to talk about your daughter."

She waited a measured beat before she spoke. "Your discretion earns you a polite dismissal instead of a call to security. Please leave."

"A fifteen-year-old girl—not at Granite Ridge, but in the theater combine—killed herself earlier this week."

Savoy-Spence's skin drained from pale to ash. She sat down heavily in one of the office's visitor chairs. Without invitation I sat in the other. She snapped her head up at me when I did that, but for a long time said nothing. Then, in a hoarse voice, she said, "Oh my God. I'm sorry."

"Her parents have asked me to look into what happened."

"I am sorry, truly. But I can't help you."

"Your daughter—"

"Mr. Smith? I can't help you." She pressed a little on the "can't."

Oh.

She saw me get it and nodded.

I said, "There's an agreement. An NDA."

Another nod.

"Can I ask with whom?"

One side of her mouth twitched up. "I'm sure you know you can't."

"Amber Shun's parents—that's her name, Amber Shun—"

"Don't. I can't talk about this and you know it."

"No NDA can stop you from talking about your daughter."

"No. I can tell you about her A's in Latin at her new school. How hard she's found it making friends. How pretty she is. But not about what happened last summer at Greenwood Lake, which is all you care about."

"It isn't, really," I said. "I hope she makes new friends soon. And I admire the Latin. But—"

"There is no but. I want you to leave." Neither of us moved, though. We sat looking at each other for a few long, silent minutes. Two tram cars passed by the window, the cables pulling them in opposite directions.

Finally, Savoy-Spence stood. She walked to the door and opened it. "And when you leave," she said, "I'd suggest you contact Granite Ridge and request a copy of my daughter's academic transcript."

"All right," I said. "Why?"

"Also, get a copy of her transcript from Fern Hill, in Bedford, where she goes now."

"Those records aren't sealed or something?"

"Her counseling and psychological records are, but they would be in any case, with or without an NDA. But the academic transcripts have to stay available, for school transfers and for college applications."

"And the schools will give the records to me?"

"Give me ten minutes. I'll call both schools and authorize the release of the transcripts to my academic consultant. I assume you can fake that identity as well as you do accountant?"

"I don't do that very well."

"It got you in the door."

"You notice I dropped it before I had to start juggling numbers."

"And you and I are the only people who know you dropped it at all." Her eyes held me steadily.

"Which is why you're not sending me the records yourself," I said. "If anyone asks you need to be able to say I hoodwinked you."

She shrugged.

"Must be a pretty ironclad NDA."

"It is. It was offered within a week of . . . what happened, and it will send Lauren and her sisters to college. And speaking of Lauren and her sisters, you will, of course, not attempt to contact any of my children in any way. They're all underage and I could, and would, have you charged with a serious crime."

"Understood," I said. "In these transcripts, what am I looking for?"

"If you're any good at what you do, they'll help you. If you don't see what's there to be seen then Amber Shun's parents have hired the wrong investigator." She gave me a faint smile. "Good luck, Mr. Smith."

# 25

Ten minutes. Plenty of time to stop at the nearest FedEx and get a box for the shooter's damn gun and its constituent parts. I couldn't FedEx to the private lab I use—illegal as hell—so I called a messenger service to send a guy to the Moonstruck Diner. Then I walked the two blocks to the diner, settled in a booth, ordered coffee and a BLT, and hoped something broke in this case soon.

Though, as always, hope soon proved to be a two-edged thing.

At first all was calm. I texted Lydia for an update and got no response. I took that to mean coffee with Madison was going well, though what defined "well" in this context was unknown to me. My coffee came; I drank it, thinking about NDAs. I opened Gmail and set up a new account. The messenger came, a skinny young guy with a Mets cap. I told him to be careful with the package, it was my grandma's china. He couldn't have cared less what it was. I tipped him and he was off. At the ten-minute mark, my sandwich was delivered. Before I started in on it I called Granite Ridge, identified myself as William Smith of Smith and Chin Educational Services, and requested Lauren Spence's academic records. "I believe Ms. Savoy-Spence has been in touch with you."

"Yes, she's sent us an e-signed authorization. If you'll just provide an email address—?"

So I did, to the new account. While I waited for the Granite Ridge transcript I went through the same process with Fern Hill. While I waited for the Fern Hill transcript I ate and examined the Granite Ridge transcript, which had arrived as a PDF attached to an email. I glanced over Lauren Spence's freshman and sophomore years, checked my email again, and opened the junior-year PDF from Fern Hill.

At both schools, A- to B grades, with a C+ in gym two semesters at Granite Ridge. Not a jock, then. A's in Latin at Fern Hill, as her mother had said, and also in English Poetry. I toggled back and forth between the two transcripts on my phone, wondering what I was supposed to be seeing.

And then I saw it.

Once I did, it was unmissable, though what it meant wasn't as clear. I wiped my hands and was about to make a call when I heard Lydia's voice in my head: *They don't call, they text.* So I texted Astrid Bergson: Important. Please call me. Smith.

She did, a minute or two later. "Hey," she said. "What's up?"

"You okay?"

"Yeah. Hanging out, you know. Trying to chill." I heard other kids' voices in the background and translated Astrid's words to mean, "Everyone's shaken up about Jacob's shooting and no one wants to be alone."

"I won't keep you long," I said. "I have a question."

"About Mark? Or Amber?"

"No. Lauren Spence."

"Lauren? Wow, that's random. Um, I don't know her that well. She's not at this school anymore, you know."

"I know. When she was, she was a violinist, right?"

"That's right. I mean, she left after sophomore year." A tiny pause. "There were, I don't know, like, rumors . . ."

So the kids at Granite Ridge weren't sure about Lauren Spence's suicide attempt. That was a hell of an NDA.

"Tell me about her as a musician."

"Oh, wow, I have no idea. I think she was in Small Ensemble. Um, wait. Hold on." I heard murmurs of a brief conversation, Astrid and another kid. Then she returned. "Mr. Smith? You can talk to Tristan Osmos. He's concertmaster in the All-Schools Orchestra."

A new voice came on then. "Uh, Mr. Smith? Uh, this is Tristan."

"Hi, Tristan. I guess Astrid told you, I'm an investigator, looking into a couple of things. I'd like to ask you about Lauren Spence."

"Lauren? Uh, Astrid said you were trying to find Mark. Like, he really disappeared?"

"I'm pretty sure he's safe. But this Lauren thing, it's connected." As I said that I was sure I was right, though I wasn't sure what the connection was.

"I don't think they actually know each other. Lauren and Mark. And Lauren, she's at some school upstate now."

Bedford. Thirty miles from midtown Manhattan in a state that's four hundred miles north to south, but to a New York City kid, Here Be Monsters.

"Doesn't matter if they know each other," I said. "Right now, it's Lauren I'm interested in. Especially her violin playing."

"Her playing?"

"Yes. Tell me about that."

Luckily for me, Tristan Osmos was a kid used to trying to get along with adults. The question obviously seemed weird to him, but he went with it. "Uh, well, yeah, she's pretty good, I guess."

"Pretty good. Not great?"

"Well, like, she was a sophomore when she was last here. Young, you know?"

I guessed to be concertmaster, Tristan must be a senior. From where I was, not so different from a sophomore; but the gulf between them is enormous when you're one or the other.

"Even still," I said. "You'd know a prodigy, I'll bet. Is she that good? Will she be, if she keeps at it? I need you to be honest with me, Tristan. I know it's just your opinion and you don't want to bad-mouth anyone. What you say won't get back to her, but I need to know what you think."

"Um, yeah, okay. I mean, like, no. No. She's not."

"Not that good?"

He took a breath. I had no idea what this kid looked like but I could imagine him squinting into space for a way to explain what he knew. "Some guys, I mean, girls too, some people, you know, they want something really bad? And if you're good at it, and you, like, put in the work, you can get it. You know? But sometimes people put in the work, they literally work their butts off, but they're not that good and they're not going to be. Not their fault, but it's not going to happen. All that work and, like, how much they want it, but they can't. They just can't."

I got, oddly, from this unknown boy, a sense that he *was* that good, and he knew it; but that he considered it inexplicably unfair that others who wanted the same thing he did and worked as hard as he did for it should find it forever out of reach.

"And Lauren," I said. "She's like that?"

"I felt bad for her. You could see how bad she wanted it. She practiced, like, all the time. She tried out for everything. All-Schools Orchestra, the ensembles, orchestra for the fall and spring musicals. I mean, like, everyone here is good, you know? You need to audition to get in. Or, like, have a portfolio, like Astrid. Or a chapbook or whatever. But there's good and there's, you know . . ."

"Yes," I said. "I get it."

"Uh, I mean, like, I could be wrong." He hurried to backpedal. "She got into Greenwood Lake. So, you know, they saw something. Heard, I mean. Heard something, at her audition. And maybe now, especially after she went there last summer, maybe at her new school, maybe it's different. Because you know, sometimes a change like that, sometimes it could help?" That was the well-brought-up boy being polite. No matter what the Greenwood Lake people heard at her audition, no matter what change she made, of venue or of teacher, nothing could do anything about the difference between good and what was beyond.

"Okay. Thanks, Tristan. Could you give Astrid back the phone?"

A few seconds, then, "Mr. Smith? Did talking to Tristan help you?"

"Yes, thanks, Astrid."

"Yeah. He kind of . . . knows stuff, you know? And this about Lauren, it has something to do with Mark?"

Maybe Mark; certainly, Amber Shun. I told Astrid the truth: "I think so. It fills something out for me."

"Good. Could you, I mean . . ."

"Keep you in the loop? I'll let you know anything I can. Thanks again."

I cut the call and went back to the transcripts to make sure I was right. I was.

If Tristan Osmos knew what he was talking about—if he "knew stuff"—nothing would make Lauren Spence the violinist she wanted to be. But there was another reason transferring to a new school wasn't going to do anything for Lauren Spence's violin playing.

At Fern Hill, Lauren Spence was taking no music at all.

# 26

I texted Lydia: I may be onto something. Call when you can. Then I
called my piano teacher, Max Bauer.

"Hey, Max, it's Bill Smith."

"No! Bill Smith, the pianist who doesn't play, doesn't practice, doesn't
come for a lesson? It's this Bill Smith?"

"I practice." I bit into my BLT, which by now had gotten a little soggy.

"And who would know this," Max asked, "since only the mice in the
walls hear you?"

"I'm famous among rodents."

"Such ears you must have, to hear mice applaud. Are you finally
calling Max to schedule a lesson? My day has brightened."

Max had had a concert career himself when he was young, but his
real gift had always been teaching. In his decades on the Juilliard faculty
he'd had his pick of the best. Other teachers—from Juilliard, from other
institutions in New York, and from all over the world—would sit in on
his master classes, and his techniques had helped shape modern piano
pedagogy.

He'd been retired for years now. He still taught at music festivals, gave master classes at retreats around the country and occasionally abroad. But mostly what he did was walk. From his home in Brooklyn Heights he and his wife Elaine would set out in one direction or another, covering ground, greeting people, giving children candy, feeding biscuits to dogs, stopping for tea. He'd spent his life staring at eighty-eight keys, he said; now he wanted to look up and see what the rest of the world held. "The Burgermeister of Brooklyn, that's who Max is now," he told me. "Strolling with Mrs. Burgermeister, greeting the citizens. Happy as a clam."

"I hate to disappoint," I said now, "but no."

"No? Your Prokofiev is that beautiful, it doesn't need work anymore?"

"It needs more work than ever. But Max, I'm calling you for help on a case."

An intake of breath. "A case? The private eye wants Max Bauer's help on a case?" He chortled. "Max Bauer, private eye! So. What can I do for you?"

"You can answer a question. Why have you never taught at Greenwood Lake?"

"Ah." Max's tone changed. Again he said, "Ah."

"You can't tell me you haven't been asked. All the summer programs must be begging for you. You've taught at Tanglewood, at Interlochen. Last year you went all the way the hell to Brevard. Why not Greenwood Lake?"

"Ah. May I ask why?"

"Why do I want to know? A couple of kids from there have run into trouble lately."

"Girls?"

"Yes, Max, girls. What is it?"

He sighed. "You understand, I can't be quoted. I'm just an old retired piano teacher. And I know nothing, really."

"What is it you know nothing about?"

"Rumors, all rumors. But they say, sometimes, some of the girls . . ." He trailed off.

"That for some of the girls, Greenwood Lake isn't really free?"

"Mmm. Put very well. Of course, people talk, always, and boys especially can be mean about beautiful girls. At first when I heard these things I dismissed them, just talk. Everything is all whispers, people shaking their heads. But I heard enough whispers to keep me wondering." He sighed. "Maybe, if I were a younger man, maybe if I still had a name to make, maybe I'd go there, I would teach and not see anything except what was right in front of my eyes. Or if I were braver, I'd stand up and denounce! But Max Bauer has gotten old. Who I am, I am already. So I don't need to go. And the whispering makes me uncomfortable, but to denounce based on whispering? No. So neither. I just politely say thank you but no when I'm invited."

"Can you tell me anything more specific? Anyone in particular, student, teacher?"

"No, nothing. Whispering. Just the usual. Men with money, they take what they want. Men without, we take what we get."

I was silent. Then, "Max," I said, "thanks. You don't know what a help this is."

"You have a case about these girls?"

Max didn't need to know about Lauren Spence. Or, if I was right, Amber Shun. "It didn't start out that way, but I think that may be what it's about, yes."

"Well, I hope you can help them. But my name, you won't mention it? Oscar Trask, you know he sues people. Max is much too old and tired for that."

# 27

I finished my sandwich, trying to will Lydia to call. Lydia's the only person who has her own ringtone on my phone—the theme from *Crouching Tiger, Hidden Dragon*, which she programmed in herself one rainy afternoon—so I gave my mental powers an E for Effort and an I for Incomplete when the phone finally rang but with its usual bells. When I checked the screen, I revised that to an F. It was Bree. I was tempted not to answer, but she might have identified Tattoo Man.

No such luck. I said, "Hey, Bree," then yanked the phone from my ear at her shout.

*"What the fuck have you done?"*

Bree prided herself on not losing her temper and also on not cursing. Whatever this was about, it was big.

"What do you mean?"

"Turn on your goddamn TV."

"I'm at a diner. They don't have a goddamn TV. What's up?"

"Mark. Somebody spilled the tea, is what. New York One is running with it already, the other outlets are calling here, they're calling the home staff, probably the neighbors and the school and the mailman. The mayor's kid's been missing for days, the mayor hasn't called the police, she's too busy politicking, what kind of a Mommie Dearest is she—this is exactly what wasn't supposed to happen!"

"I'm sorry that it did, but it wasn't us."

"It must have been! So much for discretion. I promised Carole you could keep it quiet."

"I promised her I'd try to find her son." That stopped Aubrey for a moment. I took advantage. "It wasn't us. Not me, not Lydia. But none of this has ever really been a secret. You're the one who called his friends, looking for him. Sooner or later people were going to start putting it together. Come on, you're a spin doctor. I'm sure this is the kind of fire someone like you can put out pretty easily."

"Screw you. And when some smartass figures out Mark knew that Amber Shun? Girl kills herself, boyfriend disappears, happens to be the mayor's son, wow, how juicy is that? You have to produce him, Bill."

"I don't have him."

"I only half believe you. It would be like you to find him and then fall for his bullshit and not make him go home."

"It would," I agreed. "And I still might. But I'd tell you I'd found him and he was all right, just in case anyone was actually worried. Right now, I have no idea where he is."

"Right now." A pause. "But you did, right? Goddammit, you did!"

"I'm going to have to work on my grammar, I can see that."

"Christ! This smartass bullshit—"

"—is the reason you dumped me, yeah, I know. I knew it wasn't because I was coarse."

"Bill! Dammit! This isn't a game. And it's not about getting back at me. You have to bring Mark in."

"Jesus, Bree, center of the universe much? Getting back at you isn't even in my top twenty. What about my Tattoo Man?"

"Fuck your Tattoo Man! He probably has nothing to do with anything. Get me Mark!"

"I don't have Mark and I don't know where he is. But Tattoo Man is hunting for him, too."

"Then you'd better goddamn well find him and I mean soon!"

I started to say that had been the point from the beginning but she was gone. Probably to do spin control. Luckily, as per the Oscar Trask story, spin control had long been one of her gifts.

I was thinking about the leak when my phone rang again. This time, though, it was playing "Crouching Tiger."

"Hey," Lydia said. "What's up?"

"Seen the news? To quote Bree, someone spilled the tea."

"Oh no."

"Somehow the media got tipped off. Bree just called me in a nuclear meltdown."

"She thinks it was us?"

"Of course."

"Are we fired?"

"No such luck. Listen, where are you?"

"That's why I called. Unless you have a better idea, I'm heading home to change. Madison wants to take me to a cocktail party."

"You have Stockholm Syndrome already? Do you need an intervention?"

"She said you'd be jealous."

"This is payback for the Bloomingdale's employee discount, isn't it?"

"Did that lawyer give it to you?"

"Of course not. She'd have had to like me. Whose party?" I sipped my new hot coffee. Apparently at the Moonstruck the coffee pot was bottomless.

"Oscar—Mr. Trask, for those of you not on a first-name basis," Lydia said, "is throwing a small drop-in-after-work soiree. Madison wasn't going to go but she's all excited about helping me out and she thinks people might come that I need to meet. You know, so I can have a better class of clients. Personally, I'm interested to know who's going to go all the way up to the Bronx for a cocktail party."

"Brown-nosers."

"And I guess Oscar's Riverdale mansion neighbors. Do you think it's a waste of time?"

"For the neighbors, or for you? I think your going is an excellent idea. But I need to tell you—"

"Hold on. Chris is calling."

I waved for the check while I waited, wondering how soon my face would be posted on the New York diner owners' social media pages as a coffee-swilling bum with a cell phone habit.

Lydia came back. "Sorry. Chris wants to meet."

"He does? Did he say why?"

"He didn't want to say on the phone."

"Oh, hell. That doesn't sound good."

"Columbus Park, half an hour?"

"Sure. And while I have you—I was about to call Mr. Shun, but I think he'd rather hear from you."

"Most people would. What about?"

"He said Amber had summer plans. I want to know what they were."

# 28

The sky was still gray and the pavement was still puddled but unless the rain's actually pelting down nothing can keep New Yorkers out of the parks in spring. In Chinatown pink and white blossoms blanketed Columbus Park's crabapple and cherry trees. I found Chris Chiang standing, hands in pockets, at the edge of a crowd watching a game of Xiangqi, Chinese chess. He peeled away when he spotted me.

"Heavy betting on that one," he said by way of greeting.

"Aren't you supposed to do something about that?"

"I'm investigations, not vice. Besides, they're playing for mung beans."

"Is that true?"

"Hey, that's what they told me, and who'd lie to a cop? Hi, Lydia," he said, as Lydia parted a pair of oblivious earbud-wearing teenagers to come and stand beside us.

"Hi, guys. So, Chris. What's up?"

Chris shook his head. "Nothing good. For one thing, the news is out that your boy is missing."

"Yeah, it leaked," she said. "Nothing to do with us."

"Though they're blaming us and Lydia was hoping that would be enough to get us fired," I said.

"Is it?"

"Sadly, no."

Lydia said, "Can't win 'em all. Has the mayor made a statement?"

I'd asked myself exactly that question as I was coming up out of the subway and searched the news on my phone for the answer. "Not her," I said, "but City Hall put one out. They say the mayor and her team are completely focused on the needs of the city, including the ongoing salary negotiations which are of such critical importance. She appreciates the offer of the Detectives' Endowment Association to postpone the upcoming sessions in view of the situation but there's no need."

Chris's eyebrows went up. "The DEA offered to postpone?"

"Worried about your raise, are you? Vacation days? Your pension?"

"Hah. I'll never see a pension if Straley stays in charge. But really, he said he'd postpone? Instead of going for the jugular when the other guy's down? I wonder what got into him."

"Come on," said Lydia. "It's the decent thing to do."

"Yeah. That's what I mean."

"Hey," I said. "He's your union president."

"I voted for the other guy."

"Well, it's not happening anyway. City Hall says the negotiations will go on as scheduled. Furthermore, they say, Mayor McCann will not discuss her family life with the media. However, she appreciates the public concern for her son and can assure everyone that he's safe."

Lydia rolled her eyes. "I hardly know your girlfriend Aubrey but I'd swear that was her."

"It's completely her. It doesn't say so in so many words but you could get the impression the kid's in rehab, in a mental hospital, someplace embarrassing, maybe, but not missing."

"Your girlfriend Aubrey?" Chris looked at me.

"The mayor's spin doctor," I said.

"But it's not true, right?" Chris said. "You don't know that he's safe."

"He's smart. His mother thinks he's not resourceful, but boy, is she wrong. I do think he's probably safe. But not forever. We need to track him down again."

"Again?"

Lydia glanced at me. I nodded. "That's why I wanted the gun and the tattoo," she said. She gave him the short version: Jacob Dolo, the Sundaris, Tattoo Man, Mark's second vanishing act.

It was a complicated story with a large cast of characters but Chris interrupted her only once. "Goofy?"

She shrugged.

He shook his head and didn't speak again while Lydia went on. When she finished Chris looked across the park to the benches. A singer had just begun a set of Chinese folk songs, accompanied by erhu, banjo, and accordion. "Crap," Chris said. He turned back to us. "Crap, crap, crap. That's who the tattoo belongs to? The shooter?"

"Why?" I asked. "Did you find it? Bree said it wasn't in the system."

"No, it's not. That tattoo's not in the system because it doesn't belong to a bad guy. It probably belongs to a cop."

The guy with the Justice League of America around his wrist had tailed us. He may have shot Jacob Dolo. He'd for sure held the Sundaris hostage. That made him a bad guy, cop or not.

But Chris was right: crap.

"Who?" I asked.

"Any one of a group of guys."

"How do you know?"

"I called Jon Cobb in organized crime. You met him."

"I remember."

"Even if no one with that tattoo is in the system I thought he might've seen it."

"And he had."

"But he wouldn't talk about it on the phone. He met me here. I called you"—nodding at Lydia—"right after he left. That Justice League around the wrist, that was a thing ten, fifteen years ago. Bunch of wannabe hero cowboy cops."

"Club? Secret society?"

"Not even. More like a frat, like drinking buddies. One for all, all for one, we're the NYPD Justice League, we'll clean up this city, let us at 'em. That kind of garbage. Big talkers but pretty much all mouth, according to Cobb. A few of them got written up a couple of times. Excessive force, civilian complaint, appearance of impropriety. That one generally means getting caught accepting a free cup of coffee. So on. Nothing out of the ordinary."

"Is it still a thing, the Justice League?"

Chris shook his head. "Some of them have retired. Cobb doesn't know if they even still drink together. Whole thing might have died out."

"But tattoos don't."

"Right. Even if there's no more NYPD Justice League, there's still a bunch of guys running around with that tattoo."

"But Cobb wouldn't tell you this on the phone? Nothing about it incriminates anyone. You didn't even know what there was to be incriminated in when you called him."

"Seriously? I called to find out if the tattoo was a gang thing. It's kind of obvious I must be looking for a bad guy. And all Cobb had to offer was a bunch of cops."

# 29

"There's something else," said Chris, as we stood in Columbus Park in the gray of the late afternoon.

"Tell me you found the gun," Lydia said.

"No. It wasn't bought legally in New York State and it's not registered here."

A loud groan went up from the Xiangqi table behind him. I felt their pain. "I sent it to the lab for prints. I have no hope but if they do find something I'll let you know, Chris, so you can get them ID'd."

"Great."

"The something else—it's more bad news?"

"Shouldn't be news. Now that it's out that the kid's gone, I really do have to tell Joe Lenz about him and Amber Shun."

"Crap. But yeah," I said as he frowned and started to speak, "I know you do. What are you going to say?"

"That I heard around Chinatown that they knew each other. Local girl and the mayor's son, people talk. If there's more to it than that, don't tell me."

"I really don't know what there is to it."

"I'm choosing to believe that."

Another groan from the game. Someone's strategy hadn't panned out. Spectators started reaching into their pockets, transferring what was not mung beans to other spectators. Chris kept his back turned.

"About these Justice League guys," he said. "If you figure out which one it is, and he figures out Cobb and I ratted him out, we're Serpico."

Frank Serpico, honest cop, unearther of corruption in the 1970s NYPD. A hero to New Yorkers. A leper to his fellow cops.

Lydia squeezed Chris's arm. "We'll do it some other way. Right?" She looked at me.

I shook my head. "I'm not asking you to put yourself on the line like that, Chris."

"Who the hell cares what you're asking? If I know this shit, I can't just sit on it."

"But what do you really know? What do we have? There could be a hundred guys in New York who just happen to have that tattoo. I'd bet the farm that there aren't but there could be. Plus, the Dolo shooting is in the One Twentieth." I didn't add, because all of us knew, that the chances of NYPD cops investigating NYPD cops on the basis of a single piece of circumstantial evidence, which is what we had, were bad, and on Staten Island they were worse.

"All right." Chris nodded. "I'm leaving. I'll call Lenz. Bent cops and the mayor's son. Why do I even know you people?"

He headed out of the park.

Lydia watched after him. "He's wanted to be a cop since he was a little kid," she said to me. "If we screw this up for him . . ."

"We won't. We'll find a way to keep him out of it."

She looked unconvinced. I didn't blame her.

I took out my phone, called Mark, on both numbers. Both went to voicemail. I left each the same message. "The guy shooting at you *is a cop*. Stay out of sight and call me." I looked up the number of the 120th Precinct. I blocked my ID, called, and to the guy who answered I said, "Got a tip for you on Jacob Dolo. Shooter was a cop. Justice League of America tattooed around his wrist." I cut the call before he could respond.

Next, I called Bree. Again, voicemail. I was starting to think voicemail should be outlawed but then people would just do what they used to do when I called: hang up. "Call me," I said after the inescapable beep. "You have no idea."

"If it is a cop," Lydia said, "the question is why."

"I hate to point out the obvious, but that's always been the question no matter who it was."

"Now we have a wider choice of motives, though. This can't really be about the negotiations, can it? To rattle the mayor?"

"Risking a homicide rap for an incrementally bigger paycheck would be completely nuts. That doesn't rule it out but it makes it a lot less likely."

"Mark says he doesn't think the shot was meant to hit him."

"It hit Jacob, though. And after that instead of backing off, the shooter went to Queens and took hostages. I'm not buying 'just kidding.'"

Lydia checked the time. "If I'm going to make it to this cocktail party I need to get home and change. Unless now you think I shouldn't go?"

"No, I think it's even more important that you do. Come on, I'll walk you home."

As I lit a cigarette and we started off I heard the clack of a new Xiangqi game starting up behind us. We threaded through the blossoming trees in Columbus Park toward Mosco Street.

"Did you get anything from Madison?" I asked.

"Other than this party invite, not much. I told her I'd met this lawyer for Bloomingdale's who had a daughter in private school and wondered if Madison knew her. She gave me a look like you give the people who say, *Hey, you live in New York, do you know my cousin Joe,* but she laughed when I told her it was Lauren Spence and said sure, she knew her. Or used to, a little bit, when Lauren was at Granite Ridge. Pretty, but kind of a loser. She asked did I know the crazy bitch had tried to kill herself? And couldn't even do that right? Lucky for her, her parents are shark lawyers, because they threatened to sue the music camp where she was. Oscar's camp, where all he did was try to help kids get careers. Madison was outraged. She said, 'Like being a no-talent loser couldn't possibly be a reason to want to kill yourself, so it had to be someone else's fault, right? So Lauren ended up with a big settlement and an NDA. Good thing because she'll never have a career. Now that it's obvious she can't handle stress they put her in an easier school.'"

"Fern Hill? Easier?"

"What are you, some kind of education consultant?"

"In fact, I am, but never mind. Go on."

She narrowed her eyes but I didn't explain so she gave up. "I said since she'd brought up suicide, and stress, what about this Amber Shun, she must have heard about that, right? I mean, kids today must be under so much pressure, I couldn't even imagine. Madison made a sad face. And then, because who can resist being part of bad news, she told me she knew Amber, too, and it's awful, she was a sweet kid."

"Kid? They're the same age."

"Only on paper. Anyway, I guess if your suicide attempt is successful you're a sweet kid, not a crazy bitch."

"Or if you don't threaten to sue Oscar. A sad face. Did you get the feeling she was really sad?"

"She was something—upset? Uncomfortable? But no, I don't think sad."

"Does she know about Amber and Mark?"

"Sort of. She told me her loser brother had had a crush on Amber. I said, 'Just a crush, they were never together?' and she asked if I was kidding. Still, it seemed like a great opening so I asked about Mark and all the pressure *he* must be under. She said 'Oh, yeah, right,' and switched straight into diss mode. Some superhero, but at least in those stupid costumes he doesn't talk, much better than having to listen to him yelling and screaming when he has a part. I asked her didn't she think pressure might be why Mark ran away and wasn't she worried? She said no and no. He ran away for the attention and he's really good at finding people to help him. Like that caretaker in Watermill that time. Suckers who feel sorry for him."

"Empathy, it's a beautiful thing."

"Envy. Bill, I get the feeling she's had trouble finding people to take care of her, all her life."

"There might be a reason for that. She's a major pain."

"Because she's insecure? Rick Crewe said she was still a little kid sometimes."

I stubbed my cigarette out on the park fence. "You know, that's the danger of always being the good cop. You start to believe in your own niceness."

"You don't believe in my niceness?"

"You're so nice, it's unbelievable. What else did she have to say?"

"Nothing, except how excited she is to be able to help me out. That's another feeling I have—that not a lot of people have ever needed her."

Lydia and I had reached the spot where Mosco Street hits the park. We were about to cross when I stopped.

"Hold on," I said. "She said something about the stupid superhero costumes? She knows about that? About Times Square?"

"I guess."

"I thought Vela said no one knew. That Mark didn't tell anyone."

"You're right, he did. Well, he must've been wrong."

"But Madison? Of all people to—" The light bulb went on. "Mark didn't tell her, Rick Crewe did. He's the one who knew, and he told me he filled Madison in on Mark when she asked."

"Bill." Lydia put a hand on my arm. "Madison was there getting a popsicle when Rick Crewe told us to go find Spider-Man."

I thought back. "You're right. And then Tattoo Man picked us up in Times Square."

She frowned. "No. No. I mean, he's trying to kill her brother. No way she'd be part of that."

"You sure?"

She met my eyes. "Yes. I'm sure."

"Okay." I thought. "But maybe she told someone else that's where we were going. Guilder?"

"Guilder? That's as awful as if it were her."

We crossed Mulberry in silence. When we got to her building I said, "Speaking of parents, did you reach Mr. Shun?"

"That's cold. Anyway, not yet. I left a message. I'll call when he calls me back."

"Okay. Now I guess you'd better kiss me."

"I'd be happy to, but why?"

"Because you're going to a party with Madison Guilder and Co. You might need protection. My kisses can cast magic spells."

"Oh, can they? Does Aubrey know that?"

"Of course. She was a nice person when I met her. Then I kissed her, and look at her now."

Lydia smiled and kissed me. I was lying, of course. It was her kisses that cast the spells.

# 30

After Lydia went upstairs to change I walked the rest of the way home, but I didn't go up. I pulled open the door to Shorty's. Shorty wasn't behind the bar; a moonlighting muscleman Caribbean cop named Patrice was pouring. He gave me a bourbon and said, "What is happening, my friend?" His white teeth glowed against his dark skin.

"Nothing," I said. "I'm looking for inspiration."

"Sit there," he said, nodding at the back booth. "I have seen it work."

I took the drink to the booth and sat, hoping Patrice was right. I sipped, listening to the clink of glasses and the murmurs of talk around me, watched my own fingers tapping on the incised wooden tabletop.

If Oscar Trask was trading admission to his super-selective music camp—more, to a career in music, which is what his sponsorship could mean—to underage girls for sex, I didn't have any evidence to prove it.

If someone—some cop—was trying to kill Mark McCann and that's why Mark was on the run, I didn't have any evidence to prove that either.

If someone, some cop, was trying to kill Mark McCann because Mark had evidence against Trask, what I didn't have was any link between any cop and Trask.

I also didn't have Mark.

I was trying to come up with a next step that didn't involve putting on a suit and crashing Trask's party. That was tempting, but Lydia was already going. If there was anything to find, she'd find it. My showing up would just cramp her style. Also, we could be right about Trask but wrong about Mark's disappearance having anything to do with him. Maybe we'd just stumbled over a sleazebucket in the search for a missing kid. That they had Amber Shun in common might be meaningless.

For that matter, Amber's suicide might have nothing to do with Greenwood Lake, or Trask.

It was even possible Trask actually had no interest in underage girls.

Although Imani Overbey, in setting us onto Lauren Spence, saw a connection—Trask, or something else—between the girls.

And Rick Crewe had said he wouldn't bet against Overbey's intuition.

And I myself wouldn't bet against Rick Crewe's.

Or Max Bauer's.

I took another sip. My mental powers must have been stung by the bad grade from before, because my phone rang. Lydia.

"Looking for a plus-one?" I said. "I may be available."

"I don't think plus-ones get to take plus-ones. I just heard from Mr. Shun. He said Amber was planning to go to camp this summer. A special camp, a music camp where she had to audition to get in. She did that in the fall and got her acceptance just before Chinese New Year. Very auspicious. He was so proud of her. He couldn't remember the name but he said it had trees and water in it. I asked if it was Greenwood Lake. He said that sounded right."

"Damn." I put my glass down. "Lauren Spence was at Greenwood Lake last summer. That's where she tried to kill herself."

Lydia was silent. Two Black women came in and took seats at the bar. Civilian clothes but cop swagger.

"Could it be coincidence?" Lydia finally asked. "High-strung high-achievers looking for a way out from under the pressure? Or maybe copycat? Amber, feeling overwhelmed, remembering what Lauren had done?"

"Maybe. But here's the thing. They might've been high-strung but neither of them was so high-achieving."

"What do you mean?"

"Greenwood Lake is a free ride. Prodigies regardless of ability to pay. The best inspiring the best. Tomorrow's top artists learning from today's. And so on. They have hundreds of applications. You've heard Amber sing. She was good, but she wasn't top tier."

"I'll have to take your word for that."

"And apparently neither was Lauren Spence."

"Her mother told you that?"

"No. I talked to one of the kids at Granite Ridge. The orchestra concertmaster. He said she was desperate to be really, really good but she didn't have it."

"That's not just jealousy, you don't think? One kid tearing down another?"

I thought back to Tristan Osmos's careful search for the words he needed. "No. I got the feeling if he could have made her as good as she wanted to be he would have. I'm pretty sure he knew what he was talking about."

Patrice gave each of the women cops beer with a whisky back. They nodded their thanks. One started with the beer. The other went right to the whiskey.

"If Lauren and Amber weren't that good," Lydia said, "how did they get in?"

"They'd have no problem if the deep pockets that finance the camp wanted them in."

"Trask?"

"Neither of them is all that talented," I said. "But they're both beautiful."

She paused for a second. "Oh, no. Bill, they're kids."

"Wouldn't be the first time. Take girls who don't have much hope of making it and give them a chance beyond their wildest dreams. Then ask them to show you how grateful they are."

Lydia was silent for a few moments. A Black male cop came in and joined the two women. Lydia said, "It would explain what happened between Amber and Mark."

"How do you mean?"

"Before Chinese New Year, when she got her acceptance, would be right around Christmas. When she and Mark broke up. I bet she ended it with him, like Astrid says, and I bet it was because she'd started sleeping with Trask. God, she must have hated herself. But she loved Mark. That's why she didn't do the social-media purge. And he didn't know why she ended it but he still loved her too." Lydia sighed. "I guess she finally felt like she couldn't live with it."

"Looks like neither she nor Lauren felt like they could live with it. Although luckily, Lauren did live. And ended up with a huge payout and an NDA. And gave up music."

# 31

I put the phone on the table in my booth at Shorty's. Men with money, they take what they want. Just the usual.

Andrea Savoy-Spence had said she'd have me arrested if I went near Lauren, and I had no doubt she would. I wondered, though, how many other girls had been through Greenwood Lake over the years, and who might talk to me.

My phone rang again. My mental powers must be going for extra credit. I looked; it was Linus.

"Hey," I said. "What's up?"

"Hey," said Linus, and Trella echoed the greeting. This time Woof had nothing to say. "I called Cousin Lydia before but she didn't answer," Linus told me.

"She was probably in the shower. I just talked to her. She's getting ready for a fancy do tonight."

"Cool. You going too?"

"I'm PNG with the party host. She's going to have to handle it alone. You have something?"

"A couple of somethings. One, those Instas and TikToks Lydia wanted? Lauren Spence and Madison Guilder? Madison Guilder, she was easy, nothing hidden there. I mean, like, she lets it all hang out. But Lauren Spence deleted all her old accounts last summer so we had to, you know, dig them up."

"You can do that? 'Deleted' doesn't mean deleted?"

"Dude, on the internet, nothing means deleted. Trella did a deep dive. If you go back a year, eighteen months, those two are all over each other's pages."

"Those two, Lauren Spence and Madison Guilder?"

"For reals. After that Lauren Spence's new accounts start and Madison Guilder's not in those. As a matter of fact, no one from the first accounts is. Are?"

"Is."

"Whatever. It's all new people, and not so many posts. Like Lauren doesn't know any of those old people anymore and doesn't know a whole lot of new people, either. And Lauren isn't on Madison's pages from then on, either. They unfriended and unfollowed each other pretty fast."

That the two girls weren't on each other's pages since Lauren had changed schools was understandable. But Madison had told Lydia she'd known Lauren "a little," and here was Linus telling me Madison and Lauren were all over each other's pages. Was Madison just distancing herself from the crazy bitch loser she'd told Lydia that Lauren was? Or was something else going on?

"Okay, Linus, thanks."

"But wait, there's more," Linus said. "For just postage and handling—no, seriously, dude. I found two of those phones."

I felt an electric sizzle. "You did? Holy crap, why didn't you tell me that right off? Which two? Where are they?"

"Because it's more like where were they. One of them my guy at the carrier tracked down. It's gonna cost you Knicks tickets, by the way."

"No problem."

"Celebrity Row."

"It's okay, the client has juice. Go on."

"Wow. Can I get a pair too?"

"You don't even like basketball."

"No, but I wanna meet Spike Lee."

"Linus? The phones?"

"Oh, right. Okay, that one"—he gave me the number—"the last time it was on was early this afternoon. On Staten Island. Somewhere in Clifton."

"Rats," I said. "Sorry but I knew that. That's Mark's burner. It was me he was calling. It's off now?"

"He called you? Did you actually talk to him?"

"For all the good it did me. Talked to him, saw him face to face, lost him again."

"Dude, you're shaking my faith."

"Faith is the opiate of the masses."

"What?"

"Never mind. Go on."

"I still get the tickets, though, right? I'm gonna need this guy again."

"For him. Not for you."

"Sigh. Goodbye, Spike."

"What about the other phone you found? Was that Mark's real phone, same place?"

"No. His real phone's an iPhone, not a burner, so I didn't have to ask my guy, I just back-doored into the Find My iPhone app—" I heard Trella say something from across the room. "Oh, yeah, sorry, dude, Trella says you don't need the details. Bottom line, Mark's real phone hasn't been on since Tuesday night."

"Damn. But then what phone did you find?" I felt that sizzle again. "Wait—Amber Shun's?"

"I don't know whose. Cousin Lydia just gave me the number." He repeated it back to me.

"Yes, that's Amber's. What do you have?"

"Well, turns out that's another iPhone, so I did the same thing. That one, last time it was on was Tuesday, too."

The sizzle turned into a full-blown jolt. Amber Shun had died on Monday night. "Where was it?"

"This is the bizarro thing, dude. It was at City Hall."

# 32

C ity Hall?" I said to Linus. I sat upright in the booth. "Specifically? Not just, downtown, in the area, maybe City Hall Park, that kind of thing?"

"City Hall, my dude. On Staten Island they don't have that many towers, so the best I could do for you was Clifton. But lower Manhattan has, like, a million. City Hall for sure. They have jammers and scramblers and shit in there or I could've told you what room it was in."

"Do you know who it called, or who called it?"

"No one. I probably couldn't have told you who anyway, that's what the jammers and stuff are for, you know? But there was no incoming or outgoing to jam. Calls, text, nothing. The phone was on for just a few minutes, like someone was checking something—or maybe taking selfies?—but then it turned off again."

"And it hasn't been on since?"

"Nope. I have an alert for if it gets turned on again, but since Tuesday, nothing."

"Great work, Linus. Can you keep looking for Mark's other phone?"

"I have an alert for that one, too. I'll let you know."

"Terrific. You guys are the best."

"Yeah, aren't we? Tell him, Woof."

Woof gave a loud bark of agreement.

I sipped my bourbon and thought and I didn't like what I was thinking. Amber Shun's phone at City Hall. On and off again. *Like someone was checking something.* Checking who was in the phone's call history, would be my guess. Maybe its photos, too.

And my other guess would be, now that it was off, it wasn't coming back on.

Not a guess, but something I knew for sure: Bree hadn't called me back yet. Her job was to run interference for the mayor and in theory I was high priority.

But someone in City Hall had Mark's girlfriend's phone the day after she died—two days before Bree called me in. So now the question enlarged from what was going on to who was lying about it, and to whom.

And whether Bree's fury about the news that Mark was missing was a smokescreen for something else.

I called her again. Again, voicemail. I put what I had to say in a way most likely to get her attention. "You have some seriously fucked-up shit going on in that political snake pit. I feel a strong need to tell *somebody*."

I called Lydia. When she picked up I said, "Can you talk?"

"I'm about to go downstairs and wait for the car. Madison's picking me up."

"She drives?"

"Don't be silly. She's fifteen."

"I learned when I was twelve."

"On an Army Jeep or a tank or something, I'm sure. Madison's bodyguard is playing chauffeur."

"Ahlgren? A Ken doll in cop's clothing?"

"That's the guy. So unless they're early I have a few minutes."

"Madison doesn't strike me as the early type. I just talked to Linus. He tried to call you."

"Yes, I saw that. He left a message that he was going to call you next. I figured if it was important you'd tell me."

"It's important." I gave her the rundown. I heard her lock the door behind herself and trot down the creaky stairs, but she didn't say anything until I was done. When she spoke she asked me the same question I'd asked Linus.

"City Hall? Not just downtown near there, or something?"

"Linus says not. He seemed pretty sure."

She was silent for a moment. Then: "What does it mean? Aubrey? Or the mayor?"

"One or the other. Both. Neither, but then who?"

"Mark? Or Madison? They must be regulars around City Hall. Were either of them there Tuesday?"

"I thought of that, too. No one said they were but I can check. But what would they be doing with Amber's phone?"

"What would the mayor or Aubrey be doing with it?"

"If there's an innocent answer I can't come up with it. And if there is, why didn't whoever has that phone tell us about it?"

"Here's the car," she said. "I can't talk anymore but text me if you find out anything."

"I don't guess you have time to call Joe Lenz?"

"No. You want him to dump Amber's phone records?"

"I'm not sure I'm going to like what he finds, but I do."

"I could slip away from Madison and call him once we get up there. But if you want it to get started right away, call Chris. If he told Lenz about Amber's connection to Mark, Lenz might have done that already."

I was about to hang up when something hit me. "Wait. One more thing. You said Madison told you that crazy bitch Lauren tried to kill herself. And ended up with a big settlement and an NDA. How does she know?"

"Why wouldn't she?"

"Lauren's suicide attempt was in the summer, when she was away at camp. Within a week she was locked into the NDA. None of the other kids at Granite Ridge know, it's all just rumors there. Linus says none of Lauren's old friends are on her social media anymore and Lauren's vanished from Madison's. And Madison says Lauren was a crazy bitch loser. So how did she know all that?"

"You want me to ask?"

"If you can do it subtly."

"Dude," she said with reproach.

"You stole that from Linus."

"Of course I did."

I recommended she have a good time at the party, and hung up.

I did call Chris, but as it turned out, not right away, and for a different reason. And by the time Joe Lenz dumped Amber's phone records it was more for proof than answers.

As I started the call to Chris my phone rang again. My mental powers gave a superior smirk. I looked, saw an unknown number. Once when that happened it had been Jeffrey Guilder, but once it had been Mark. I answered in a neutral tone.

And by God, it was Mark this time, too.

To my, "Bill Smith," I got, "Uh, yeah. It's Mark. Mark McCann."

I wanted to say, *Oh, not one of the other forty-seven Marks I'm looking for?* But what I did say, with as much calm as I could pull together, was, "Mark. Good. Where the hell are you?"

"Um, in the Bronx. I got off the subway at 231st Street. Then I saw the news, in a bodega. About me."

Crap.

The Bronx—the ritzy part, Riverdale—was where I'd told Tattoo Man that Mark was heading. I'd pulled that out of the air. But even a blind squirrel can make a huge mistake.

"What are you doing up there?" I put a finger in my non-phone ear and leaned over the carved names and hearts on the scarred table.

"I need to tell you. God, this is so fucked up. But the news. My mom. This is bad, right?"

"You mean, will her career be ruined if you don't come in?"

"I guess I sort of do."

"Yeah, well, I guess it sort of will. Mark, for God's sake, we can deal with whatever this is about but whatever it is, it's getting worse every minute you're gone."

"Not for everyone."

"No? Well, for your mom, for sure. And probably for you. And some of your friends. The Sundaris, guy with gun, remember?"

"He's really a cop? The guy who shot Jacob? Your message said. Was he the same guy as at Ashok's? I mean, what the fuck?"

"I don't know if he's the same guy but I'm betting. Or else there are two of them, which isn't good either. Listen. You have someone seriously pissed at you and it's not going to get better. You can't just keep running away." I softened my voice. "Mark. Let me help."

"I . . . Shit. Oh, shit, what am I going to do?"

"Okay, I'll tell you what you're going to do. You're going to stay right where you are—are you safe?" Christ, Smith, you should have asked that sooner.

"Yeah. I'm in the park. I can just kind of hunker on a bench. Except now my photo's on the news."

"What park? Where are you?"

"Ewen Park. By Riverdale Avenue? There's a playground."

"You're actually in Riverdale?"

"Yeah."

Great work, Smith. "Stay there. I'm on the way. You have a mask?"

"Mask?"

"A COVID mask."

"Um, no."

"Sunglasses?"

"I'm wearing them."

"Good. No one followed you?"

"I don't think so. From Queens? No. I mean, I'd know by now, wouldn't I?"

Yeah, because he'd have taken a shot at you. "Okay. Stay there. Leave this goddamn phone on and answer it if I call but otherwise don't answer and don't call. Text, nothing. Anyone. Can you manage that?"

"No one has this number. I bought the phone just now, to call you. I bought a blue hoodie, too, and threw out the yellow one."

Smart kid. "What about the other two phones?"

"I still have them. They're off."

"Leave them off. Stay where you are. I'll get there as fast as I can."

I bolted out of the booth and clonked my half-full glass on the bar. "Save it or dump it, Patrice. I've got to go."

"Might have to drink it." Patrice grinned. "Stop it turning to vinegar."

I keep my car in a lot two blocks from Shorty's, pay extra so it's always up front. Under most circumstances the subway is the quickest way around New York, especially in rush hour; but those circumstances don't include trying to get from Tribeca to a corner of the northwest Bronx before a homicidal cop tracks down a fifteen-year-old kid.

I sprinted to the lot, swiping through my call list for the number I wanted. I tapped it as I hurried through the gate.

"Chris Chiang."

"It's Bill. Where are you?"

"In Chinatown at my folks', why?"

The attendant handed me my keys. Sliding behind the wheel, I said to Chris, "I'll pick you up."

# 33

Chris was waiting on Canal and Baxter. He jumped in my car and I screeched a U-turn to head west.

"You're not serious," he said as he buckled in. "You have a fucking gumball?"

Gumball is cop for the rotating red light with siren that an undercover car, outing itself, slaps on its roof to clear traffic away. As I had done before leaving the lot. They are, of course, not legal for civilian use.

"What do you think I need you for?"

"I was hoping it was my legendary two-fisted bravery. My incisive logic. Or at least my sparkling personality." Chris thumbed his phone and spoke into it. "Detective Chris Chiang, Fifth Precinct, traveling north in a civilian gray Audi, license number—" He looked at me, I gave it to him, and he repeated it to his dispatcher. "No backup requested yet. Will advise." He ended the call, pocketed his phone, and said, "You're determined to get me canned, aren't you?"

"On the contrary. You're going to be the hero who finds the mayor's kid."

"Finds him doing what?"

"I hope, sitting still and being invisible like I told him to."

"You know where he is?"

I glanced over. "I know where he said he was."

"Anyone else know?"

"You mean Tattoo Man? I don't know but I don't think so. The kid says he wasn't followed."

"Or anyone. Where's Lydia?"

"Actually, also heading to the Bronx. Same general area, Riverdale. She and Madison Guilder are going to a party at Oscar Trask's estate."

"They have estates up there?"

I swung right to head uptown. "They probably don't call them that. Just, you know, huge houses with swimming pools, rolling lawns, gardens, servants. That kind of thing."

"Sounds estatey to me. How come Lydia got invited and you didn't?"

"You really asking?"

"No," he said. "No, I guess not."

"Okay, now, Mark was the good news. You want the bad news?"

"I never do and somehow you always give it to me anyway."

I told him about Amber's phone.

"Goddamn," he sighed. "Any idea who had it?"

"None. Did you call Lenz, to tell him about Amber and Mark?"

"I had to."

"What did he say?"

"Sounded a lot like, 'shit.'"

From then on we didn't talk for a time. Chris wondered out loud if he should call Lenz to tell him about Amber's phone, but Linus and Trella had bent the law to find it. "Lenz is dumping her phone records right now," Chris pointed out to himself. "He'll go for last known location as a matter of course."

"Why didn't he do that before?" I interrupted the conversation.

Chris turned toward me. "Because she was a model minority suicide. Not the mayor's son's girlfriend."

She was Amber Shun, I reflected. The whole time.

After that I focused on weaving through the rush hour traffic. About half the other drivers pulled over to let us go by—some by only an inch or two, but hey—or delayed jumping their own lights until we were through the intersection. The other half must've been out sick for emergency-vehicle day in Driver's Ed.

Still, the gumball gave me enough of an edge that I could stick to city streets all the way through Manhattan, avoiding the inevitable jams on the highway.

Somewhere in the west nineties my phone rang. I hit the hands-free and answered.

"It's me," Bree said, sharp in the air. "What the hell is your problem?"

"The last time Amber Shun's phone was heard from, it was at City Hall."

"Amber Shun—oh, the girlfriend. What do you mean, her phone was at City Hall?"

"She died Monday night. Her phone was briefly turned on at City Hall on Tuesday. It hasn't been on since. Do you have it?"

"What are you talking about? Me? Are you insane? I didn't even know she existed until you told me."

"Your boss?"

"What? Why would she?" Pause. "What are you accusing her of? You're treading on thin ice here, Bill."

"Someone had that phone. Were either Mark or Madison down there on Tuesday?"

"No."

I sped up through a yellow light. "Someone else, a friend of either kid, someone from one of the schools?"

"If they were they didn't come to see Carole and no one checked in with me. How do you know the phone was here?"

"My techies traced it."

"Oh, for God's sake. City Hall has all kinds of high-tech blockers and jammers and things. The point is to screw techies up. They don't know what they're talking about."

I said nothing.

"Okay," she said. "Now hear this. I don't care where that girl's phone was, or is, unless it can find Mark. That's what you're being paid to do, you remember that, right? You any closer?" Short pause. "Okay, that's what I thought. I'm going into a meeting. Call when you have something useful to say." She hung up.

"You didn't tell her you *are* closer," Chris said once the air in the car had settled.

"She didn't give me much of a chance."

"You really used to date her?"

"Haven't you ever made mistakes?"

Chris grinned and shook his head.

The other thing I hadn't told Bree was that the shooter was a cop. Now that the news was out that Mark was gone, I wasn't sure what good Bree knowing that would do.

Or what harm.

Where Manhattan gave way to the Bronx I took the Broadway Bridge over the Harlem River Ship Canal. From there it was just a half dozen blocks to 231st Street, which dead-ends into Ewen Park. I sped up the street, swept onto the sidewalk, slammed to a stop. Chris, cursing, jumped out when I did. We charged up the steep hill. I didn't know about Chris's conditioning, but myself, I was running on adrenaline.

After adrenaline, of course, there's always a crash. This one came fast, when we hit the playground and saw it was empty.

"Goddammit," I said, gasping, hands on knees. Chris was breathing heavily but not panting. That answered the conditioning question. I fumbled out my phone, called back the number Mark had called from. Voicemail. "Mark!" I coughed. "It's Bill. Where the hell are you?"

No pick up, no call back. Chris went off to circle the playground's fence to see if Mark had secreted himself behind a dumpster or shrubbery. As breath returned I automatically reached for a cigarette, then decided that was the stupidest idea I'd had in a long time. I was slipping the pack back into my jacket when Chris came trotting over.

"Nothing," he said. "Now what?"

I shook my head.

"Sure it was him?" he asked.

"Completely."

"Well, you think he was playing you? Sending you up here when he's somewhere else?"

"Why? It's not like I was hot on his trail and he needed to throw me off. I had no idea where he was and he must have known that. Why call at all? Also," I thought back to the brief conversation I'd had with Mark, while I was staring at carved names on the tabletop, "he sounded miserable. He sounded scared."

I looked around. Enough oxygen must have reached my brain finally that I could have a thought. I took out my phone again. "I told him to leave that phone on in case I called. Maybe he did, even if he's not answering it." What I was thinking was, if he had left the phone on, maybe it could be traced. I called Linus.

"Yo, dude." I heard the familiar speaker echo. "You reading my mind?"

That stopped me. "What?"

"I was about to call you. Your phone's on."

"Of course it—" It took me a second. Not *my* phone. "Wait. Amber's?"

"That's the City Hall one? Then no, the other one. Mark's, right? Just turned on. The iPhone, his real one. Not texting or calling or anything, but on."

"Where?"

"In the Bronx."

"He was supposed to meet me in Ewen Park by 231st Street but I don't see him. Can you tell if he's here?"

Click click click. "No. I mean, yes, I can, and he's not. At least, the phone's not. It's about a mile north. And kind of west."

Oh, shit, I thought, and said so. "Shit. Look up Oscar Trask's address. Is the phone near there?"

More clicks. "Kind of like Staten Island, that part of the Bronx. Not so many towers by that address. But yeah, near there. Can't pinpoint any closer for you. Sorry."

"I'm afraid that's good enough. Thanks, Linus." I hung up without waiting to hear from Woof.

# 34

C ome on," I said to Chris, and took off, charging back through Ewen Park to my car. This slalom was all downhill so I was still breathing when we got there.

"In case you're interested, I'm way over running around after you," Chris said as we buckled up and I started the car.

"I'm way over running around," I said. "That was Linus."

"Yeah, so?"

"Mark's phone is on." I was breathing, yes, but apparently not yet up to long sentences.

"Linus found it?"

"Close enough. It's somewhere near Trask's place." Hah. Short sentences but two in a row.

"Is that where Mark's going, you think? Why?"

I realized Chris didn't know the theory Lydia and I were working from, the one Max Bauer had all but confirmed: Trask, Amber, Lauren Spence; the music camp and the young girls with more ambition than talent.

Before I could tell him, we came to a stoplight. "Hold on." I thumbed my phone, called the phone Mark had called me from. "Don't do it," I said to the voicemail robot. "Mark, wait for me. I know you're going to Trask's and I know why. I'll meet you there."

"Don't do what?" Chris said when I put the phone down. "Jesus, you think the kid's armed?"

"I don't, but just in case. Even if he's not, I'm sure Trask's got a professional-grade kitchen with some outstanding knives." My breath returning to normal, I filled Chris in as we drove up the hill, across the highway, and under the canopy of new green leaves on old trees into one of New York's most wealthy, least known neighborhoods.

Riverdale as a whole is like a lot of areas in the eighty percent of the city the Times-Square-centric call the "Outer Boroughs." Apartment buildings, shopping streets, schools, parks, elevated subway lines, and houses ranging from rows of attached stud-framed two-families to rambling old homes with front and backyards. Each borough has its highest-income area, though, and the part of Riverdale we were snaking through now was the Bronx's. It had no real name, was always just referred to by locals as "down by the river."

*Where does Oscar Trask live?*

*Down by the river.*

*Ah.*

Here you found the oldest estates, the grandest houses, the biggest trees. Three-car garages that held luxury autos, and lawns that sloped to the Hudson. Views from flagstone terraces across to the Palisades, where tonight's sunset, coming soon through broken clouds, was likely to be spectacular.

Some of these places were home to old WASP money and some to more recent wealth. Trask's fortune was new, his mansion an old and showy mock-Tudor on a broad stone base. We could see it from the street, just barely, standing regally behind its wrought-iron fence. I drove past it, slowed for a look.

From where we left the car you couldn't see the house at all. It's not that I was trying to be discreet. Just that both sides of the street were parked up with the cars of The Invited. I snuck the Audi in among them, snuggled it up to the topiary boxwood lollipops of a neighboring estate. I doubted the neighbor would object; he was probably at Trask's soiree.

If this area had had blocks, we'd have been about two away, but the old-world leafy splendor didn't allow for that. No sidewalks, either, so we fast-walked along the badly paved road. Potholes, a privilege of the elite. Keeps the proletariat from speeding through the neighborhood. I called Mark's new burner again as we went. "It's Bill. I'm here. Back off. Wait." Then I called his iPhone. Same no pick up. Same message.

Would he check either phone? If he did, would he do what I said? If he didn't, what the hell *was* he going to do?

Which was the question he'd asked me when we'd talked. *What am I going to do?*

"I could call for backup," Chris said. "Although . . ."

"Although is right. We don't know what the kid's up to. There's a crowd of civilians in there. Plus Lydia's there, and Madison Guilder's bodyguard. And now that I mention it, who knows how many other armed bodyguards for how many other VIPs? The best thing we can do is find Mark before he makes a move. Not call in another whole thundering herd of guys with guns."

"Okay, but just to remind you, that thundering herd? We're the good guys."

We stopped at the iron gates, swung wide on their granite gateposts. At the far end of the long gravel driveway, men in suits and women in cocktail dresses strolled along the terrace with champagne glasses in hand. Music floated toward us, Beethoven, an early string quartet, nothing too taxing for the ears of the elect. The performers were high school students, I'd bet. Prodigies.

"Looks like a nice party," I said. "Let's drop in."

"Wait." Chris tapped his knuckles on the bronze sign affixed to one of the gateposts. "'Greenwood'?"

"Yeah. This place, the camp, his firm. Not sure which chicken or egg came first."

"His firm? This asshole is Greenwood Holdings?"

"That's where all this comes from." I spread my arms. "Wealth beyond imagining."

"Yeah, mine. Greenwood Holdings is where Straley locked up the DEA pension fund."

# 35

I stopped too, stared at Chris. "Straley invested the DEA money with Trask?"

Chris nodded. "Worked great for a while. Now the market's slipping but Straley says don't worry, kids, I have everything under control. No one would care except by everything he means our pensions. Most of the Board wants to move the money somewhere safer but Straley and his boys still claim Greenwood will make us rich. Bulldog Straley, never wrong no matter how wrong he is. I'll tell you this for free, if he doesn't get us a big giant contract he's toast." He shook his head. "Stubborn bastard."

Stubborn?

Or something else, something a lot worse?

Because there it was, my connection. Between Trask and the NYPD.

Straley's money—okay, not his, money he controlled, but chances were it smelled the same—was in Trask's hands. Straley had left it there even when the market started to fall. His refusal to move it was creating a threat to his prestige, his power, and his position as DEA president.

That he was digging in so deep might be accounted for by a bigger threat, the one to his ego that would come with admitting he'd been wrong.

Or by another: the threat to his standing as a free man, if what he'd gotten in return came to light.

"Chris?" I spoke slowly. "Tattoo Man may not be the only dirty cop in this case."

He took a moment. "You're saying Straley?"

I nodded. "And he may be here. If you want out—"

"Dirty how?"

"Underage girls. Supplied by Trask."

"Under—" Chris glanced to the house and back to me. "Honey traps?"

"Not quite. That would imply Straley didn't know how young they were. I'm thinking more of a quid pro quo."

Chris took a deep breath, met my eyes. "Explain it."

I could see what Chris wanted: to know if my suspicions were worth risking his career on.

"Trask has access to beautiful, talented, ambitious young girls."

"Amber Shun."

"And others. Lauren Spence. He promises them the moon. All they have to do in return is be nice to him."

"You told me this. I believe it."

I nodded. "Or, meet a friend of his, maybe two, and be nice to *them*. Straley's a friend of his. Straley has access to a lot of money. He invests it with Trask and all *he* has to do is leave it there. No matter how much sense it would make to move it, no matter how much pressure he's under."

Chris looked at the house again.

"I don't think it's only Straley," I said. "I mean, not only dirty cops. Trask's investors have a reputation for inexplicable loyalty."

Chris swore under his breath.

"But something goes wrong," I said. "Amber Shun kills herself. Mark McCann runs away. And a tattooed cop starts hunting for Mark."

Chris swore again, more loudly. "Mark knows. That's why he ran and that's why he's here."

"I don't know how much he knows but yes, I think that's why he's here."

"All right," Chris said. "We going in or not?"

"You don't have to do this. I could be way off base. If you don't—"

"If *you* don't stop talking we won't be in time."

"For what?" I said as for once I was the one following him as he trotted through the gate.

"For whatever the hell trouble you're about to get me into."

# 36

Ordinarily thoughts like the ones I was thinking wouldn't even be spoken aloud until a massive investigation had been done. Times and dates. Interviews and witness statements. Correlations, corroborations, confirmations. These speculations were such stuff as lawsuits were made on. As Max Bauer had reminded me, *Oscar Trask, you know he sues people.*

And as I'd told Chris, I might be entirely wrong.

But right or wrong, if I'd put the pieces together like this, Mark could have, too. And if I were Mark and thought someone had driven my girlfriend to suicide, and I'd made my way to the someone's home, I'd have come prepared to kill him.

The music, though still soft, grew in volume as we approached the house. Beethoven had given way to Mendelssohn, not exactly Easy Listening—that would be beneath Trask—but like chocolate that's more sweet than dark. We made it as far as the terrace, ignoring a few curious looks directed at our get-ups—me in chinos and Nikes, Chris in jeans and black cop shoes, both of us in leather jackets—but at the door a young woman in a short black dress and high red heels declined to pass judgment. She just smiled and asked for our names, readying her finger over her iPad.

"We're not on the list," I said. "Tell Oscar it's Bill Smith. He invited me for a drink."

The young woman looked concerned, probably wondering if letting us in or keeping us out was more likely to get her in trouble. She turned away and whispered into a Bluetooth headset. Beside her a flush-faced giant with a straw-colored fade glared at us, clearly hoping the order would come back to chuck us in the Hudson.

Chris muttered, "Screw it, I'm going to badge us in," and reached into his jacket. The giant stiffened. Before Chris got his ID out the young woman turned back, smiling uncertainly.

"I'm afraid we can't locate Mr. Trask at the moment. If you'll just wait here—"

"Detective Chris Chiang, NYPD," Chris said, flashing the badge. "Not a good idea, waiting. Where's he supposed to be?"

"Um. He's, like, the host. He's supposed to be, like, everywhere." Her cool, along with her elocution lessons, went flying out the window.

"Well then." Chris strode across the threshold, me right behind. The giant advanced but Chris, with a scowl and without stopping, stuck his gold shield an inch from the guy's pink nose.

"Hey," I said to Chris as the guy backed off and we strode in, "Good work. Very cop-like."

We entered the wide double-height entrance hall, where two huge Hudson River School paintings dominated the wainscoted walls and a heavy staircase ran up from the back. On the first broad landing, in front of the stained-glass window, the string quartet was stationed, performing in the flickering light from multiple standing candlesticks. As I'd suspected, the musicians were teenagers: a boy on cello, girls on viola and violins. All of them, unsurprisingly, attractive.

Chris surveyed the scene. "Split up," he said. Full cop now. He pointed me to the right, toward the dining room and kitchen wing. "This floor first, then go up. I'll take there." He nodded left, the living room. "If Lydia—" He stopped, because Lydia.

A knot of partygoers in front of us had swerved as one, like a school of fish, to head into the rooms on the left, revealing what they'd concealed: not just Lydia, but Ahlgren and Madison Guilder.

"What the fuck?" Madison said, folding her bare arms. She wore gold, strappy sandals and what looked like an item of royal blue lingerie. "Who let you in? Who's he?" She scowled at Chris. With her eyes still on him she spoke to Lydia. "Did you invite your clown partner? And who's his clown partner?"

Lydia wore a red dress with cap sleeves, a tight-fitting top, and a wide skirt. Over her shoulder she carried a small red purse on a long gold chain. No doubt it held her phone, her keys, and her .22. "I didn't invite anyone," she said, looking a question at me. "That's Chris Chiang. Chris, Madison Guilder. And Detective Ken Ahlgren, NYPD."

His name really was Ken?

Lydia, I knew, had done the intro that way to give Chris the lay of the land without blowing his cover, since she didn't know what we were up to. But Chris played it straight. He showed his gold shield. Ahlgren shaped up, opened his jacket to show his, on his shirt pocket. He nodded at Chris, but stayed beside Madison.

From the corner of my eye I saw the front-door giant watching us. He seemed to relax, probably figuring he'd handed us off to Ahlgren and so his work was done.

"Your brother's here," Chris said to Madison. "He's looking for Trask."

"What the actual fuck are you talking about?" Madison snapped.

"Where would he be? Trask?" Chris hardened his voice.

"You checked the rooms?" Ahlgren said. I remembered how alien it had been when I'd seen Bree go into professional mode. Now Lifeguard Boy was doing it, too.

"We were about to," Chris said. "Though the staff did, just now, and they couldn't find him."

"Is Herb Straley here?" I said.

Ahlgren looked at me curiously, but answered. "Yes. You're thinking backup?"

"No," I said. "Trouble."

"Hey, big shot. I asked you a question." Madison had a pout on her face and a whine in her voice. Not being part of the conversation for ninety seconds was driving her to a meltdown.

"If we don't find Trask before Mark does, Mark may kill him," I said. "Clear enough for you?"

"You're fucking high. Or you're just crazy," Madison said, but she looked at Lydia.

"No," Lydia said. "It's true." Not that she had any more idea than Madison did what I was talking about, but as always, she had my back. "If you know where he could be—"

Madison paled. She glanced from Lydia to me, then to Ahlgren, maybe for reassurance. Ahlgren nodded.

"He has a den," Madison said. She spun on her pointed toe and glared impatiently over her shoulder, to tell us to stop dawdling and follow her.

# 37

The entire west wall of the cathedral-ceilinged living room was glass. Very un-Tudor, but a hell of a view of the lawn, the woods sloping away, and the Hudson beyond. The setting sun striped the sky purple and orange and cast a warm light on the well-dressed guests with their cocktails and canapés. Murmurs, clinks, and laughter spun up to the ceiling and bounced down again, almost drowning out the music of the string quartet.

Madison seemed to know exactly where she was going. She cut through the crowd like an icebreaker, the rest of us bobbing along on the waves she made.

"What's going on?" Lydia whispered to me as we went.

"Just what I said. Mark may be here, he may be armed, and he may be planning to kill Trask."

"May be?"

"Mark's phone is on. Linus pinpointed it to pretty much here."

We stopped and we shut up as a sharp right brought Madison to a wall of books. *Don't tell me*, I thought, but yes, she pressed on a leather-bound volume—Proust—and with a click the section of bookcase in front of us swung a few inches ajar. She put a practiced hand on the edge of it and pulled it just wide enough to slip through.

I wondered if the staff had checked this room. I wondered if they even knew about this room.

Lydia slid in after Madison. So much for the small craft. Chris hauled the bookcase open wider so the barges could follow. Once he, Ahlgren, and I were through and no one was holding it open, the door noiselessly closed behind us.

Madison had called this a den, a concept closely related to man-cave. What I glimpsed from the half-opened bookcase, even before I got into the room, told me the place actually had a different emphasis. The bed, the bar, the carpet, the giant TV screen, and the walls' silky quilted soundproofing implied more intimate, less solitary pastimes.

Once inside it was clear that even if the staff did know about this room, they hadn't checked it. Oscar Trask was indeed here, sitting on a brandy-colored leather recliner. He had a glass of champagne by his side and looked calm and relaxed, which was impressive since Mark McCann sat perched on a stool at the bar with a gun in his hand.

# 38

Ahlgren yanked Madison behind him. It was automatic; the guy was a trained bodyguard. Though I'd have bet that when he got this gig having to actually use his training was the last thing on his mind.

Chris, Lydia, and I all stopped. "Okay, Mark," Chris said quietly. He showed his badge. "Put down the gun."

"Mark?" Madison said, peering around Ahlgren. "What the fuck?"

Chris took a slow step toward Mark. That cleared my line of sight. Motionless, off to the right, sat Trask's good buddy, Mark and Madison's dad, Jeffrey Guilder. And not alone. On a sofa with his arm around a halo-haired Black girl who, wide-eyed, pressed into him. Olivia, Astrid's friend. She didn't really know Mark, she'd said. But she knew Madison.

Guilder jumped up, leaving Olivia on the cushions. "Okay, Mark, that's it. Dammit—"

Mark swung the gun to him.

"You!" said Chris. "Sit down!"

"I'm his father!"

*And you were shivering in your boots until people showed up you had to swing your dick for,* I thought; but I let Chris handle it.

Chris handled it. "Sit the fuck down before your *son* shoots someone!"

Chris had a mighty glare. It lowered Guilder back onto the sofa like a tractor beam.

Madison spoke, a tentative, "Daddy? What are you doing here?"

"Having a drink, honey," Guilder said. He slid away from Olivia. "Just having a drink."

Madison's eyes went to Olivia, who was biting her trembling lip. "Livvy?" It was a question, but Olivia looked away and Madison didn't continue. What was there to ask?

Mark had been frozen, watching us all pour into the room. Now he jumped down off the stool. He held the gun two-handed and straight out. "For fuck's sake, Maddie!" he said. "What do you think he's doing here? Goddammit, where did you guys come from? Why? *Why?*"

"To keep you from doing something you'll regret," Chris said. I wondered if that was a line they taught them at the academy.

"You should have stayed out! You should have left us alone!"

Mark swept the gun around. I looked at it, engulfed in his hands. Small, blue-black, automatic. Hard to tell the make or model. Where had an Upper East Side kid like Mark gotten a gun? Who'd be dumb enough to sell a weapon to the mayor's son? And where had he learned to hold it, to steady it, to shoot?

Our eyes met for a long moment, Mark's and mine. He broke the link and swung the gun to Trask.

"Mark," I said. "This is a risky game."

"It's not a game." Mark's voice rasped. "He was going to tell me about it. He still is."

"Mark—" Guilder couldn't resist.

"Shut up!" Chris barked at Guilder. "Did I forget that part?"

"He was going to tell you about what?" I asked Mark.

"What he's been doing. He needs to tell me."

"I don't really," Trask drawled. "What I need is for someone to take the gun from this child before he hurts himself."

"No!" said Mark. "Don't try it." Holding the gun on Trask, he said, "All of you, I know you're armed. Except my sister, because in that dress? Take your guns out and put them on the floor. One by one. Mr. Smith, you go first."

"If I don't?"

"You think I won't shoot him? Like he deserves?"

I nodded and did as Mark said. Lydia had moved slowly away from me, toward Guilder's sofa, spreading the floor as she had at the Sundaris'. She threw me a raised eyebrow. I gave a tiny headshake. She took the .22 out of her purse and put it on the Mondrian-esque carpet. That brought Lydia an interested look from Trask, and that brought me a flash of what Mark must be feeling. Next was Chris's service .38, and finally Ahlgren's, though getting him to surrender it took a nod from Chris and a jiggle of Mark's gun.

"Careful there," said Chris. "You don't want to shoot anyone by accident."

"No, I want to shoot him on purpose," Mark said. "But I want him to tell the story first."

"I don't tell bedtime stories," Trask said.

"I think you do nothing but," I said. "Tell stories to get girls into bed."

Trask looked at me with raised eyebrows. "How do *you* do it?"

Madison gave a high-pitched giggle. *Come on, Madison*, I thought, *don't lose it.*

Trask sighed. "Honestly, people, this is out of hand. The boy's on some sort of drug. He's delusional and he needs help. Now," he turned to Mark, "it was one thing when it was just the three of us"—he waved his hand idly at Guilder and Olivia—"and you thought you could shoot me and get away with it. You probably wouldn't have shot me and you certainly couldn't have gotten away with it, but I saw you thinking it. But now there are guns all over the floor and seven witnesses. You take a shot and four people will grab their guns and be all over *you*. Madison, I trust"—he smiled at her—"would have the sense to hang back. So I'm going to get up and walk out of here. Let's go, Madison. We'll get a drink and let these people clean up this mess."

"No!" Mark shouted as Trask started to rise. "Not with her. Not with my sister, anymore."

I caught Guilder's frown. He looked from Madison to Trask.

Mark's voice and his hands on the gun were shaking.

"I don't tell stories and I don't take orders from children. Or really, from anyone." Trask, standing, held his hand out to Madison. She reached to take it but Ahlgren pulled her back.

"No!" Mark said again, sounding more desperate. "You think he loves you, Maddie, but he doesn't. He doesn't even like you. He's using you. He's poison. You'll die."

"Oh my God, Mark," said Madison, in bored tones such as only a fifteen-year-old girl could offer. "Could you overact a little more, please? I'm not sure everyone's getting it."

That kind of talk was dangerous. Mark's eyes skipped from Madison to me. *Come on, Smith,* I thought, *help the kid out.*

"You think Mark's being melodramatic," I said, "but one girl's dead and one is lucky to be alive. Friends of yours, Madison. Lauren Spence and Amber Shun."

"Yeah, sad, but what's your point?" Madison shrugged. "That has nothing to do with Oscar. And by the way, they're not my friends."

"Not close friends, no. I imagine not a lot of people are close to you. Not the way people get close to Mark. The way Jacob Dolo is close to Mark."

"Jacob? Why are we talking about Jacob?"

"Because someone shot him this morning. Mark was with him. They were trying to shoot Mark."

Madison cocked her head, frowning. "Someone shot him? They were trying to shoot Mark? Excuse me, but what the fuck are you talking about?" She looked not at me, though, but at Trask. Trask shook his head, raised his hands in a gesture of both innocence and impatience.

Guilder's frown deepened. He opened his mouth but I jumped in. Guilder was not a guy we needed to hear from right now.

"Jacob will be okay," I said. "But Amber Shun was close to Mark, too."

"Being close to a delusional boy is obviously dangerous," Trask said drily.

I ignored him. "You hated that, Madison. That Mark had that. So you stole Amber away, to give her to Trask."

Trask laughed. "My God, you're suffering from delusions, too. I think I'd better call my security people. And my therapist."

"No!" That was Mark again. "Everyone just stay where they are!"

"It's okay, Mark," I said. "I'm sorry we busted in and screwed up your plan, but we don't need the recording. There's enough evidence. We can do this a different way."

"Recording?" Trask threw a sharp look at Mark.

"That was the plan. Mark wasn't really intending to shoot you. He was going to scare you into confessing that you forced the girls into sex. Lauren and Amber."

"Other girls, too!" said Mark.

"He's recording all this. That's why your phone's on, am I right, Mark?"

After a second Mark gave me a nod. He didn't lower the gun, though.

"Forcing—Oscar doesn't force anybody! He doesn't have to! Are you crazy?" Madison aimed that at me but again kept her eyes on Trask.

"You don't *feel* like he forced you, Maddie," Mark said quietly. "He's a snake. He probably told you you were beautiful. He told Amber she was beautiful."

"My God, she was!" said Trask. "And so's Madison. Does that constitute force these woke days, telling a woman she's beautiful?"

*And Olivia*, I thought. *She's beautiful, too.*

"You said you had important friends who wanted to meet Amber, because she sang like an angel." Mark's voice was bitter. He glanced at his sister. "It's the same thing, Maddie. I bet I know what he told you. He made you feel like Dad would be proud. Didn't he? Proud of you for being irresistible to Oscar Trask. So special."

"You have a filthy mind," Trask said.

"But he isn't," Mark said. "Are you, Dad? Proud of her for sleeping with Trask?"

"Sleeping—" Guilder couldn't contain himself. "Jesus Christ, Mark. You do have a filthy mind. You do need help." He looked at Madison.

She was staring at the carpet.

"Madison? Look at me."

Slowly, Madison lifted her head, met her father's gaze. Her eyes were moist.

Guilder stared. He snapped his head to Trask. "Oscar? What the fuck?"

"Dad, just shut *up*!" Mark's voice was ragged. "Look at you, cuddling on the sofa with Olivia. Such hypocritical bullshit." With a nasty grin, he said, "Anyone might think you were a lawyer." He moved the gun to Guilder.

Red-faced, Guilder sneered. "Oh, for God's sake, Mark. You're not going to shoot me."

"You don't think so? Why not? Because of what a great dad you are? I wouldn't miss you and Maddie would be able to stop fucking your friends to impress you."

"Guilder." I spoke calmly, but let my eyes meet Mark's. "This isn't a courtroom. It's a hostage situation. He wants you to shut up. Maybe you should do it."

"He's insane!"

"Yeah," Mark said. "Yeah, I am. So you shut up." He grinned again and waggled the gun. "And you," back to Trask, "you'd better go ahead and tell the story."

I waited for more bluster from Guilder but his jaw tightened and he said nothing.

"There's no story." Trask managed to sound wearied, put-upon. I was impressed. "None of this is true. There's nothing to tell."

"Yes, there is." Madison's voice was soft and toneless. "That is what you said. How proud Daddy would be. You said it about looking for Mark, too. That Daddy would be proud if we found him ourselves." She turned to me. "I told him you were going to Times Square. He sent someone to follow you. Is it my fault Jacob got shot?"

"No," I said, though I wasn't sure it wasn't. "We lost that guy. But that tells me where he came from, so thanks for that."

"This is all bullshit!" Finally, some emotion from Trask. "Madison, what are you doing, trying to prove you're as crazy as your brother? I don't know what you're talking about, I never sent anyone anywhere, and for the record," looking at Mark, "since you're recording, I never slept with the Shun girl. What happened to her had nothing to do with me. She was headed for a great career but she couldn't handle the pressure. Her death was a tragedy."

"Her death was a tragedy but there would've been no career," I said, partly to turn the room back to me, to dial down the current a notch. "Just the lies you told her. The bedtime story. Although I believe you that you didn't sleep with her. She was one of the ones you saved for your friends."

"Friends?" Mark spat the word out.

"It's okay, Mark," I said. "We can take it from here. He's not going to confess and you're not going to shoot him. But there's enough evidence for an investigation. It'll be slow but he can't hide."

"How do you know I'm not going to shoot him?" Mark demanded, extending the pistol straight out at Trask. He closed one eye, homing on his target.

"Because," I said, "that's not a gun."

# 39

Lydia was the first to catch on. She bent, scooped up her .22, snapped it back in her purse.

"What?" Trask said. "*What*?"

"Three-D printing," I said. "Amazing what it can do. Replica pistols, piece of cake. Jacob Dolo's really good at it. He made that for you, right, Mark? That's why you went to Staten Island. To pick it up."

"You son of a bitch! You punk!" Trask was shouting. His red-faced fury told me how scared he'd really been. "I'll kill you!"

"I'll kill *you* first!" Guilder shouted. "You and my daughter? You bastard!" He lunged from the sofa. Ahlgren body-checked him.

"No one's killing anyone," Chris said. He stooped for his gun, slipped it in his shoulder rig. Stepping toward Mark, he said, "Come on, we'll put all the toys away and see where we are."

Ahlgren retrieved his gun, too. The temperature in the room started to fall. Trask and Guilder were both quivering with anger but neither moved.

Mark looked at the pistol in his hand. "Sad but true." His voice was relaxed, no longer shaking. He grinned at me. "I knew you knew."

"And I, et cetera. You were pretty good, by the way. The unhinged kid. New role for you?"

"No time to rehearse. Total improv. It was okay?" He lifted the gun, drew a bead on Trask again. Trask snarled.

And that was almost it.

Everyone breathed.

But the bookcase door flew open. Bulldog Straley burst in. Behind him, Bozinski, his Doberman, service revolver in hand. Seeing Mark holding the gun on Trask, Bozinski swept his to Mark.

I barely had time to see, as Bozinski's wrist slid out from his cuff, the Justice League of America circling it.

Shouts of "NO!"

One shout was mine.

Then a flash of blue silk.

The bang-whine of a shot.

A loud "Shit!" from Mark.

Not because he was hurt. Because he was staring at Madison, crumpled on the floor, blood soaking her dress.

Madison, obnoxious, provocative, disdainful, and cold, had taken a bullet for her brother.

# 40

M adison!" shouted Guilder. But he didn't move.

I launched myself across the room, tackled Bozinski as his
second shot went off. Did he believe Mark's gun was real? Maybe. That
he had to be stopped from using it? I'd have put money that that was a
no. But it made a hell of a good excuse to finally kill someone you'd been
after. *"Hey, I'm really, really sorry I shot the kid, but he was waving a gun
around and no way it looked like a toy. I mean, everyone saw it. Am I right?
Amazing what they can do today, huh?"*

I crashed Bozinski right into Straley, and we all rocked back onto
the bar. The tinkle of glass mixed with the aroma of aged whiskey. *Now
there's a waste*, came the thought as I stretched for Bozinski's gun hand.
From the corner of my eye I saw Ahlgren kneel by Madison, whip off his
jacket, press it to her side. She tried to sit up. He gently pushed her down.

I bent Bozinski's arm back, squeezed the pressure point in his
elbow. He yelped, twisted, and with his other elbow slammed me in
the neck. Straley, pinned between Bozinski and the bar, flailed around.
His granite fist found the side of my head. Probably by accident, but
what did that matter? Breath came hard, vision went wild, and my grip

264

on Bozinski's gun hand loosened. I made another weak lunge for the gun and missed it by a mile.

"Mark!" I managed to bray. *Duck, kid.* I waited for the next shot.

"Don't shoot!" Straley shouted.

No next shot.

Bozinski let out a yowl and bent forward.

I looked up from my attempts to breathe and saw why.

Lydia, in Bozinski's pause after Straley's order, had spun-kicked her spike heel into his ribs.

Straley shoved the crumpled Bozinski into me. Instead of pushing I pulled, yanking Bozinski's arm to keep the momentum going. Bozinski staggered. He stayed on his feet but he dropped the gun.

With a sharp blow to the side of the neck, Lydia dropped him. She kicked off her heels to make her fighting life easier.

Another shot exploded. Not Bozinski this time. Wheezing like a hole-punched accordion, I looked up to see Trask cowering on the far side of the bed and Chris with his hand on Straley's arm. "It won't help to shoot him," Chris shouted in the Bulldog's face. "It's all on tape. About you and Amber Shun."

Mark had apparently heeded my telepathic advice and lunged behind a chair. But he was an actor and knew a cue when he heard one. His hand with his phone rose into view, waving back and forth. What Chris had said was bullpucky, of course. Nothing on Mark's recording implicated Straley. But it was excellent bullpucky and deserved reinforcing. I said to Straley, "Think hard. If Trask lives you can fight him in court, say he's lying, whatever. If you shoot him, what's on the tape is a dying declaration. As good as sworn testimony." That was even less true than what Chris had said. A dying declaration, to be useful in court, has to be made when someone knows he's dying. Anything on that tape—if there had been anything—would be hearsay whether Trask lived or died.

But Straley didn't strike me as the kind of cop who'd spent a lot of time reading the law.

"Mark!" Chris yelled. "Throw your gun out here."

Mark did.

"Okay," said Chris. "The civilians are unarmed. Anyone gets shot now, it's a bad shooting. You need that, Bulldog? I mean, you already stopped Bozinski from shooting Mark. Obviously you know how bad this could be."

Straley hesitated. "Fuck you. All of you." He lowered and holstered his gun. I could see how badly Chris wanted to take it off him, but he didn't have the authority. "I wasn't shooting at that asshole," Straley said, directing his jowls toward Trask. "The kid had a gun. My gun went off because Smith pushed me. I don't know what kind of shit he's been saying," nodding at Trask again, "but if he told you I had anything to do with that dead Chinese girl he's talking out of his ass. Everyone knows he's a friend of the mayor's. He's trying to—"

"No one knows that because it's not true," I said. "And how do you know she's dead?"

He stared. "Fuck you, Smitty. We all get the suspicious death reports."

"You're in admin at One Police Plaza. All that important union stuff. You telling me you read all the reports, all precincts, every morning? Besides, the detective who caught this one didn't think there was anything suspicious about it. He called it a suicide. So there wouldn't have been a report."

Straley stopped. With a glare that could've burned through rock, he clamped his huge jaw shut.

"But," Mark said, standing up, grinning, "he didn't say not to shoot. That was me."

I turned to him, so I was looking at his mouth when Straley's voice yelled out of it, "Don't shoot!"

Straley turned purple.

Guilder jumped up. He seemed confused about why, though. Be the concerned father and rush to his bleeding daughter? The protector, and punch out the guy who shot her? Or go for the throat of his buddy, who'd taken her to bed? Which would play better in accounts of what went on here?

He may have made his choice, but he didn't get to follow through. Mark, in Guilder's own voice, said, "Sit the fuck down!" Guilder froze. Then, quoting Chris, and in Chris's voice, Mark said, "Before your *son* shoots someone."

Guilder snarled, "You stupid little punk—"

Chris grabbed Guilder, pushed him down on the sofa. Olivia jumped up off it.

Mark turned to me and winked.

"Hey," said Ahlgren, still beside Madison, "would someone go out there and show EMS where we are?"

"They're on the way?" said Chris.

"Ow," whined Madison. "That hurts."

Ahlgren, pressing his jacket to Madison's side, grinned. "Sorry, Princess. But it's okay, you're a hero."

She tried to push Ahlgren away.

"No, no, no. Now stay still." Ahlgren looked up at Chris. "Yeah, on the way. Can someone go?"

It seemed Lifeguard Boy, while we were all socking each other, had called it in.

# 41

Lydia glanced around her. Chris, radiating authority, nodded. He was junior to two of the other three cops in the room, equal in rank to the third, but there was no doubting who was in charge.

When Lydia slipped out the bookcase door, cocktail party sounds spilled in. They stopped when she pulled the door shut behind her. I wondered what the guests, blithely unaware of what had just gone on in here, were making of a disheveled barefoot woman emerging from the bookcase wall. Well, just wait until she opened the front door and guided the cavalry in.

Bozinski moaned and stirred. Sharply, Chris said, "Don't get up." Bozinski blinked, peered blankly at the ceiling. Chris's command was probably superfluous.

Chris seemed calm but I was sure he was boiling. Bozinski had tried to kill Mark and Straley had tried to kill Trask but there was no way to prove either and they both outranked him and no one was going to be arrested tonight.

Why? I suddenly wondered.

Not why no arrests. They would come, though later.

Guilder would deny any involvement with Olivia, which might be true; this might have been their first evening together. He'd jettison Trask as a client, of course. Trask would for sure be charged with the statutory rape of Guilder's daughter. How much had Guilder really been unaware of, how much had he turned a blind eye on? Whatever the truth of that, he was going to have to act the betrayed and angry friend, the fierce and protective dad. Launch immediately into what the mayor had called his high dudgeon mode.

Eighty-sixed by Guilder, Trask would get a new lawyer who, seeing the writing on the wall, would advise Trask to sing. If I were Trask my song would be about coercion, how powerful guys like Straley strong-armed me into a life of badness. Chances of that being true were, in my estimation, zilch, but shit would fly in every direction and Straley would get jammed up, along with God knows how many more of Trask's investors, friends, and, hell, party guests.

Straley could see that coming. That's why, just now, he'd tried to kill Trask.

But why had Bozinski been after Mark?

I looked for Mark and found him kneeling beside his sister, holding her hand.

"I better not have a scar," she said to him, in a voice weak but steady.

"Come on, you know you want one," Mark said. "A bullet wound? Are you kidding me?"

"Jerko."

"Jerkella."

The bookcase door swung wide and Lydia strode through at the head of a uniformed, transceiver-crackling, apparatus-hefting parade. No cocktail party noises poured in this time. They'd been replaced by the sounds of excited people jostling for position, holding up cell phones, each eager to be the first to know, and report on, what calamity had taken place.

Ahlgren, without prompting, stood from Madison's side. He beckoned to one of the three armor-vested cops who'd just arrived and they went to the door, taking on crowd control.

Two EMTs dealt with Madison and another set knelt next to Bozinski. The remaining two uniforms looked confused about what to do and I couldn't blame them. Chris spoke to them, casting the occasional glance at Straley, who muttered "fucking lies" and something about shitheads, but otherwise just stood scowling.

Lydia walked over to where Olivia was huddled against the wall, crying. Lydia sat beside her and pulled her close.

Trask clambered to his feet, only to sway and drop down again, not back on the floor but on the edge of the bed. He took a minute. Then he emptied his champagne glass, drew a long breath, and stood. He headed for the door.

Chris stopped him.

"There's been a shooting," Chris said. "You're a witness. We need you to give a statement. Talk to that officer."

"Don't be ridiculous. I don't give a shit what you need. I have guests. *They* need to be reassured there's no—"

"Talk to that officer." Chris turned his back.

The officer said, "If you'll step this way, sir."

I wondered idly how they teach cops to make "sir" sound like "asshole."

Trask sputtered. He looked around, got no traction. Visibly fuming, he stepped that way.

Unseen by Trask, Chris grinned.

An EMT gently shooed Mark away to insert a needle in Madison's arm. Mark stood, turned, and saw Bozinski, lying on the floor, with EMTs buzzing around him. Mark stared, and Bozinski stared daggers back. I headed toward them, prepared to step in if Mark moved on Bozinski; after all, the guy had tried to kill him, and had terrorized two of his friends and shot another.

But Mark made no such move. He turned slowly and found his father. Their eyes locked. When the connection between them broke, it wasn't Mark's doing. Mark, who never looked at anyone, held his father's gaze until Guilder turned away.

Then Mark deflated. Feeling behind him for the edge of the bed, he dropped onto it and shuddered once like a car when the ignition's turned off.

Post-show blues. If you considered that the curtain had gone up when he'd left home Tuesday night, this had been a very long show.

I sat next to him. He didn't look at me.

"Mark?" No answer. "Why did you leave home?"

He glanced blankly up, then back to the floor. "What?"

"Tuesday night. Why did you leave?"

He shrugged. I got the feeling he wished I'd go away but I just waited. Finally, he said, "Like I told you. To think."

"About?"

He took a deep breath. "I knew about Amber and Trask. I didn't know she was . . ." He trailed off, lifting his eyes to Straley. With a sudden flush of color in his face, he yelled, "Bastard."

"Okay, Mark." I grabbed onto his arm. Straley was glaring, hard-jawed, our way. No question he'd come charging over, fists swinging, at Mark's next outburst. It would be a pleasure to see rank-and-file cops grab and restrain him, but I had more important things on my mind.

"If you knew about Amber and Trask," I said to Mark, "what did you need to think about? Why not just go to the cops? Or tell your mother, at least?"

Mark's gaze shifted to the gurney Madison now lay on. "Because," he said, and paused, "because I knew it was her."

"What was?"

"Madison, who got the girls. For Trask. Lauren, you know, Lauren Spence? They were BFFs, Madison and her. And Amber. Probably you were right, what you said—that was because she was my girlfriend. And other girls." He gestured to the corner of the room where Olivia sat with Lydia. "Her and Olivia, they just got to be friends these last few months."

One of the cops crouched down to speak to Olivia. They could take her statement about what went on here, but they couldn't question her about anything else until she had a parent with her. I wondered if anyone had been called.

"Madison would say how cool Oscar was," Mark said. "'You really need to meet him, he can help you so much . . .' I think she believed it, that she was helping people."

Madison having been decorated with tubes, bandages, and an oxygen mask, the EMTs started to wheel the gurney out of the room. Mark looked at me again. "How could I tell anyone? Everyone would blame Maddie. But, like, it was her fault, but it wasn't her fault. You know? I mean, I shouldn't even have let Amber meet her. I knew what could happen. So sort of, it was my fault, too." He looked at the gurney disappearing through the door. "Will she go to jail?"

"Madison? Mark, she's fifteen. She won't get time, she'll get counseling. She's a victim like those other girls."

"A victim?" He smiled. "She won't like to hear that. But she'll like not going to jail."

Ahlgren stuck his head back in the bookcase-door. He caught Chris's eye. "Going with her," he said. Chris nodded.

I spoke to Mark again. "So you were thinking you had to keep Madison out of the whole thing."

Mark turned from the door. "Like I said. I don't think she meant to do anything bad."

"And you came up with a plan."

He nodded. "I thought, if I could get Trask to confess, to Amber and Lauren at least, then no one would ever have to know Maddie had anything to do with it."

It wouldn't have worked out that way, but there was no point in saying that now. "So that's it?" I asked. "You left home to think about how to keep Madison out of it, and you came up with this plan, and that's all of it?"

"Yeah. What else should there be?"

"You didn't know anything else about Amber's death?"

"Anything else? Like what?"

"Hear that, Bozinski?" I raised my voice and turned to the Doberman. He'd shoved the EMTs away and hauled himself as far as a sitting position. Right now, folded in on himself, he was leaning against the quilted wall.

He turned to look at me. "Hear fucking what?"

"All that time and trouble chasing after Mark," I said, "and he couldn't hurt you. He didn't know you'd murdered Amber Shun."

# 42

That the room went completely silent was probably my imagination. Lydia, Olivia, Chris, Straley, Guilder, and Trask all turned to me. Mark looked up from staring at the floor and frowned. Bozinski scowled. The EMTs, who had a job to do, took the opportunity to try to open Bozinski's shirt and check his heel-stab.

"Beat it!" Bozinski twisted away from them. "What the hell are you talking about, Smith?"

"Yeah." Straley stepped forward. "What the hell are you talking about?"

"Here's how I think it went," I said. "You two guys had a little too much to drink one night—or maybe at lunch, up in Straley's office, who knows?—and Bulldog, you started to complain that that Chinese chick didn't want to play anymore. That one of these days Trask's buy-offs and NDAs were going to stop working. That that was a pussy way to take care of things, anyway. It was time for someone else to step up. Right?

"And Bozinski, you heard that for the soft order it was. So you stepped up. You took Amber for a drink someplace—a Coke, the kid probably didn't even drink—and talked to her, like you were a nice guy. Maybe you

274

asked her what music she liked, what TV shows. Maybe you even commiserated with her about Straley. Lousy boss, you said. Difficult guy. You said you were sorry she'd gotten mixed up with him. And somewhere in there, after she'd dropped her guard, you slipped Valium into her Coke. When it started to work and she didn't know what was wrong with her you helped her out of the bar, helped her walk, helped her into the park. Did you tell her it was all going to be okay? I bet that was what you said while you put the rope around her neck."

Bozinski was staring at me with wide-eyed rage. "You stupid—"

"What?" Mark jumped up. I grabbed and held him. He struggled in my grip as he yelled, "She didn't kill herself? You fucking killed her? You motherfucker—"

"All right, Mark!" Chris crossed the room and gripped Mark's shoulders. "I don't want to arrest you but I will."

"Me? *That* shit—"

"I know. Give us a chance."

Mark clamped his jaw shut. He shrugged off Chris's grip and mine, but he stayed where he was.

Straley had been staring across the room. Now he saw his opportunity. "Fuck!" he said. "Fuck, Bozinski, did you do that? You son of a bitch, did you—"

"Screw you, Bulldog," Bozinski shouted back. "I'm not taking the fall for you."

"Fuck you." Straley addressed the room at large: "I swear, I had no idea what kind of shit he was up to."

"Jesus," I said. "You guys are damn quick to throw each other under the bus."

"I don't—"

"Doesn't matter, Trask's got a bus you'll both fit under." I looked over at Trask, but he'd hit the teeth-grinding "no comment" stage. "Anyway,

Bulldog, that hound won't hunt"—I had to admit I was kind of pleased with that—"because of her phone."

"Whose phone? What phone?"

"Amber's phone."

He gave a disgusted shrug, as though he had no idea what I meant and didn't care, but he wasn't the actor Mark was.

"It was turned on in City Hall the day after she died," I said. "I thought it was Aubrey Hamilton who had it, or maybe the mayor. But you and Bozinski were in City Hall for the contract talks that day. He took it from Amber's backpack the night he killed her, and he brought it to you. To make sure nothing incriminating was on it. Good doggy."

Bozinski snarled, which kind of proved my point.

"Did you manage to unlock it?" I said. "Or did you just smash it and hope no one got curious about why it was missing? Doesn't matter much. Lenz is dumping her records right now." I could have stopped there but I pressed on. I wanted everyone in the room to hear all this so that Chris wouldn't be alone in what he knew. "But Bozinski, it turned out you didn't take care of things very well, did you? Because the next thing that happened, Mark disappeared. And you were afraid you knew why. Amber must have talked to him, you thought. Told him about Straley. Maybe you had a girl or two yourself, maybe Amber knew about that, too. Who knows what the hell she told him? You didn't know what Mark knew, but he had to go."

"You fucking idiot!" Straley roared. "You tried to take out the mayor's kid? Are you too stupid to live?"

This time, it seemed to me, his rage was real.

# 43

Aubrey and I met for coffee again, as we had a week ago, but this time at the Square. I watched her slide into the booth, morning sunlight falling on her honey hair.

"You did a great job," she said with a smile. She ordered tea; I was already holding a cup of coffee. "The mayor's pleased. I wouldn't be surprised if you became her go-to PI."

The mayor, at the moment, was back at her desk at City Hall, after having spent a day jockeying with her ex-husband for time at their daughter's bedside at NYU Langone. Madison refused to see her father, consented to a brief visit from her mother, and finally demanded that they both just go away. She said Mark could come if he wanted to. He had.

No McCann or Guilder had given interviews. Mark and Madison, being minors, were off-limits to the press; the mayor's office had asked that the family's privacy be respected at this difficult time; and Jeffrey Guilder was probably blowing a gasket trying to obey his attorney's order to keep his mouth shut.

Reporters had been all over everyone else, though. They camped outside the mayor's home, tried to talk to Rick Crewe and Imani Overbey.

From Crewe, a friendly smile and a wave, from Overbey a cold shoulder, and no comment from either. Journalists had contacted the Sundaris, Joseph Tamba, Emilio Vela. One enterprising reporter had even found Mrs. Binney. Tamba had been the smoothest but they'd each offered some variation on how glad they were that the mayor's son had been safely reunited with his family. Clearly, they said, Mayor McCann loved her family as she loved the city and they could tell she wanted the best for both. These thinly-veiled references to the quids they were hoping for in return for their quos had been further explicated for the mayor at our debriefing, where Lydia laid out the various requests we'd received. McCann had nodded and written in her leather-bound notebook.

"Uh-huh," had been my only comment to Lydia when we left. She suggested I withhold judgment. "Uh-huh," I said again.

Then two days ago, the mayor's office had announced it would be sponsoring the renovation of a park on 144th Street, including facilities and funding for an after-school enrichment program. Yesterday the NYPD, while assuring the public that the safety of tourists and visitors would always be paramount, revealed a new approach to street performers that would be "wherever practical, more observational than confrontational, in keeping with modern policing standards and in support of the artists' rights to self-expression." I wondered how soon the MTA would announce track work to speed up the new trains it was no doubt planning to add to the Queens lines, and how many additional Legal Aid lawyers the City was going to fund to process new immigrants and asylum-seekers.

The Detectives' Endowment Association contract talks, meanwhile, had been postponed, as the DEA put together a new negotiating team. Straley had not been arrested, but Bozinski had—not by Chris, but by a team from Internal Affairs—and Straley had resigned as DEA president. He'd said, as one does, that he'd obviously be cleared of any wrongdoing but he didn't want to become a distraction at this critical juncture. The truth was, he had no time for anything but huddling with his lawyers on ways to dodge the boulders thundering downhill at him.

"McCann's certainly taking the high road," I said to Aubrey, sipping strong diner coffee. The mayor had refused to comment on Bozinski and Straley, saying the situation was a law enforcement matter and she had every confidence in the NYPD and the DA's office to do what was right.

Bree's smile was sly. "She'll get virtue points for that. Not to worry, other people on the team are whispering. Carole will end up with the DEA right where she wants them. Too bad the whole thing couldn't have been kept quieter, though." She made a face as she sipped Lipton's from a thick cup. "But Carole understands that wasn't your doing."

"Sorry. Keeping things quiet, that's your specialty, not mine."

Sweetly, she tilted her head. "I guess."

"Yeah. Too bad you couldn't spin this one out of existence, too."

She raised her eyebrows.

"You knew," I said.

"I knew what?" She was still smiling.

"About Trask and underage girls. When he was your client. That's what his ex was going to spill, that's why the big settlement and the NDA. When Madison started spending so much time with Trask you must've known why. McCann didn't see it because it didn't happen around her. But you knew just what was going on."

She lifted her teacup and looked at me over it, the smile softening. "I couldn't—"

"Don't bother. Don't make excuses and for God's sake don't try coming on to me. You let Trask go on ruining girls' lives for years, so Carole McCann wouldn't find out what you'd taken care of for him. She'd have fired your ass. Oh, damn, that was coarse, wasn't it? Maybe she'd even have started an investigation. Because she's principled. You told me that."

Bree stared, and now it was a hard stare. "They were allegations. Nothing more. My job was to protect my client."

"And whose job was it to protect his victims? Including your boss's daughter?"

She clinked her teacup down on the saucer. Again, no lipstick had come off on the rim. She said, "Are you going to tell her?"

"No." I gave her a few moments to relax and then said, "I'll leave that to you. McCann's smart. You told me that, too. What happened to Madison, Amber's murder, Bozinski shooting Jacob when he was hunting Mark—as it comes out, the mayor will begin to see that it all goes back to you." Her face paled. "But you're a pro." I stood, dropped a ten on the table. "Maybe you can find a way to spin it."

As I had when this began, I left Aubrey at the table and pushed out of the cafe. I headed through the sunshine to Chinatown, where Lydia was waiting.

# Acknowledgments

Big thanks to:

Josh Getzler

Steve Blier, Hillary Brown, Susan Chin, Monty Freeman,
Charles McKinney, Jim Russell

Patricia Chao

Jackie Freimor

and especially Chris Chiang and Cheryl Tan.